Salvage

Salvage

Gee
Williams

ALCEMI

First impression: 2007

© Gee Williams, 2007

*This book is subject to copyright
and may not be reproduced by any means
except for review purposes
without the prior written consent of the publishers*

Published with the financial support of the Welsh Books Council

Editor: Gwen Davies

ISBN: 0-9555272-0-1
978-0-9555272-0-3

Printed on acid-free and partly-recycled paper.
Published by Alcemi and printed and bound in Wales by
Y Lolfa Cyf., Talybont, Ceredigion SY24 5AP
e-mail ylolfa@ylolfa.com
website www.alcemi.eu
tel 01970 832 304
fax 832 782

for David

from WHAT IS IT WITH WALES?

...the place brings out the passions in me just as surely as a few days in the Med dampens them down. Suddenly, what I love I'm crazy over (its green heart, its Orphean tongue, its wild fingers poking the Atlantic) and what I hate....

cal.brinkley@ guardian.co.uk

PART 1

Chapter 1

"**D**olphins! Three dolphins!" someone shouts from the sand.

On the almost empty beach a few heads turn. It's getting toward the end of one of those strange days that have occurred here off and on for a couple of months now – ever since the storm. There's an unseasonable nip, a borrowed chill that must be flowing down from the north-east. And no sun: over the sea, morning and afternoon, a pigeon-grey sky just teases with a shilling-piece, an old coin bit of brightness.

Here's extra moisture rolling in from the waters of Aberhiw Bay and up over the land, even though every stone and slab is already slick with its own sweat. The air feels like something that has to be inhaled strand by strand. It's an impediment to more than movement. The bark of a dog falls onto rocks a few feet from its origin. A woman calls to her loitering companion to hurry and, at first, he fails to react.

"Dolphins! Look!"

"There – three dolphins!"

Whatever they are, they are superb: bewilderingly speedy and vital. In the heaviness of the afternoon, in the mauve soup of the sea, they are the streak of drama that every wave-watcher has craved.

They are not dolphins but porpoises, common porpoises – though these days far from common – and there are more than three. Seven black-backed, white-bellied pulses of heat in a cool ocean. There are five adults: four females and a young and backward male. With them are two calves, born off the coast of Africa last year. As the porpoise-unit sweeps back towards the arm of the bay (the small whiting shoal, their object, has reformed in the deeper water at the base of the cliff) two of the females plus a calf breach and the watchers' "Oh-h!" carries along the tide-line. Then another female and her calf reveal themselves.

The fish are caught in an instant. They are the poor, battered remains of a much larger bait-ball that, far out above the four hundred foot chasm of St George's Channel, have been set upon by true dolphins. This bay – Aberhiw Bay – is small and comparatively shallow, although bulging with the just-turned tide. The route to the open sea is the neck of a bag. To their hopeless prey, the porpoises – back and forth, under and over – must seem able to tighten it at will. Nothing escapes the genially wide mouths. Fish are halved or quartered, still alive or beheaded with a snapping flick of teeth that borders on the virtuoso. Only the backward male is reduced to swallowing fish whole. Soon all that's left of the whiting are their platinum scales, ash-keys of the deep, falling to the bed of silt.

On the shingle, the couple and the dog-owner wait out the period of discouragement.

"They've gone, haven't they?"

"Is that –? No, no. Ah well."

"What a sight, eh?"

The dog is lured away from its rancid crab shell. The couple link hands and turn in thought from the disorderly land's edge to the surety of home. The last, lone walker of the tide-line straightens up and rubs an aching spine with one free hand. In the other he holds (to be stowed carefully away, now, before the rucksack is shouldered) a small, glass vessel. Old, or at least unusual: once the squat little thing would have held a salve of some sort, would have come complete with – a glass stopper?

For people and creatures alike the bay is becoming a past place.

The porpoise school has already sampled the current along the outside edge of the eastern rocky outcrop. It's colder, more limpid than the bay's contents and carries an assortment of debris from around the point: branches torn from deep kelp-woods, plastic containers, a board of tropical timber....

...*But what's this? A flapping blue sheet, from which rope dangles. It holds a precarious shape that the young and backward male cannot help but deflate. He turns and performs a complete somersault, over and through the hanging stream of tiny bubbles that he has just created. But the females are intrigued by something else. A shadow – no, not a shadow. A bony but still substantial entity, it's rising now from far beneath them, coming up on the strong surge of water that's the peak of the tide.*

Playfully one of the mothers nips its flank.

Any languorous swimmer's a mark for the mob. But this set-upon creature leaks a fetid signature more bitter than squid-ink that the porpoises recognize. The primary female's anxiety spills out amongst the group, inciting the babies' whistling. A calf-less sister orbits the stricken diver and plunges down to nudge it upward in a reflexive action, part challenge, part jest.

But this swimmer will not be helped. A mere tweak, a hint of contact, has it spraying particles of its outer layers, the whipping up of a milky cloud of itself which, rather than deflecting the predator, is a magnet for tiny fish. These stand off and hover. They dart. They probe the intricacy of its flowing structure, the soft and the gristly. The sweetly enticing and the inert.

The wide extent of its grin.

Stupidly the thing seems diverted from its own, original plan. It spins on its axis and drifts inshore. When the rotation's stilled, it lies along the top of the current, its own length deep. Content, apparently. The tiddlers and fry, startled into dispersion, come sneaking back and new recruits are added to the flotilla. Bronze pollack and gurnard and baby wrasse. They blossom as shimmering, motile wreaths around each of the four limbs until turbidity wraps them into a single smeared event.

The tattered kelp has soon caught up with and overtaken the whole entourage. It begins a leisurely re-descent to the lobster floor and the black flicker of eels. But by this time the murderous posse that's a porpoise school is half a mile distant. They have the bulk of Bardsey Island in their sights… where they have breached the herring gulls settle, gleaning scraps.

Chapter 2

You don't walk a cat. Nobody does. Yet it had begun on that same beach for Elly Kent, with someone walking a cat. Elly was exactly a week too early for the dolphins. They were only irregular visitors to the bay: she would have needed uncharacteristic luck to meet with them. Or at least that's how she would have described it, believing herself to be constitutionally hexed.

But afterwards she'd remember much else that was stand-out-strange about the holiday, that free week at the cottage.

She considered it a phenomenon that they should be granted Richard's cottage at all... *not* Richard and Pippa's cottage, note, which might have been normal usage for any other couple. This was *Tŷ Awydd*, according to the smart, gold lettering. This was Richard's cottage – the tasteful little bolt-hole that they'd heard so much about but never banked on seeing. Because that was Richard Congreve all over. He needed you to *acknowledge* what he had although that need was rarely potent enough to make him want to share it. "Wonderful weekend. Can't beat Wales if you get the weather. Wasted on the Welsh. You must come down for a day. It's two hours from Chester, max. I keep thinking, Elly and Martin'd love it here."

This was as much as Elly expected, as Richard's second season of ownership flowered and began to fade.

... and then, even this expectation diminished. Richard was Elly's husband's oldest friend. In their troubles he'd been Martin's only friend. But some novelty now entered the relationship. Without warning, the crack appeared as a change of tone, though only she would ever have noticed the fissure: "Can't tell you, I'm afraid," Martin responded to some innocuous question. It was about doings at the hospital where, since their return to England and thanks to Richard, Martin now worked. After a fashion. Martin's high forehead, indelibly pigmented by a foreign sun, puckered with the realization. "Not seen Richard all week."

As he lounged back with his book, Elly noticed the cheap dark trousers, bought especially for his new job, were already bagged at the knees. A striped cotton shirt gaped open across the tanned neck and the lightly-fuzzed upper chest. No formal clothing could contain her husband for long. The reading matter, Martin's trusty shield against the world, was raised again.

This coolness spread. "For a Chinese? I don't think so – he seems not to have a moment to spare these days."

After all the years of patient Sancho Panzadom, maintained by postcard and letter and then email, after all those years looking forward to the pause in whatever important trip Richard was breaking into just to visit them, her husband began to speak about his best friend in a dissociated, an offhand manner.

Richard had done *something*.

As Elly ploughed studiously through the heaped forms on her desk top in the 'Women Into Work' Portakabin and a stray bar of brightness worked its way through the Venetian blind, she thought she may never get a glimpse of *Tŷ Awydd*. Well, what did it matter? She'd seen the world. But she would find out what had provoked the rift. Childhood allies in a new school, teenage *mates* on the prowl – a thirty-year friendship doesn't go bad overnight. Whatever this is, it must be throbbing away like an abscessed tooth in the back of his mouth – and my husband's no stoic. He'll have to have it out.

But she hadn't. Martin, always close, now kept secrets for a living. It, whatever it was, could neither be forgiven... nor revealed.

Sudden as a thaw – and just as this irritating old alliance seemed on the brink of dissolution – came the offer of the holiday.

What to pack for a Welsh summer holiday? When you've been accustomed to serious warmth, more than you think you'll need.

Still stalled in England, Martin was returned triumphant from his third search for the car keys and, at last, about to open the hatch of his mother's car. Elly lingered beside it but with an ill-grace. From an adjacent garden the radio cricket commentary filtered through a screen of copper beech and on the gravel sat a heap of luggage, battered from its numerous skirmishes with baggage handlers throughout the world. Only the model design of the small Ford they were loading up gave away the year.

Otherwise it could be nineteen sixty-nine: she'd been born that year.

Or nineteen eighty-nine, married then....

Unease was beginning to spread though her, a sensation that had nothing to do with inappropriate clothing nor missing keys. Yet overhead the sky remained a hard bright blue, while the shadows of the trees out on Edens Drive shortened. Preparation for travel, there was its origin. So often they'd packed up, moved on or been about to move on, and stood together in this way at stations, airports, or in sweltering streets waiting for taxis. Not necessarily happy – not always filled with optimism – they'd been care-less, deep down. Both sure of the other. They'd had a buoyancy about them a cancelled ferry or the absence of that English-speaking contact couldn't puncture.

Now she could feel, or convinced herself she could feel, Marjorie observing them from some vantage point high up in the apex of the house. Needing to become exuberant for show, she tapped Martin's shoulder playfully and obviously to draw him around. "Hey, Martin! Welsh summer? What d'you reckon, an oxymoron, or what?"

He wasn't listening, draping a canvas bag across the spare wheel now, so as to prevent its grime getting to his new boots. Then – as an added precaution – he padded out the space with a plastic carrier of journals... now a couple of books....

Her instincts had been proved. Marjorie's head was a bobbing pale sphere against the inner shade of the master bedroom. Watching.

If Martin was aware of his mother he chose not to look up. "What are you taking – to read?" he asked Elly.

"Me? *To read*? Nothing."

"Uh-huh." He left her standing there.

Elly looked up. She chose *The Collected Saki*. Waved it at Marjorie.

16

Or, she thought with a shiver, this scene could be taking place in nineteen ninety-nine: off to Goa then.

Goa had cured Elly of books: the writing of them.

Yet Goa was *the* place for fiction. So little about this pocket of India could be believed. Religion? Its population had faith in Allah, but also in Our Lady of Miracles, in Buddha, Bom Jesus and Vishnu the Preserver. Money? Nowhere else had Elly seen business conducted with such loud-mouthed persistence – nor had she been given so many gifts. Her newborns, her people, must be able to make their entrances, improvise their stories on this stage. Within a month she'd cast the young man, Christopher, on the run from his London childhood. (He has Martin's fair colouring and Martin's brown birthmark on his left hip – which will just be visible as he swims illicitly in the pools of the tourist hotels after dark. It will be a Martin-ugly foot probing into the circle of a floodlight and watching the water fleas dart towards the bait, before stroking away). Christopher steals mangoes from gardens and begs a fish from out of the nets being drawn up on Caranzalem Beach. A cough develops, a persistent cough that he will never be free of again, and he notices it first as the poor, just-caught *bangra* sizzles on the heat, the surprise in its popping eye. He will find, any moment now, Lakshmi – Lakshmi who looks so very like Ruth in outline, but with a longer more delicate neck, no husband.

Hour after hour, in a school-room so completely filled with heat only strict immobility could prevent its being in the constant forefront of the mind, the real Martin and a class of twelve year-olds chanted *And when the folk there spy me, / They will all come up to me, / With 'Here is the fiddler of Dooney!' / And dance like a wave of the sea.* Elly had heard them at it – had heard the unbroken voices cry out in un-requested repetition: *And dance like a wave of the sea! And dance like a wave of the SEA!...* all the little headmaster's favourites: Yeats, this term.

Ruth cleaned. And hour after hour Elly rattled away at the story that would never be finished, on the opus which would end up rotting in a heap picked over by illiterate children. When the dust had been swept between the joints in the sissoo wood boards and the new mildew wiped from around the window panes, at Elly's insistence, Ruth made the tea.

Pungent kerosene vapour, filtering out to where Elly *tap, tap, tapped,* was a signal that Ruth's duties had been performed for another day. Beneath Elly's fingers Lakshmi eludes Christopher's reach, giggles and slips from the room as Ruth steps out onto the creaking veranda. For that instant Ruth is a usurper, Lakshmi real. Then Elly and Ruth settle to drink from pewter mugs – English objects that have been slipped into the kitchen by the headmaster himself. But beside Ruth's mug there is a cloth and bits of cutlery for polishing... and these she'll pick up and handle in exquisite caramel-and-cream hands, without pausing in her speech – or loss of attention if she is the listener.

Ruth lived far beyond the school in an ochre-walled hamlet that had been engulfed by the capital and yet was without electricity or a dependable well or even a name. She lived in a corrugated-iron cabin, smaller than the bungalow she had just cleaned and swept, with her husband, two daughters, a son, her mother-in-law, her sister-in-law and her husband's ancient uncle. As the weeks passed and Elly's interest flattered the girl, who was younger than Elly by several years, they discussed Ruth's small tribe and their territorial difficulties: the daughters, "old enough to be useful" but who often ran away rather than watch their small brother. Uncle Bikram, who could not be dissuaded from spitting on the polished cow-dung floor and whose shameful gobbets must be removed constantly to avoid her mother-in-law's displeasure... and Ruth's modest but outrageous ambition: to save enough for the adored son ("my Michael,") to enter the school where his mother was a servant – as a pupil. Ruth's Catholicism could not unbind her from her lowly *Shudra* caste. Even after death she might be refused burial amongst the patrician corpses that lay around the little Church of Our Lady of Succour – but for her son there was this slender hope of extrication by learning.

Of the husband little was offered unless questioned. *What does he do?* He was a gardener. He watered the lawns and spindly palms of the hotels on Dr Atmaram Borker Road: morning and evening. For the rest of the day he circulated among the villas of wealthy, Portuguese-speaking Goans in Fontainhas and the western suburbs of the town.

He owned a bicycle. Elly had glimpsed him riding at immense speed through the swirling dirt, pounding the pedals from garden to garden with a selection of his own tools strapped in a leather harness to his back. A sinewy little man, darker than Ruth, beneath his fawn patina of dust. Whenever Elly mentioned his name Ruth's mouth began to twitch and her hand flew to cover it. *Did she love him?* Ruth giggled, threw up both hands and tugged the tangerine scarf over her sleek black hair... *He works very hard,* was the answer – when she could control her laughter.

Finally, after several near-misses, they came to the heart of the problem.

They were eating apricots, apricots big and syrupy as nectarines. Elly had bought apricots to share and the juice streamed out of them, threatening their clothes and then seeping into ears and hair as they threw back their heads to avoid it. And with the shrieks and excitement and the overwhelming gush of sweetness, the stone was revealed in Ruth's meagre dessert: sex was the problem. In the land of the *Kama Sutra,* in the land of graven cavortings, where neither gods nor goddesses seemed averse to a spot of voyeurism, sex was the problem. No time for, no privacy for, sex.

Once every few weeks the mother-in-law and sister-in-law would be cajoled into taking Uncle Bikram in the weird wooden contraption that passed for a wheelchair, over to see his last remaining friend – a friend who, though wizened as a tortoise neck and older even than Uncle Bikram, still sold roast jackfruit seeds on a pitch near the multi-coloured brilliance of the Mahalaxmi Temple. If Ruth had been sufficiently submissive and her husband sufficiently filial, they would take the children with them. For maybe one whole hour on a Sunday evening, the house would be unoccupied....

But so many things could happen to forestall this erotic hiatus. Uncle Bikram might fancy himself ill at the last moment and refuse to enter his conveyance, a daughter in sheer naughtiness might have chosen that moment to disappear, one of the husband's many employers might have demanded emergency pruning of their casuarina bushes (Sunday meaning nothing to the non-Christian among them). But worst of all, Ruth confessed, the wretched man could find himself just too exhausted. Bathed and hopeful they would lie down, hand in hand in the shaded room: but Ruth's urgent whispering is answered with a snore.

Ruth was recalled with affection. But the gentle brown girl could mutate without warning into a provocative icon, ever since Elly's return to England. The memory of Ruth flagged up how that return had been to a corner of Marjorie's house. No squabbling children, no unmarriageable sister-in-law, certainly no elderly uncle spitting on the floor... just her and a husband and Marjorie, never more than a wall-width away. A configuration that, as Ruth warned, "is very bad for the love."

But they'd just been thrown out of Goa and love was the last thing on their minds.

Chapter 3

Richard's two-hour drive took them three, Aberhiw being perched on the thumb of the long peninsular the Welsh call Braich y Pwll. "The Arm in the Pool", Martin informed her. Brilliant sunshine at the border gradually gave way to layers of thin cloud seeping from the west, and then denser heavier stuff. Six o'clock, mid-summer and by the time they should have been getting close to their destination, there was a suggestion of fade in the green fields glimpsed through high hedges. Tired and tense, they backtracked and missed turnings.

At last, Richard's fisherman's cottage. The dry lane ended with no hint of beach or boat, merely the pint-sized building in a neat walled garden, everything done in smooth grey rubble: the cottage, its boundaries, the path that lead to its gloss-painted door. Further on, scrub willow and elder blocked the view and beyond that... an immense, empty sky. Only sand showing through the sparse toupee of the lawn gave a clue to location.

"It's OK, yeah?"

Instantly rattled – why should Martin need to wring a bit of credit out of the situation, even now, even for an estranged best friend? – Elly wondered out loud, "What's made The Master of the Queen's Medicine give us the place after all this time? Over a year, is it, since he got it?" No immediate response expected or offered in the narrowness of the entrance. An old leather chair mere inches from the inward swing of the door forced a left swerve into the centre of – the parlour?

"Yes," Elly managed, dropping into the offending chair, "it's OK. *Small...* funny sort of second home for someone with all those kids, isn't it? But, no it's nice."

Martin's sigh was audible.

Against the fall of evening they put on every lamp, pried into each of *Tŷ Awydd's* four rooms. Everything was clean. Stone walls were white-washed and unmarked... the slate floor's irregularities were sufficient to hint at age whilst presenting no hazard... everywhere was a quaintness just overlapping convenience. A set of six Victorian angling prints hung either side the deep window recesses but modern blinds could be pulled against the unaccustomed real darkness. More yet to poke fun at and still enjoy before bedtime: a wok and a steamer under the butler's sink, a secret door in one corner of the bedroom revealing a shiny new shower-tray and an old willow-pattern basin fitted into the eaves....

Tŷ Awydd was without a television. Elly was mortified. Since their return from Goa, she'd developed a serious pap-tv habit. How could she last the seven days without the attention-grabbing, consciousness-numbing magic show to accompany drink? It was all right for Martin who could dissolve into a book, almost any book. But, "I've found it," Martin called as she brought in the leftovers from the glove-box. He opened a corner cupboard from which the set could be extended outward and turned to face in any direction. "Neat, huh?"

"It's the last place I'd've put it."

Oozing success in the exaggerated gesture, he clicked it on.

Celebrity Shootout – blurred but recognizable – got under way in the corner of the room. Shannon Pike, the weather girl, appeared around the corner of a graffiti-covered house and scanned the empty street. Elly knew that street and where the house was located: at a crossroads in the centre of The Deserted Village. A week ago, the weather-girl had taken refuge in it.

But the prey was turned hunter.

Poised in her hand is a pantomime pistol. If metallic, it looks as though it ought to weigh several kilos but she handles it as though it were nothing, a mere extension of the arm. Somewhere heavy footfalls crunch a friable surface – the director cuts to a shady alley, a rubble-strewn garden. In close-up the weather girl's eyes darken with suspicion. The ray-gun is brought into play.

"It's not him," Elly can't help but tell him.

"No?"

"It's that Comedy Shop guy. The one that's put on all the weight. Barry Thingy."

They freeze as though they themselves are caught in the sights of some specially-devised weapon, their fate about to be determined.

Shannon springs out with a shriek like a wind lifting slates. She fires and the pale moon face of the comic is splashed brilliant red. The carmine dye obliterates his anguish, fills his mouth and then the deep runnel between two chins.

"How did you know?"

Elly dropped to the sofa, laughing and hugging a cushion to her chest in delight. "Because it finished last night. Shannon won. It mustn't be big in Wales. Funny."

Chapter 4

Yet on the night of their arrival nothing more sinister than a sprinkling of dust on the kitchen crockery had occupied her attention... So, here we are, Elly thought – me and Martin: well-used to conflict resolution, the winkling out of denial... usually it's other people's but it was the technique that mattered. Just turn inward, focus the healing beam on the life-ingredients. Money and sex. Sex and money. Prioritise this element, downgrade that. Add a dash of seasoning to a stale mixture that can still prove palatable (those mugs would need running under the tap before she could concoct some sort of bed-time drink).

Except I don't cook.

Fresh streams of water brought up a ceramic shine that caught the light. They really were very pretty, these mugs: a jaunty pattern of anchors – *anchors!* – on a background of deep blue. She had the oddest feeling that she could stand there for an hour concentrating on nothing at all but that single pigment. The most perfect blue glaze every achieved – and so many ravishing words associated with it, bice, syenite, lapis lazuli. None of them were quite on the mark for this one, except that *cobalt* square of uncurtained sky... space and time alone was what they lacked. Yes, that was it. Seven days, six nights in good old Richard's cottage where good old Richard must bring his current squeeze that she (being a friend of Pippa) wasn't meant to know about. That would do it.

Gulls screaming from the chimney pots were the alarm call. If Martin dreamed, he woke, as usual, with nothing to report. Elly blinked at him, ruffled his hair. He blinked back, his face so close each tawny eyelash was separate. He raised one eyebrow which could always make her smile. That expression of his – shy or sly? She decided not to notice. Yawned.

They rose, showered and dressed, overly-polite in talk. *No, go on you go first. I'll go and – no, I'll make some more then – of course. Soon as you're ready.*

No rush.

Yeah, no problem.

No worries.

The breakfast they'd brought with them over the border was consumed formally at the table.

"Should I do chocolate, as well as coffee – or not bother?"

Martin considered for a comical length of time. "Not really worth it – unless, you want, you know –" He dipped the remains of his croissant, scattering flakes that gave away its lack of youth. When Elly leaned across to brush debris from his chin, he flinched then tried to evolve the movement into something else. Shoulder stretching.

Here they were in another country – another country *again* – with leisure and the need to take stock. A therapist and a charity worker, a dream team. Who should begin? Elly knew who – it would be her or nobody. Where might it end? Well it must end next Saturday. That was one thing to be said for a holiday: it had clearly defined limits. Once friends and relations had smiled on their constant wanderings. "You two – you're always on holiday," they'd joked. But really had they ever had what other people called a holiday? Away – somewhere other than home – for no good reason. She thought not.

Silence fell over the muesli box and the coffee pot. Having failed to find a jug, the open milk carton sat between them. Elly leant back in her chair and looked around. Richard and Pippa's earthenware had become, since last night, immune from sniping. Richard was just Richard – charming, acquisitive and too successful to hide it all of the time. Yet there *was* an off-note quality to the cottage that troubled, more than just its unused air.

Maybe it lay in that suggestion of iodine. She was aware of it now, even over the breakfast smells… *but that's nothing but seaweed… just rotting seaweed… stranded on some close-by rocks and warming up as the sun gets going – if I don't like – if I'm going to start complaining, I shouldn't be accepting free gifts.* Sunlight leapt in through the single casement at the sitting end of the room. "Much better than the forecast," she suggested. *We could look for that beach.* She ran through the statement again in her head. *That* beach managed to connect itself with their absent former-friend in a way *the* beach did not. *That beach Richard mentions as though it were a private facility he's had tacked onto the cottage....*

She chose: "D'you fancy a walk on the beach if we can find it?"

Instantly he looked up, ran his fingers through the crisp waves of his hair, smiled — the scene progressed.

A pity not to....

Specially when you can't rely on its being....

They were away, backs turned to Aberhiw's centre, such as it was, and into an adjoining lane where *Y Mor* was indicated. "The sea," Martin said, "the sea."

"Thank you, Iris Murdoch."

Ancient tarmac petered out almost straightaway. An unadopted path led them past lemon and pink cottages and bungalows to the deep cut of a stream where fuchsia bushes and red hot pokers from riotous, weekenders' gardens were invading both banks. A Sunday morning inertia lay over all. "Soon," Martin said.

"That's a promise is it?"

He shrugged. Warm jackets, taken off in the shelter of the lane, now demanded to be put back on as a stiff, salt breeze caught them in the face.

Another sign for the easily discouraged — *Porth Aberhiw.*

"I hear it," Elly said, excited despite her heavy mood. Its voice was the hiss and rattle of waves flinging extra stones up onto a fine, clean shingle beach. The last low buildings passed, the scrub gave way suddenly to openness in a great, splayed V of ultramarine and white and a mobile dazzle that was its own colour and no colour at all. The stream they'd followed had cut a notch in the low cliffs through which they'd walked. Martin smiled his indulgent smile as though having arranged, personally, the spectacle of sharply curving coastline under a *bice* sky and the watery smudge of their coming together.

"Aberhiw Bay," he said.

"Much more of that sort of thing and the week'll just fly by.

Anyway, it's... mm-mm... lovely." She'd been looking for a better word but there really wasn't one.

"Somewhere in these cliffs there's a burial chamber – or, no, at least, a cave and burial site," Martin offered in all seriousness, "and back from the beach, but nearby – possibly connected, possibly not – there's a standing stone."

"Shall we just walk then, this morning?"

"We could."

They stumbled across ankle-turning stones the size of baking potatoes to gain the hard, gritty sea-edge: no sand, here, but shells, battered and splintered on their way to becoming sand.

In Goa there had been a beach with the beautiful name of Siridao where the sand was dark and the pale shells big and preposterous. Who could take them for real? They'd been sprinkled for effect by a cheesy film director. They were a lazy man's emblem of the tropics. But these workaday Welsh shells, with their childhood echoes, were unexpectedly fascinating.

"That's a cockle," Martin said, watching her turn it over and run a finger tip along its ridges.

"Everybody knows that. But how about this?"

"A whelk."

"Really?"

"Yeah."

"And this?"

"A scallop – a big one."

"Like you eat?"

"Of course like you eat." There was a hint of mockery now, but a good-natured sub-species that she could respond to.

"It's –" she was about to say *perfect*... slip it into the pocket of her jacket perhaps, but now she saw the lack of symmetry where one flared edge had been ground away.

She dropped it and walked on, head down. The shells were a torment to the eye: fawn, pink, mother-of-pearl – every second, every step showed a new selection from which one perfect, intact cockle, winkle or scallop carapace could be lifted. But it was an illusion. Once picked up each miniature house was revealed as derelict: a whorl broken off and jagged, an entire underside pulverised and rough. The desire for just one single intact mollusc-case became intense.

They'd covered a mile or so when around a jutting cliff strolled a family: elderly mother, grown-up son, weak-chinned and downcast-looking, with a small child of indeterminate sex on his shoulders... ("Divorced," Elly whispered to Martin even before they were close, "access weekend.")... *and the cat.* The odd, incomplete family grouping was made up by a huge, striped familiar, big as a Scottish wildcat. A bonsai tiger.

"Chush-chush-chush," the woman called and a name Elly couldn't quite catch. Martin nodded to the man. Already tall, the addition of the child on his shoulders gave his silhouette monstrous proportions against the brightness at his back.

Suddenly she didn't want to meet any of their eyes, instead bending to stroke the cat's body, a body elongated, it seemed, especially for her touch.

Safely past, Elly took a lungful of ozone – a stimulant though corrosive. Begin, she told herself. Tell him what needs to happen if you're to stay together, get some sort of plan going... how to make it come about. "If you could just – firmly – explain to your mother," she began.

Cruel really: a sucker-punch. As anticipated, he tried to turn it aside with a joke. "I don't think a trained negotiator from the UN could explain to –"

"No! I mean it. While we have to live with her, I want you to tell her not to come into our space."

"Ever?"

"Don't be stupid. We have the annexe – OK? That was the deal – our own door. What's the use in being separate if we're not able to keep her out? If *I'm* not able to keep her out? Martin, let's just face it, Marjorie and I can't stand each other. We never could. I don't know why." She did, of course. "Perhaps it's my fault." It certainly wasn't, Elly was satisfied of that. "I keep thinking I'll just get used to her." Another lie. "But I don't."

"Yes – yes, of course." Martin's shoulders dropped.

They were walking into the sun and his grey-green eyes were

screwed up against the glare. At thirty-five the lines around them were just starting to set, pointing down to a thin-lipped, almost feminine mouth but, despite the forehead's freckling, ageing well, just like Marjorie. Unexpectedly Elly felt her too-easily quickened temper subside. Love, she noted dispassionately, that might be doing it... still working away at the most unlikely of tasks, here whittling down a hated memento into something dear. "You look very like her – sometimes, you know."

Martin couldn't, of course, be expected to catch the sudden change in the atmosphere, the unseen barometer clawing its way back up.

Annoyed, "I can't help that, can I?" he muttered.

She took his hand, not retaken after her attempt to woo the cat.

"No, I know you can't. I meant... sometimes I have to remind myself. You move your head, blink that way when you don't like what somebody says to you – and it's her to a tee. But it's not her. You're nothing like her. I mean... well done, you."

He burst out laughing: almost convincingly but they both knew. It was the sort of laugh you make with just the mouth-parts and the lungs. "Well, thanks a bunch."

They were alone again, just as they'd thought they wanted to be, walking over an abandoned excavation of drying sand where a child had half-built a moated castle, pallisaded it with lolly-ice sticks. Further up the beach, there was a deep cleft beneath an overhang of crumbling rock. Martin's promised burial chamber (so unimpressive he had failed to pick it out himself) showed an entrance no wider than a front door. They slowed and tried to stare into the gloom. "D'you want to look?"

She answered by making towards it and then half way there halted, changing her mind... there were blackened patches visible just inside the cave's doorstep where fires had been lit – perhaps where teenagers had brought beer, smoked a few spliffs, quarrelled, had sex. Twenty years ago they had done it – not here but places like here. She could still relive individual acts of coupling, on nights that stood out as perfect in their mix of sensations, in their emotional tinge: the liquor's acid residue on the tongue... the stored heat in the rocks... Martin's longer hair falling across his face in the flickering light as he ran his hands over her sides, her stomach, up again to breasts that were hardly formed.

They were old enough now to have children who could be up to the same sort of thing. But here they were, still living like children themselves – not bad in the sense of wrongdoing, but wrong. They were children having to fall back on a parent's largesse, in a parent's house – in part of a parent's house... Ruth's plum lips mouthing *very bad for the love.*

Ahead the sand was split by worn wooden groins held in steel retainers rusted almost through on the seaward side. Martin helped her over a barrier that was both failing and yet an impediment. "She's lonely I expect. She's never had any friends, that's the trouble."

"I wonder why that is? Could it be because –"

He was waiting for her to continue. He must've seen her tongue's flick and presumed it was an attempt to rephrase – with extra venom – the coming tirade.

"What on earth is *that?*" Elly asked, pointing.

Something... some bright thing was nestled into the angle of stone and rotting plank. Elly watched as he stooped, picked it from the pebbles and then with a "Uh! Shit!" of disgust dropped it again so that it lay at her feet. "Jesus wept! No, don't you touch it!" But it was too late. Elly had it and was turning over – to examine properly in her palm – a ring, a gold dress ring with three stones in a heavy setting.

A natural impulse would have been to hold it up to the light... wonder about the two supporting gems... *diamonds? Yes, certainly diamonds, look at them sparkle as they catch the sun, only real diamonds do that, don't they? And the big stone, the big, square stone the colour of cyclamen – what sort of precious stone comes in blush pink?*

All this they would do and say but not until later, not until they were back at the cottage with the door shut and the morning sunlight already fading as the mist rolled in off the bay. For the moment the two of them stood, quietly fascinated by the ring, and the pale bony finger to which it was clinging.

"Oh-oh." Elly let go of a used-up lungful of air. "It is, isn't it? It's a real finger."

Gently Martin took it from her. The three slim carpel bones remained articulated on grey threads of connecting tissue; the ring was caught somehow between two and three, having worked itself into the joint. Nail and flesh were long gone. What there was could have been a bit of chicken carcase, pecked over by birds. "Yeah it's a – woman's finger."

"Or a man's."

"It's a woman's ring," he pointed out, reasonably. Three stones, a slim gold band, a slightly jazzy-looking setting with extra gold buttresses filling the space between huge main and smaller supporting stones: a woman's ring.

"Can I see it please?" Elly felt that it was hers already. She had seen it – or if they had seen it in exactly the same instant it was her hand that had closed and held on to it.

"Do you want it with or without the finger?"

Elly glanced guiltily up and down the beach but they were alone. "Will it come off?"

"Oh, yes," he said.

"Perhaps we shouldn't though...."

"Why not? Oh, I see." He only needed a look at her thin, intent face. "Evidence. I see. You're thinking where's the rest?"

This was one other reason for loving him, Elly realised. His saying *You're thinking where's the rest?...* and raising one eyebrow at her and joining in the grin that was now winning control over the set look of repulsion.

"The rest of the fingers or the rest of the body? And what's so funny?" she demanded, hypocritically.

"I don't know... it's bits, I suppose. I mean a whole body is serious but – bits are... sort of –"

"Van Gogh's ear?"

"That's it! Doesn't mean death necessarily... just a –?"

"Boating accident."

He slipped an arm around her waist, the trophy into the pocket of his fleece. "We could take a walk up and down," he looked about. "Christ, we've come a good way!" As so often on a shoreline the normal measures of distance seemed to have faded out. Now they saw the mini-estuary with its deep-cut stream where their walk had begun was a curving mile or more away, the pink and yellow bungalow chimneys invisible. "We should do... say, ten minutes in each direction? Really look for any... other parts."

He stooped to the task, choosing to go on ahead and leaving her to follow or re-examine their tracks; either way, Elly felt, maximising his own chances of an another discovery and diminishing hers.

But there were no others. Braced internally against a grisly find, they became tetchy with disappointment. ("What about – oh, it's just broken glass!" "You're meant to be looking for a body not treasure trove!") All that scanning and toe-poking and nothing else that had once belonged to a living woman presented itself. All that Elly came across – and almost because she craved something else now – was a chalk-white, finely-carved spindle shell. The spindle was the beach's top-of-the-range trinket: five decreasing spirals each incised and further decorated, rococo fashion. It was absolutely blemish free but she tucked it away without mention, felt it enfolded in a bed of tissues – a second prize. The sun had been welcome an hour ago but with a real task to perform it seemed a burden on their bent backs and craning necks. Martin abandoned the fleece, checking for the ring-finger as an afterthought, having flung the jacket carelessly over one shoulder. Twice they encountered solitary walkers and straightened up with gratitude for the relief. They exchanged complicit grimaces. To be involved in something vaguely disreputable held its own charm.

"Why don't we sit over there, have a proper look at the thing?" Martin suggested. They chose a big, comfortable stone each at the base of the cliff and he produced the ring.

"Where's the – you know?"

"God! It's come off." Martin dug deep into the inside pocket. "Here it is."

The digit, unembellished, seemed the more pathetic. "I wonder who she was? I mean, she is dead. Probably dead. I know she's dead."

You're dead and gone, she told the unknown woman, *and I'm sorry for you. I really am.* But it was a message in a bottle, really, not involving the heart. The finding of the ring was too exciting not to push all else to the region of the barely-felt. It was the ring now sending cold in tremors up through the backs of her thighs. "I've got the shakes now."

32

The waves seemed to have transfixed Martin. Elly could feel the draw of their restlessness as a pressure on her own eyes. Finally, "You know, I think she's dead too," he said. "Let's take it back to the cottage... there's no point in staying out here, is there?"

The sun had moved off to warm other interiors, leaving in deep shadow the room they'd breakfasted in.

Elly waited patiently for Martin to lay the ring down.

"Should I put it on the table, d'you think?"

"Why ever not?"

Now the smile was sheepish. "It seems unhygienic, somehow."

"Wash it then."

They rose together and lathered their hands under a flowing tap. Elly was teased by glimpses of the ring as it slithered in Martin's grip.

"Don't lose it down the plug-hole!"

"Too big for that."

It was all she could do not to snatch it off him. She told herself it was Martin's right to take charge of it, burdened as he was by a pocketful of finger-bones but she wanted it... had to have it again – and now. "Let me see!"

Obediently he dropped it onto the gingham cloth, shining and wet as though plucked straight from the sea and not the soiled beach. He'd been sharp in his estimation of size. Once she slipped off the worn eternity ring that had been her mother's, the found ring was loose around her finger. Wearing the ring, her own hand became another woman's – a woman who, when glancing down, had been perfectly at ease with a big, show-stealing jewel.

"Two diamonds," she said taking it to the window to catch them with the natural light, "have to be, don't they? Nothing else flashes like that." He nodded, mesmerised. "But... but what's this big one? The pink one?"

"Dunno."

"Well, it must be a precious stone. It's square but if you look closely it's a complicated cut, all faces and different angles. Surely that must mean quality – you know, workmanship. It might be a pale... um, amethyst maybe? No, *too* pale. But you wouldn't put a piece of glass – paste, you know – you wouldn't do that, not in between diamonds."

She realised that to make him play she'd need to hand it over. Reluctantly she slid it off and passed it across. How heavy it was; it caused an excited, greedy stir in her. Nothing so weighty could be without worth. "Hold it up to the light. You need to take it to the window. See what you think."

But Martin's movement opened up a new perspective across the room.

From a selection of silver frames propped up on a fragile side-table, Richard watched her. Multiple Richards. Richard and the two elder boys – a couple of seasons smaller – all three posed against a Disneyland backdrop. Richard, dark-suited but bizarrely draped with his stethoscope, leaving the viewer in no doubt the presentation, so professionally snapped, was some sort of medical award. The most disturbing of the three was of Richard and Pippa. One arm protectively about her small plump shoulders, his manner suggested something patronising, something nephew-and-doting-auntie, famous-actor-and-fan about it.

There were no toys. At least, if the cottage contained anything to keep three little boys amused, then it was well-hidden. This was meant to be the Congreve family's second home and yet there was that air about it: staged, as though it were for another purpose altogether.

"No toys," Elly said. "Pictures of the children but no toys."

"Fantastic, isn't it?"

She looked from her absent host in the photographs to a Martin still enraptured by their find. "Yeah, fantastic."

Had Martin ever strayed... ever had a proper, sustained affair? That solitary, admitted faux pas in Ireland could hardly be held against him. But men never grew out of wanting Beauty, did they? If she edged forward, Pippa and Richard disappeared – her own reflection replaced them in the picture glass. Her hair needed a trim. Straight from the sea-damp open air it had formed a straggly, hennaed halo of half-curls and tufts.

There was that thing Pippa had told her, about looking in a mirror, and how one day every woman sees a female relative there, an ancestral portrait, looking back... a great-aunt was it, Pippa had seen? A completely crazy great-aunt.

"Yes, it's – I don't know, more than fantastic," she agreed, "or, maybe it's exactly that. I can't take it in... that we found it. I mean, who'd believe it? We found it. What are the odds against, huh? If you lost something out there, you'd never find it again... not if you went straight back out and – and *really searched*." Even as she spoke the words the luckiness of the find, the incredible against-all-odds-ness of it, ran through her like a strong drink.

"Tell you what, I'll buy us a pub lunch. We can –" he paused. "We can think what to do over a ploughman's. Suit you?"

Even that *think what to do* had bad connotations. But "OK," she said, "Give me a minute. I'll tidy myself up."

Once he would have countered, "You look fine. I'd take you into The Grosvenor just as you are."

"No rush," he said.

Psychology Today was offering THE END OF ANALYSIS in anxious block capitals. Martin disappeared behind it.

Chapter 5

"What you got there?"

Guilt being a public emotion Elly cringed. She saw Martin's startled head-turn and made an involuntary, only-just-aborted, grab for his hand. But the woman behind the bar – a small Russian doll who could barely see over the taps – was looking beyond them to where a young man had just entered the Maeswyn Hotel, a black-and-white collie pup beneath one arm.

They could relax again in their private, horse-brassy corner. Although it was high summer the Maeswyn was the sort of thick-walled old place that wouldn't heat up till the end of August. Stone flags under the soles of their light shoes felt colder than the early morning shingle. They huddled in their thin clothes next to the fire.

"Go on, then," Elly whispered. "Let's have another look-see."

After a quick check around, Martin produced the prize and set it down on the beaten copper of the table-top. Two halves of lager hid it from the rest of the room and the colour of beer now kindled the central stone to a fiery strawberry. Perhaps because it had grown in her imagination as they'd completed the half-mile walk – studiously discussing anything but what each was thinking – the ring itself seemed smaller now.

"How can we...?"

"What? Keep it?" Martin offered. "I can tell what you're thinking."

"*No* – what I was going to say was, how can we do anything, you know, public-spirited with it now?" A couple of tourist-types passed rather too close on their way to the winking games-machine. Very casually she let her hand fall so that the ring disappeared from sight. "I mean, if it's a piece of evidence – to a crime, say or just an accident –

if it is, d'you see what we've done wrong?"

"Yeah, I know."

"We've disturbed the scene, haven't we? *Washed it.* DNA, or whatever – we've washed it off."

"I said, I know."

"Why did we do that? Whose idea was it, yours or mine?" She knew it had been hers, as did he – a double bluff in the blame-game. *Go on Martin, how will you put it? I'm afraid, officer, that my wife insisted we wash the thing. Needed to have a good look at the treasure trove. Well yes, she did want to hang onto it, as it happens, keep schtum... of course, I had to persuade her to....*

"It'd been in the water for – well, a good while, surely? Long enough for the finger – the flesh, I mean – long enough for that to... be gone. There's just bones and the gristle. I bet it's bristling with DNA, gristle. Can it really matter, us washing it? We did it, anyway." He was sticking to that *we* as to a lifeline – even as an expression of new, deeper seriousness crossed his face. "Maybe," he leaned in, "we did it because we were already tempted to keep it? Subconsciously we'd said to ourselves: This could be for us. Too good not to be. How about that?"

"You've started work, again, I see."

"But it's true, isn't it? Neither of us said to the other, 'Oh no, put it back down! You stand guard and I'll go to the police' – did we?"

There was something about the intimate moment that made her recoil. She had seen that intense grey-green stare before. The professional eye-contact: no hint of the judgemental, all pure attention and distant kindliness. It was acquired – on *Counselling, Module B23.* They'd rehearsed it, together, for his practical assessment.

Across the dingy bar the old fruit machine chortled; its acolytes raised a sudden shout that had every head turned in their direction. A pause – and then came the money-rattle payout that was the signal for an insincere cheer to limp around the pub.

"You'll want to be spending some of that, lads," called the doll from behind the bar. The collie pup was ensconced in front of her, between its owner's pint and an ashtray the size of *Tŷ Awydd's* sink. The young animal cowered at the raised voices around it and she resumed her petting of the silken-head with fat doll's fingers, the modest windfall dismissed.

A cat and now a dog and a found ring. It was a fairy story.

"So, we meant to hang on to it? Is that what you're saying?" she pretended to ask. Two could play at the *we* game. Implicate him, make it harder to do what she didn't want. In response he just nodded and gulped at his drink, throat exposed, so that she could note the liquid's progress.

"Why didn't you get bottles? I bet that stuff's vile."

"Have you seen how much the *Stella* is here?"

"We could've had Snakebite, then."

"Would they know what it was?"

There was a patch of stubble beneath his jaw-line which a slapdash holiday shave had failed to harvest. She found it unexpectedly touching.

"Look," he said, putting the glass down, "I think what you're holding there is really worth something. A lot. And the other thing I think – the other thing we both think – is that it came off a body. Someone drowned, I'd guess. We could do a trawl through the back papers. There must be a local paper. We've got the week. There must be a library somewhere that has the Aberhiw Review or something. Of course, she may not be missing now. The rest of her could have turned up – I don't know. I suppose it could've all happened years ago – and miles away? We wouldn't necessarily –"

"Not miles away, surely."

"Yes. It –" He couldn't say *she* now. "It could have been caught up in a boat's propeller or fishing gear. It could've been –" he grinned queasily as a warning of what was to come, "eaten by something. Passed straight through. What I'm saying is we wouldn't necessarily have heard about it, would we? I mean you tend to hear about missing persons and murders but not so much in the way of accidents. Or just a snippet –"

"A forty-year-old woman from Stoke-on-Trent drowned after getting into difficulties while on holiday…"

"What made you say Stoke?"

"I don't know."

"It's that sometimes people'll come up with something like that and it'll be because they've read or heard a real piece of news without registering it."

"So how does this affect things?"

"I don't know. I'm just saying...." he pointed towards the glowing coals of the fireplace as though the new idea he meant to introduce had come that way. "We could try and find out, I suppose. There's something about flotsam and jetsam... some law. Though, of course, this is complicated by – What about that policeman-bloke you used to know? Couldn't we get in touch with him, unofficially somehow?"

"Josh? You mean Josh. Are you *serious?*"

He took another peek at the chimney and shook his head again. "No, of course not. Incredibly stupid thought. Either we hand it in – *now* – or we keep it, and keep quiet until we find a way to sell it."

"How much?"

"Ah! You know what Shaw said – we've established what we are, we're just discussing our price."

"*How much?* Come on – I mean if it's just a few hundred," she let the implication go, ashamed.

For answer he gently turned her hand over and took the ring from the table. Glancing around once – but the pub's focus was at the bar with the collie pup now sharing attention with the columns of pound coins being counted before an admiring crowd – he took the ring and positioned it so that the big pink stone was outermost. Carefully he ran it down the length of the empty half-pint glass and turned it to display the result: a deep score-mark.

"That's a diamond," Elly said, "surely?"

She was bent forward, above the golden glow of her own untouched drink. So this was avarice, was it? You knew these concepts but you never really *knew* them. Not until one of them came over and whisked you onto the dance-floor. "A diamond," and she added, "as in a girl's best friend," without meaning to wound. "And yesterday I thought my favourite colour was blue."

"What? Anyway that's a bloody huge pink diamond. It's got to be worth –"

"Thousands?"

"Got to be."

What a glitzy gift it must once have made, this obvious unit of sexual currency. And what on earth could he, its giver, have expected – demanded – in return? Adulation, pain or more like, its infliction? It must've been something unusual, rather than cheap, old love'n sex. Which were on free issue.

A sense of superiority to both giver and recipient emerged across her face, a grimace that was almost a sneer.

They had never cared about money.

The words ran through her mind as cleanly and discretely as though spoken out loud, although she knew for sure they had not been. Everything was so much sharper than just a couple of hours ago: beer and perfume, someone's greasy snack – the blue check of the shirt of the man she was with, the nacreous shimmer of its white buttons... That other person, the one seated miserably over a finished breakfast in a loaned cottage, she seemed a less-fortunate sister now. *They had never cared about money.* Very distinctly she heard Marjorie's voice: *Of course, it's only money.*

Of course she, Elly, cared about money – about never having money and about having money just occasionally when Marjorie dribbled a little of the promised future Shop in their direction. And the corrosive blaming of Marjorie, spending Marjorie's money and hating the banker when all she was doing was what almost anyone would do in her position. Enjoying the privileges she felt entitled to by the state of her current account.

"Do you think," Elly asked, "it's worth, you know, *house money*? If we just kept it – for a while... see if anything happened or we heard anything – and then sold it, somehow. I have those bits and pieces Mum left me – there were a couple of rings, you remember, mentioned in the will? Who's to say this wasn't one of them? We could go to Boodles, maybe. No. Amsterdam! No – London, realistically. Get it valued."

He said nothing.

"It's not as if it's the sodding Koo-i-noor, is it?"

"Cursed, you mean?"

"*Famous*, I mean. As in trouble for us... All right, if not house money... flat money, then? Or just... something for the slacker's fund, at least," she pleaded.

Martin polished the central stone on his sleeve and held it up between their two pairs of eyes. "I would say... I'd say it might be worth *that* much – enough, anyway. Maybe a lot more than enough." He was miserable with the realisation, Elly could see. It meant that the weight of a decision was falling across him like a yoke. As if there wasn't a full load balanced there already, in the shape of guilt and regret. He was, after all, The Man Who Destroyed Books (well her book), The Man Who Ate Futures, The Man Who Emptied The Slacker's Fund. "Then again, we owe it to her, whoever she was...."

The fruit machine winnings had given the day-trippers a rapid entry into Aberhiw society. The girl sat on a tall red stool, her bare legs curling and uncurling as she chatted to the barmaid and fed crisps to the pup. Her partner was aiming darts inexpertly, in contest with a white-haired old boy.

Not only the two participants had money riding on the outcome, she guessed.

What must the locals make of Richard? Driving up on a summer Friday in his shiny car that was longer than the cottage was wide, chivvying a giggling girl ahead of him, ducking under the door lintel to the chink of bottles – she had a sudden, very complete vision of herself and Martin, sitting up in Richard's absurd four-poster that almost grazed the ceiling: their blue mugs of cocoa, their defeated, half-apologetic expressions. *It was the only thing to do. Neither of us would have felt easy about... not in the long term. All right, we have problems and it's very tempting. But... I mean, you can't just keep something like that....*

Firmly she removed the ring from his folded fist and looked into the stone's interior. Triangles and lozenges of light could be made to flicker across its surface by the slightest realignment of its perfect geometry to the dim overhead lamp... but its pink was the blush of her own finger-tips or some other natural thing. It was made of earth and air and sun, just like herself. There's no way she was giving it up.

"Are you drinking that?"

"Not if you want it." She pushed it over – watched as he downed it.

"I'll just get you another," he said contritely.

Of course! It was the Chimp and the Sweets all over again. One of their favourites.

One night Martin had come home full of the scientific paper he'd found. It concerned the behaviour of lab chimpanzees and an experiment involving the giving of sweets. On Martin's pale photocopy, an adult female chimpanzee was in the act of reaching across a white void towards a grey, anonymous hand. With its pieces of candy. Much to the surprise of the behaviourists the animals had learned to count proficiently. Offer any ape a hand with five sweets in it and another with three: five won every time. Complications arose when the candy was hidden from view. Count out ten sweets, show the chimpanzee in question eight being loaded into a paper bag and then offer it a choice. Either take what's in the open hand – or the bagful.

The project's most gifted primate still went for what was on show.

Martin, and then Elly, loved the story, unwinding it for discussion this way and that way... using it to explain the impulsive consumption they saw around them. But so often the teasing out of the Chimp and the Sweets ended, for Elly, with the same private conclusion: the chimps were far from stupid. They put their money on the short odds. The sweets in the hand. Candy in a sweaty palm was at least real and sweet. On the tongue the pleasure might be transitory but it was never snatched away.

Elly took a drop of spillage from the table top, ran a finger-tip over the ring's main stone, brightening it further. Every few seconds the thing seemed to compel one or other of them to do something with it. When she looked up Martin was standing there. "It could get us in the shit, you know? Or in my case, even more in the shit," he just had to add.

Leon, the boy had been called, that boy in Goa who had caused Martin all the trouble. Although trouble hardly covered what Leon had caused them. It had meant a spell in jail for Martin following a conviction for assault on a minor. Their diminishing capital was alchemised into debt. Worse, an inexact amount of debt to Marjorie and un-repayable now... up till now.

No way I'm giving this up. No way, Jose. Not on, Leon.

The boy that had caused so much. The boy that had brought them here, however indirectly.

"How about this?" she offered. Without any provocation, she felt so tender towards him suddenly, she could have taken him in her arms, there and then. It was a tidal rush, going out for miles, exposing the lifeless sand-dunes, but always surging back in. You could find no explanation for it. Just as on that grim night he'd asked, *Why d'you love me, Elly?* — and she'd had no answer except *If I could get my hands on young Leon's neck, I'd kill him right now.*

She barely touched the frayed cuff of the old blue check shirt. "How about we go for a walk tomorrow morning — just like we did this morning, yes?" The tone was a deliberate maybe-this, maybe-that.

Hurry on now, that was the thing to do, don't see his eyebrows coalesce, the mouth forming some contradictory thought. "You know you said how we made up our minds *before* we knew we'd decided anything. Well we could leave it to chance. OK? Not decide. Do the walk again. And, say I find one perfect spindle shell? Then we'll keep the, er, object. If not we'll do the right thing — hand it in."

Chapter 6

As so often happened for Elly, easing into sleep – hardly aware of the transition – was paid for by an awakening in the early hours. Martin's low larynxial snore wove in and out of the steady beat of the waves and the flexing of timbers above her head. She was awake – and not under a familiar roof. It was Richard's roof.

Without needing to consult the watch just within hand's reach, she knew it'd be somewhere between three and four. She slid out of the bed and let the room's cold air dry the light dampness coating her chest and arms and back. Another moment and goosepimples germinated but when she clutched her own body, she felt the undersides of both breasts still hot and moist. Martin's shirt hung from the top of the part-open door and brushed her face. In an automatic movement she slithered into it but – undecided between fever and chill – left it unbuttoned, flapping.

In about equal proportions she craved a cold drink and a pee; that would require her making her way down to a little lavatory cupboard next to the door to the outside.

Every stair creaked. Below, when her feet found the slate kitchen floor, the light switch went on like a pistol shot. Martin's breathing couldn't reach here. In this new, true silence only an echo of a hiss intruded as another batch of sea made its way up or down the beach.

The darkness, pressing on each of the three little windows in her line of sight, closed in the space to doll's house proportions. She noticed again the kitchen's single black beam that Martin's hair had brushed against – and must be low enough to take the top of Richard's head off. What on earth had possessed him to buy a place where standing up needed forethought?

The ring was where she had left it on the tiled sill behind the taps; its ghostly owner had forgotten it after some domestic task – she had placed it carefully in the exact centre between hot and cold....

Elly picked it up and slipped it on.

The lavatory opened outward. In her weariness and unfamiliarity she had no automatic system to guide her movements. She stood for a moment, defeated by the puzzle of the door – her bladder adding its own complaint to her muddled mind – and then, pulling it towards her, thwacked her bare toes.

"Fuckfuckfuckfuck." She slumped onto the wooden seat, sitting in the semi-darkness and crying softly. Something told her it would hurt less and for half as long if she kept it dark. She made fists and beat on the walls.

The tears were exiting via her nose now. "Fuckfuckfuck," she sniffed.

In a while, she was able to massage one foot with the other – and only then recall why she was sitting on the lavatory at all. Relieved, she stood up, fumbled for the light cord, sat back down. The tiny, cream space came into being, revealing the basin with brass fittings and over it, a driftwood cabinet.

Aspirin.

Her toes, apart from a slight redness, gave no indication of why pain from them still shot up her leg in intermittent pulses.

Paracetamol. Codeine. Best of all a mixture – in big soluble tablets – definitely not up to swallowing.

Richard's medicine chest held a single sachet of Johnson's *Baby SunCare,* cotton wool buds, a bar of Pears soap and a new toothbrush and toothmug, still in their wrappers... naturally. A professional mother, such as Pippa was, wouldn't leave down here anything the boys might get into after lights out. Although almost empty, containers of detergent, bleach and some noxious substance to unblock drains, were held in a locked box under the kitchen sink. Martin and she had laughed at the cryptic Pippa-note that had come with the cottage keys: **Small Yale – All Dangerous Goods Held Here.** Suddenly, just as she was about to slam the worm-eaten door, she saw it: a single white tablet pushed into the corner next to the mug. Held up to the light between finger and thumb it showed its A imprint. But in the simple transfer from eye-line to mouth, the prize shot away, pinged against the basin and disappeared.

"Fuckfuckfuckfuck."

She dropped to the cold of the slate floor and let her fingertips search.

Nowhere.

"Fuck." It appeared she was destined to spend the entire week searching for one thing or another, fucking shells, fucking body parts, fuckingly uselessly small doses of insufficiently fuckingly strong pain-killers –

Her hand glanced against rather than touched the object. It was lodged next to the white curve of the lavatory and nestled so close in, the constant elliptical shadow had concealed it in the windowless room.

A minute glass bottle, complete with stopper and a mere trace of something – yes, something still liquid – inside. After a moment she sat back, resting thighs on calves and the injury to her foot forgotten.

After another moment, she started to grin.

"Martin! You've got to see this!"

Always he took an exasperating period of time to wake. Half-upright in the bed, shielding his brow with one hand from the very modest wattage of the lamp, he was still not really capable of taking it in. The swollen eyelids threatened to seal again at the next long exhalation. "No, stay with me. Look what I've found," she pleaded. She wiggled the bottle a few inches from his face. "Behind the loo. On the floor. What about this, eh?"

With a massive effort Martin focused first on her lips, then on the bottle. The hand not engaged in blocking the light took it from her. She was content to let it go. "Who would've thought it? Huh? You couldn't make it up." She slid off the bed and walked around, hardly noticing the cardigan she was picking up and pulling around her shoulders, the sleeves she was tying in a slip-knot across her exposed breasts. "Richard Congreve – the Resector General – playing away from home and not content with that –" she turned toward him. Some things... you just had to be looking at each other when you said them.

If he recognised Elly's expression it was too late. As she said, "Martin – no, don't!" he'd raised the unstoppered bottle to his nose and sniffed.

From around the bed, four or five feet away, there was just a hint of that fetid underarm/old shoe-interior combination that she'd never smelt herself but had heard described. Then Martin gasped, "JesusChristaliveElly!"

He dropped the thing onto the quilt cover and slumped back in the bed, eyes rolled up, dead to the world.

PART 2

PART 2

The sea's humour is wicked, an ogre's peevish child put in with puppies. Where will the teasing end – and with what? Seemingly playful, genially suave… and then the casual blow is delivered. With a push, a pat, it can throw a delicate structure straight out of itself: an egg, guts and shell combined, against a brick wall. Or it prepares a landing for the unprotected. But the landing is deep in grey cold. What lives down here has had a million years to learn the trick of it. The general level of incivility is outrageous considering the only wealth is bodily integrity. Theft is the norm.

This poor voyager now, lounging in the bay, has been the butt of more than one prank.

The land has been denied it for several days. Water has taken over the entire circle of its world. And just when grown used to its new daily routine, and as it is on the point of shedding its earth-clothes like a glove, the coast reappears with suddeness. It is a huge panel of gloom and noise – and grows bigger, nearer and more dense and demanding by the hour. "Come to Mother!" the land calls to the tumbling shape over the thrash of the waves. She throws out a pair of rough, welcoming arms.

And comes up below: to snag on anything trailing and impede progress, to relieve the pilgrim of further goods in skin. In return the neck and shoulders are draped with mock-laurels, in this instance slime-green bladder wrack and brown ribbons of furbelows.

i

"I suppose you do remember? Do you Martin? What it was Richard did?"

This was from Elly, my wife.

Shocking, to be challenged thus, in the mantrap of the car. "Let me just —" I stall for time, negotiating a pair of bikers with care. Under those visors could lurk middle-aged nostalgics or full-blown psychopaths.

'What Richard did' – to be honest, I thought we might have shelved that one. What with her finding Richard's amyl nitrate. Having the best jibe ever at the Arch Enemy's expense. (*Fancy our Richard needing a chemical leg-up for weekend leg-over!*). My getting out of my skull on Richard's stray popper, without meaning to. Elly falling onto the bed – because once she started laughing she just couldn't stop – and that laughter filling not only the room but the inside of my entire body for the first couple of minutes. Like a drum roll with me as the drum. Who could blame her?

These are the things I can remember.

The smell. Then laughter. Then lightness – by which I mean an unannounced *swish-sh* of anti-gravity. A giant's fist grabs hold of me and flings me smartly back up the slide. That was it. *That* was the event. Poppers are for keeping the rush, not for giving you one.

And then Elly, at intervals through the next half-hour or so, demanding, "What are you feeling?"

Not *how,* note.

"Wonderful."

"Really?"

"No – a bit crap now – oh, no good again. I think it'd be better if I was doing something."

"I'll bet."

"Why don't you get back in here? Pity to waste it."

"You're *such* a romantic, Martin… anyway it wasn't meant to be like this."

"You could – yourself, you know?… then you won't notice."

For a second I thought she might go for it. She put the re-stoppered bottle down next to the lamp. "No thanks. I think you'll find the best bit's pretty well over. You'll have a filthy headache in the morning."

"Yes, matron."

In the shower room I heard her running the tap. She reappeared, wiping her mouth with the back of one hand – rough, it looked, for her. What a buzz.

"Come on!" I said. "What am I meant to do with this?"

She smiled sweetly. "Sleep on it."

Her getting out of the sweater and my shirt and only then turning off the light brought up another bout of palpitations – and anyway wasn't this what we were here for? She snuggled down beside me, her cool, bony little backside against my hip.

"How come you knew – like straightaway?" We'd seen most things between us but it wasn't as if we were clubbers or ever had been.

"The punters. At work," she said. "Keith gave a kid the push only the other week for selling E, good old diazepam and amyl nitrate. He did poppers – in the glass vials, you know? – but these dinky little snifters, they're more the thing."

"Bit of a limited range, then."

"He did *E, amyl nitrate and diazepam*. That means up – oh yes! oh yes! oh yes! – and down. Work it out."

"Right. Christ! What must it be like to have that sort of constitution? You won't be thinking in the long term, naturally but – "

"Can shift any amount apparently."

"You don't say."

ii

"Can shift any amount."

"Of what?" Elly wanted to know.

"Sorry – it was what you said. The night of the popper."

"Don't change the subject. I was asking what Richard had done. Apart from stimulants to heighten sexual performance –"

"Well heighten pleasure, anyway. I wouldn't have minded checking that out."

We'd thrown Richard's guilty little bottle into the sea – which Elly had agreed to at the time and then, a day later, seemed annoyed by.

But somewhere in one of those battered cases behind us, other small objects rattled, loose as boxes of teeth.

Fine – so what had Richard done?

I opened my mouth. Shut it again.

And my sermon today, ladies and gentlemen, is on the subject of memory.

Mine. My inability to manage it.

There are days when I'm sure Elly has told me an important thing, whether meaning to or not. But I can't for fucksake remember what it is. I *feel* it's there, somehow, lodged amongst all the other material I have in store, the Elly Files. But there the little bugger goes – a puck of an idea slithering out onto the thinner ice until, crack! It's gone, down into the murky, unchartable depths. I'm afraid, of course – and with good reason. There's every chance I'll be caught out, find myself floundering down there in the ooze.

Forget the puck. Forget the whole ice-hockey scenario. It's too dramatic. What I fear is – what happens is, I just sort of come to; I surface between stations, a traveller without a valid ticket. Elly's challenge is made – and what? A sort of slow-motion blur is all I can come up with. Previous scenes sneaking past in peripheral vision, unnamed halts on the line – or worse, what I can only describe as an Adlestrop moment.

Adlestrop, that poem by Edward Thomas. It's a good example of what I'm on about. It's a backdrop without a play.

The time? 'One afternoon.'

The place? Has to be the Oxfordshire/Gloucestershire border.

The season? High summer. I could continue: conditions excellent and likely to remain so with just that hint of high cumulus, the fair weather cloud. But the occasion for all this detail is that '*no one left and no one came/ On the bare platform.*'

Up and down the deserted halt the inner eye roves – and all too often in my case there's not a face it recognizes. Stalled without meaning or explanation in a stifling railway carriage. I can take in and remember mainly the process of *being me*. Everyone else's business is pretty much a mystery.

In my counselling job – in my *new* counselling job – I manage by keeping notes. Not something you can do with wives. They tend to take umbrage. And no amount of practice and effort can alter it: what will and won't be classified as worthy of recall. Tennis, for instance. It's a pretty meaningless duel of movement and pause, parry and thrust. The body's occupied in fulfilling its function and, unusually, the attention's properly involved in direction and support services. As opposed, say, to drifting off elsewhere, creating a more palatable *now*. Tennis will stick. There are matches I can replay perfectly in my head, point by point to the last double fault – time of day, time of year, atmospheric bloody conditions, etc, etc.

So it's on the way home. It's after the holiday and we're thrilled with the souvenir of the holiday – excited. I know I am. We're just the other side of Bangor, and I'm not a bit surprised to have Elly come out of her long silence with, "I suppose you do remember what it was Richard did?"

Straight out with it. Messing about, not on the agenda. Perhaps it was the knock-on effect of the find, because with Elly everything's connected to everything else. For instance: near miss on the high road coming home from the theatre caused such an extreme bout of rudeness to Marjorie, I thought we'd have to make other sleeping arrangements. (I told Marjorie she'd had one too many although she hadn't – she'd elected to drive). Was it Arthur Miller had wound her up or a brush with extinction? Both, of course – and the discovery of Marjorie having a nose about in our kitchen. Alibi? That *Tarte-florette Marjorie* as a 'nice surprise' for the next day.

Did I remember?

Ahead the A55 turned that few degrees north to have us facing the sea for an instant. The pain of afternoon sun on wet Lavan Sands caught me across the retinas. Then we were back on course for Conway – though in the not-so-distance, the red brake lights were flashing on with perfect, regular periodicity.

"May," I said, "Yeah – I'm sure it was back at the beginning of May. Or April."

iii

Cool for springtime, but calm with none of that thin, unpredictable blow off the Dee that can make the Parkgate courts my least favourite. I was ahead. I was about to take him, now – finish him off after a patchy but nearly pleasurable four sets and nothing but defeats already this season (although we'd hardly played that much, his being *so busy*). He'd dropped two services games. He was three games down in all and we were at thirty-love when I said what I said. The first serve? I'd caught that just perfectly, early and right off the centre of the racket. It touched down at Richard's feet for a nano-second and then it was a blur across the doubles court and into the netting.

"Oo-oo," Richard had mocked with a camp wiggle.

Great shot, Martin, another Richard acknowledged – only in my mind, you understand. I admit to the sad-deluded-matiness of this fantasy.

He flounced across and took up position, carrying it off well because despite his height he was spare and sinewy as a Masai… and moved with their loose-jointed, physical arrogance. Richard and the Masai, they give the impression they're moving through a world they made.

If I start my bounce-bounce-bounce routine I know I'd get something like, "Come on then, Venus, let's see what you're made of."

I mis-timed the throw up, took it too quickly and sent the ball high and slow over the net. All he had to do was take one step forward and with that vicious backhand put it away. But he didn't. He thought about it, actually moved the back foot, dithered, leaned away from the oncoming serve and hit it out, off the wood.

"Sapping your strength, is she?" I said. "Don't expect any sympathy from –"

"What did you say?"

"You heard."

He was upright, all six-foot-two/six-three of him, and there was never much to be gleaned from Richard, expression-wise. Certainly nothing I caught as I tried to hurry the game on, preserve my momentum.

"Come on," I said, turning side-on. I still thought he was taking it OK.

"What do you mean by that? Who's been telling you – what?"

Now I had to look at him.

Why is it, do you think, the British are so poor at tennis (I mean at the higher levels of the game) and so good at strangely disparate activities such as mountaineering, horse-jumping – snooker, for God's sake? It's this face-to-face business, in my opinion. We've no real objection to beating the shit out of anybody *so long as we don't have to look him in the eye as we do it.*

Richard advanced to the net and stood glaring, tapping one open hand with the racket head, then tapping along the cord itself.

There's a favourite line I have from *The Friends of Eddy Coyle* that goes, "You had to be there." It encapsulates all the later difficulty you'll have explaining the inexplicable. Great movie. Fine performance, Robert Mitchum's.

Well, you had to be there. You had to see Richard. I'd hardly looked at him objectively for decades but Elly tells me he's 'a bit of a handsome, nineteen-fifties-ish brute'.

My opponent towered over the net and, of course, me. His rapid breathing and hair darkened to the colour of old rope suggested we'd just finished a long rally, which we had not. Slowly, he pointed the head of the racket at my chest as though it were a weapon. Kept it there. It was absurd. It was absolutely bloody ridiculous – but to a walker up on the old railway line (now the country park) it might *just* have looked as if my opponent had made the journey to the net to acknowledge superior play.

As I said, only in a parallel universe and with another Richard.

There wasn't any question of playing the next point – or was there? I took up station, bounced the ball once, twice, three times, four times and glanced up – just casually – as part of the service action. He hadn't moved. Even now it would be possible for him to let the moment go: to smirk, back off with his hands raised saying, "I had you going then, eh?" – even if the anger were absolutely authentic and fresh, he could still manage it. Almost everybody can, if it's worth the doing. Richard was always just this side of acceptable when pissed off... there'd be the flicker of something really dangerous as the frustration surfaced – and then it would disappear. I'd seen it happen with friends, other doctors, nurses. I'd seen him come close to frightening people who the next second were falling victim to his charm. If this sounds too intimate – especially after that *Get you!* – it's nothing sexual, nothing fraternal even, just absolute familiarity. I've known him for thirty years, seen him in every situation including fucking a girl called Brandy we'd picked up... he'd picked up. An Australian girl who liked to share. Once, when Elly and I were living on Cyprus and he'd invited himself to stay, he'd caused a bar brawl that had us both (me and Richard) in the cells overnight.

Because? Because he was enjoying himself and there wasn't any reason not to. No reason he could see to break off staring at some raven-haired daughter of the south with only a hint of a moustache. And he got away with it. He gets away with everything. Me: nothing. Next morning the little *astinomikos* served us coffee and figs, slapped Richard on the back. Winked. Called him '*poli kako pethi!*' Very bad boy.

"Don't arse around," I suggested. "I've got the beating of you today. I can feel it."

"What d'you mean, *she?*"

It was a still and dry afternoon but the Parkgate courts were deserted.

"So what's the word now round the hospital? What are *you* saying, Martin? What do you mean by *she?*"

"You know –"

"No. You tell me. Who's *she?*"

I wanted to laugh – laugh out loud with all the deflationary aggression of a teenager. But I couldn't do it. Because an angry man's always to some extent ridiculous to a cool one, and because on Richard's rigid body the anger was obvious as a girl's blush, I should have been able to pull it off. Something stopped me.

Under the tirade, the dangerous breathing through the nostrils, there was something else. There was this other, deeper well of anger. It was connected with what was happening now, but not about it. That's what I thought at the time and what I still think. Too powerful for a mere facial spasm to give it away, Richard's adrenalin coursed

58

through his entire frame, registering everywhere.

I threw the ball up carelessly and lobbed it over his head and straight out of the court. It was so quiet I imagined I could catch its impact amongst the bronze heads of sycamore along the footpath – and then its fall to earth. New and bright yellow, it'd lie amongst last year's leaves for a child or dog to find because neither of us was going to retrieve it. Neither of us could now.

You had to be there. Walking forward, nice and slow, is what you do in this situation. Offer attention, withhold judgement; I had it in my head that it'd all come out into the open, whatever had been going on with Richard for a while now.

"You've gone quiet." He leans right over the net at this and while I'm still thinking *Christ you're looking a bit jaded mate* – which he was, his eyes bloodshot and the skin around his eyes mottled with red – he grabs the front of my shirt and yanks me forward.

"What the fuck d'you –" I get out. But he reverses the handle of his racket and jabs it up under my ribs. And for a count of ten, there we are. Standing eyeball-to-eyeball, I can smell his sweat, his breath, a sweet-sour whiff of digestion gases and toothpaste. From a distance it could still have looked as though we were fooling around and – this is the really infuriating aspect of it – I still wasn't sure that we weren't.

It was getting a bit hard to inhale. And painful. He'd know more about that than I would being a physician but also less about, being the inflictor rather than the inflictee. I shifted, brought up my shoulder and then my left arm into the equation and sort of pushed/shrugged him away. Punching him square in the face would also have been an option, especially as he was without a hand to defend himself at this point. But I didn't – and then he let go of my shirt and retracted the racket handle. He said, "You tosser, Martin," under his breath. It was only at that precise moment I was convinced it had been for real.

I turned and walked off to the gate and kept on going.

I was halfway along Edens Drive, half-way home, when he caught me up. Of course, his Jag was parked next to my rust-bucket in the front of my house so there wasn't a choice. If it hadn't been for the sound of footsteps and the puffing coming up behind me, his scent alone would've announced him. It was sharp and clean, but still unpleasant

– like grapefruit peel. He veered out and took the grass beside me. Edens Drive is one of those roads with wide, tree-planted verges that the residents meticulously maintain to thwart the council.

I didn't expect him to speak. Whatever he was riled up about needed more than a few minutes to dissipate – and it would be unbearably patronising for me to attempt small-talk. We stalked along beneath the avenue of limes both of us, I guess, willing every next house to be the one.

Home's a big, red brick, half-timbered job, similar but not identical, to some of its distant neighbours. Impressive. Even Richard, with his Georgian villa, fancies it: "If Marjorie ever feels like selling, you'll give me first refusal, eh?" My mother, that's Marjorie, owns the house. Elly and I live in Servants Hall – kitchen, sitting room, back stairs, bed and bath. We got there easily enough: by having nowhere else to go on account of my being a useless pillock.

I walked around to the side door and unlocked it, glad Elly wouldn't be home till after six. Nor was Marjorie's new blue hatchback on the gravel in front of the garage – an added piece of good luck. Only when I'd pushed the door wide and then stood back did I actually look at him. "D'you still want that shower?"

He was paler now, a more natural colour and breathing less noisily. "Yes." He went in first, dropped bag and racket onto the tiles and ran up the stairs as though it were a perfectly normal end to a perfectly amicable game. Usually I'd have gone to what we called the kitchen – a tiny former pantry still with its butler's sink and brass taps – drunk a pint of water and waited till Richard reappeared. He'd have a gin and tonic on the go by the time I came down, together with some Gershwin or Scott Joplin, nothing too heavy that's for sure.

Today I went through to the front of the house, Marjorie's domain. It smelt of beeswax, whereas behind me last night's takeaway still lingered. I made for the main bathroom at the top of the stairs.

My intention was to shower and to be down to hand Richard his drink – and say, "OK, so who the fuck's rattled your cage?" But when I came back through the heavy oak door, the bag and racket were gone. I stared for a moment, stupidly. The rectangle of black and white floor tiles were dirty and cracked and empty. Apart from myself, the house was empty too.

Counsellors get angry, counsellors get depressed, have unresolved childhood issues and occasional sexual dysfunctions. Fail to come to terms with grief. When I found Richard gone, I prowled those rooms I could think of as legally mine and fumed. The match had been *all but won* – and my remark, if not innocuous, then hardly the formative stuff of a major strop.

Wearing you out, is she? A tantrum, that's all it was. And this from a man who could so easily, who *had* so suavely on many an occasion, boasted of much the same thing I was enquiring into....

The wet towel thrown half-over the radiator in the bathroom, the body-wash bottle containing nothing but a few suds left empty in the bath, the cap of the body-wash bottle still in its soapy mass on the window-sill, the shower curtain malevolently positioned to drip straight onto the wooden boards – all this, with ferocity, I cleaned up. I cleaned up after Richard so Elly wouldn't have to do it later. But I did it with fonder feelings toward my wife now; in fact I wiped down and polished up almost in the spirit of atonement – because Elly now disliked and distrusted Richard, expressing it through a covert, just-giving-you-a-hint sort of spitefulness. And as I squeezed out a flattened, granular pitta bread affair that had once been a sponge mop but whose absorbency now had to be taken on trust, I shared her vision of him. And why didn't we get a mop that mopped?

Back downstairs in our small sitting room I found that Richard had poured himself and downed at least a couple of drinks before his departure: an opened tonic water sat in a moist ring on my CD player, a thick, used tumbler beside it. The Gordons was finished, on its side and on the floor. I picked it up by the neck. Holding it up to the light there were exposed a complete set of Richard's prints against the green glass.

Still sweating, then, even after his shower.

I flopped down onto the sofa and turned on the news because to find reading matter would mean getting up again. Six o'clock. Any moment Elly might walk in with that tight, pleasant look on her face, expecting to find Richard and me there – Richard loftily welcoming, as though it were his house. But not this Friday evening.

It's a bloody, once-a-century ill wind-up blows nobody any good. Elly, at least, would be pleased....

Sleep – now there was an idea. That'll show her – I mean him though, don't I? Go to sleep, stop being Martin – stop being *you tosser Martin*.

Finally inactive, my shoulders began to register as aching, with the left one, my service side, my fending off attackers side, leading the way. Then a deep muscle in the back of one thigh joined in. The fingers of my racket hand are stiff when I try to massage the thigh muscle. Tomorrow I'd have to relive the match whether I wanted to or not, prompted by discomfort at every small movement.

The obvious thing to do was to prepare for it by getting good and pissed off now. Start feeling black all over again about our situation here in the delightful Edens Drive – and then there was the ageing bit, the game going off relentlessly year after year no matter how fit you tried to stay. Suddenly I was wide-awake. *Rage!* Gut-wrenching, obscenity-spitting rage that I hadn't had the presence of mind to smack the bastard, knock him down on his arse, spread him lengthways on the court – and then made him receive serve.

Now depression, I should explain to you (if you ever find yourself sitting across from me in my cupboard in the hospital basement), depression can be a road we chose to turn into. Physical discomfort, a trivial disappointment – either can be its street sign. If I'd ever played tennis professionally – as I had once dreamed of doing – I'd be veteran-class by now. Instead of which here I was: one brilliant win at Eastbourne seventeen years ago to look back on, pissed off at being done out of a victory over a same-age vascular surgeon who kept himself in only reasonable shape.

But it wasn't just that.

On the TV screen, the newscaster's familiar frown disappeared. Suddenly we were across the Channel. In a Parisian street, perhaps even as Richard and I had made our way companionably up to the courts a couple of hours ago, someone had taken a pot-shot at President Chirac ('of France' it being ITV).

One image jostled the next as the quickly edited footage unrolled: long shot of a boulevard with its mutilated plane-trees, then a close-up of cobbles, a uniformed back. As always happens for me (and, I guess, for anyone else who knows the city) a corner café instantly presented itself as *the* one. We've all got *the* one. In my case it's where Elly and I had had that student birthday-dinner of *crepes de marrons*. Chirac's ugly, ancient, bewildered face flashed across the screen as he was hustled into the darkness of a car by tough young body-guards.

It could be worse. I could be as old and befuddled and irreclaimable as Chirac.

Although I tried to follow who and where and what else was going on, that single phrase from the voiceover "…or the unresolved anger of powerful forces," instantly sent me back to thirty-love, two match points and Richard's blazing march to the net.

There was no way I'd be telling Elly.

"Elly'll just love this, I thought," I finished deftly to the Elly seated beside me in the car. I overtook a coach the size of a pantechnicon filled with grimacing, leering teenagers.

I'd divulged about a third of the above. A quarter, maybe. "Then Richard offered us the cottage – to make amends – and I thought, why spoil it? So, Richard storms off 'cos I beat him and take the piss about his current bit on the side. No need to do you out of a break because of it."

I'd done well. I'd done extremely, unexpectedly, unusually well. Elly was quiet. Bangor was far behind us. The A55 that took you all the way to England seemed as if it might be only *partially* clogged ahead.

And when she did speak it was just, "So d'you know who this new girl is? The one that's wearing him out?"

iv

"Then Richard offered us the cottage," I'd said to Elly.

Not straight away he didn't.

On the following Monday morning I was on my way across the hospital car park, having left the Fiat in its reserved space. As usual I was trying not to notice the haggard relatives of terminal patients and the shell-shocked parents of cancerous children, all trapped in the lengthy search for parking spots. Even this observation sounds a note-too-far on the sympathy scale. Already I thought I could detect the raised voices of a brewing disturbance on the far side of the barrier. Ah yes, those waiting to be admitted to three acres of solid, stationary metal were being prevented by someone unlucky enough to have both an ailing loved-one and a substandard pound coin.

To be caught up in acute misery seems to have less of a knock-on effect on normal life than you'd imagine. If you're inclined to irritability and lacking an effective anger-control mechanism, a death sentence pronounced on your wife or the production of a malformed baby will certainly not be the occasion for inner peace. I've watched with my own eyes the father and uncle of a recent still-birth leave with a miniature TV and MP3 player, stolen from a couple of the more successful mothers on the same ward. Perhaps they felt they were evening up the score – which brought me neatly round to Richard. I could go for days, a week, perhaps, without coming across him during work hours. But such a week certainly would end with my seeking him out or a royal summons through Nancy, his secretary, to join him for lunch.

My office, located on what's called the lower mezzanine, seemed colder and darker even than usual. Though I could tip the blinds to minimum occlusion and turn up the radiator I knew my malaise at just being there and sitting at my desk was mainly to do with the previous Friday's events. Being back in Richard's domain. My hand hovered over the phone and landed again onto a pile of scribbled notes awaiting electronic metamorphosis. A few vigorous spins in my chair failed to delight. Finally, I tried looking – really looking, again – at my print on the opposite wall.

It was Henry Raeburn's *The Reverend Robert Walker Skating*. The low winter light touches upon the ice-skating vicar's ruddy cheeks and the healthy pink flesh of one ear. His grey hair falls neatly about his collar and the brilliant singularity of his white cravat. It's brilliant because although this is a frozen scene, the grey Scots sky has turned everything icy to burnished bismuth. Above the ice glides our cleric in complete relaxation, one black-coated arm across his breast ready at this very moment to swing out and follow through the next perfectly balanced step. There never was a man less in need of counsel.

The original's in the National Gallery of Scotland. This poster was a present from Elly on the day I'd been given a bit of office-space and they'd made my half-time post permanent. If I could be anyone on this earth I'd be the Reverend Robert Walker, skating forever across a metallic Duddingston Loch. Deliberately I've maintained my ignorance of the real Robert Walker. If he were subject to the stale, smelly, familiar little trials of existence, I'd rather not know. To me he's all those confident extinct clergymen rolled into one. The ones God never seems to have impinged on overmuch except to provide them with an income. Certain and content in his sureties, a bachelor and probably celibate, for the Reverend Robert Walker skating is religious ecstasy and sexual *denouement* rolled into one.

Even as I dialled I was leaving it to the moment to decide what I'd say, how I'd play it. Anything was possible.

"Hello Nancy," I said, "It's me – Martin. Is he in?"

"Already in theatre, I'm afraid. A patient – should've had elective this morning I mean, but came in last night and tried to die on us in the early hours. What time is it now? Nine-thirtyish? Himself has been in since seven. No knowing when he'll be out. Was it – something?"

"No, no. I'll try later."

"He's got a full list," Nancy warned.

"Right."

"I don't think he'll manage lunch if that's –"

"No, no. Thanks Nancy. Bye. Yes… Bye."

I considered texting Elly to see if she might want to snatch a bite somewhere cheap. It being a change from routine, it'd need careful wording. I pictured her, already bent over the keyboard in the training centre Portakabin, the first mug of coffee cooling on its beer-mat. I wasn't intending to do it, was I?

Further dithering was denied me when the phone rang and I was summoned upstairs to *'please come and see what you can do with Mr Brinkley'*.

I retraced my steps, then up and along – be in the right mood and you can imagine the hospital as a huge liner. Its old-fashioned balconies suggested deck after Art Deco deck rising towards the 'funnel' of the air conditioning tower. The good ship Deva, sailing the Sea of Sickness to the Blessed Healthy Isles – not. My journey was taking me out of the hold, away from the engine room and noxious boilers to the better class areas, high up and fore. The trolley-rattle of rowed specimens could be the pursers out dispensing treats.

Mr Brinkley was a rodenty little man in his seventies, by the looks of it and hunched up in the relatives' room. He was occupying only part of a mock-leather chair that I couldn't help noticing someone had taken a Stanley knife to over the weekend. Its grey stuffing now sprouted between Mr Brinkley's black-clad knees. *He was actually wearing a suit.* It was pin-striped and so ancient the trousers had turn-ups – and it went with an unpressed shirt and a greasy-looking tie. A shocking outfit. The bereaved usually presented themselves in sportswear or combats, spaghetti straps, Nikes, six-inch heels. That's what I was accustomed to. On Mr Brinkley's feet were a pair of leather brogues, cracked and friable, with the mud from recent spadework still trapped in the stitching and still breaking into clay matchsticks and falling onto the floor as it dried.

The instant I'd sat down I'd become conscious of an overpowering whiff of tobacco smoke being passively emitted by Mr Brinkley's person. It might mean nothing. In all likelihood it hung about him always, in clothes, hair, skin and breath. I could have mentioned it – was in no doubt that the staff nurse who'd summoned me would have: *You are aware this is a no-smoking area?* The filthy deliciousness of the scent almost irked me into complaint – but I have a fuzzy relationship with the cigarette. A reformed addict myself and working in a setting where the weed is officially detested, I come across punter after punter saved from violence or self-harm through lighting up.

"Sorry about this," Mr Brinkley said as soon as I was seated. Although he spoke to me – was obviously aware of my coming in as an event specifically connected with himself – he made no move to look me in the eye. "I don't know what's the matter with me, doctor – I'm not usually – you know."

His thin, stubbly face made up for the rest of his body's immobility by working like crazy over every word. Up went the grizzled eyebrows, in went the cheeks. An extra twitch of the top lip finished off the sentence. There was a trace of Scouse about his speech, an accent that always gives cause, or at least always gives me cause, to anticipate a joke. But I'd already been well-briefed by Staff Nurse Doran. Mr Brinkley wasn't about to launch into stand-up.

He'd just killed his daughter.

"That's all right," I told him, "no need to apologise. This is a bad time, yes?"

After thirty seconds or so, I tried, "This is about as bad as times get, isn't it?"

Beyond the closed door a couple of light blue shapes passed across the obscured glass panel. A muffled few words ended in laughter.

About suffering they were never wrong / The Old Masters: how well they understood / Its human position.

Mr Brinkley's human position was doubled over and petrified on a slashed vinyl chair while above his head hung in brightly coloured, if not illuminated script, the Hospital Canticle.

- **Please keep this area clean and tidy**
- **Please do not monopolise this area**
- **Please do not leave valuables and property in this room (The Deva Hospital Trust cannot accept responsibility for any loss or damage of personal property on Hospital premises)**
- **This waiting room is not intended for overnight stay**
- **Smoking is prohibited in this area**

I counted ten in my head. And then another ten. "We often wonder what it'll be like – times like these. But I doubt we can ever get it right. No one can really know how they're going to feel."

Another decimal count was underway, but before I'd gotten to its end I found a private fume about Richard was poised to interrupt. Even if, as Nancy claimed, he'd been down in theatre since dawn, he could be up here by now, on his way to exactly here – could be about to open this door, because there was always some cock-up going on. You could depend on it –

"Mr Brinkley," I said, "You made a decision for um, for Cal

– Calwen. You've done what you thought was the best for her because you're her father. And that's what you've always done, I expect. Yes?"

His jaw set and his eyes unseeing, he nodded – which was a start.

"I'm not a doctor, by the way. I – well, I try to help when people lose someone close to them. Like you – now."

Lose someone.

Passed on or worse, passed over, fell asleep, slipped away. I can't stomach any of these. Even in the mouths of the bereaved, they offend. But to lose someone seems about right. The people we genuinely love, we possess. We keep them closer than a credit card, safer than the keys to the Porsche. When they're stolen, our lives are ransacked, the locks are all forced and shit's smeared all over the bedroom walls.

"I'm sorry about what's happened to Calwen. But I suppose everyone has said that, haven't they?"

Another nod and a small, strangled sob very nearly got out before he rammed it back down. The bobbing Adam's apple. The straining force. It brought to mind a lead ball, rodded into the barrel of a musket.

"Means nothing, though, does it?"

No response this time. How powerful old-fashioned good manners can prove. Richard mentioned it to me. He sees it a lot.

"It means nothing because what's happened here, it's just between you and her. Last night when she was brought in, the consultant – the second doctor – he explained, didn't he? That even last night, Calwen – the daughter you've always done the best for – that *that* Calwen was gone. He explained that, didn't he?"

Another slight inclination of the head jerked out a tear to run down an immobile face.

"And you're her father, so you sat with her all through the night because – quite right, no one should decide anything in the dark… in the middle of the night when they're tired and can't think straight. Yes?" I expected weeping to at least get a foothold at this point, but he, Mr Brinkley, was a tough one, tougher even than the work-scarred hands and the broken eye-tooth suggested. "And this morning you did exactly what was best for Calwen. You had a bit of time together without all the machines and the stuff that can get in the way. You held her hand and then you let go. You tried to find the best thing for her – and you did it."

There'd be no more tears. He looked up at me for the first time and wiped the traitorously full eye roughly enough to do it damage. "Right," he said as though I'd made some proposition. "Right. Yes. I – I think I'd better be on my way now. Things to get sorted. Thanks." He reached down out of sight and came up with the forbidden pack of Silk Cut and a big old chromium-plated lighter. Then he stood up and edged past me and walked out, a bit of grey fibrous material clinging to the back of both trouser legs.

Staff Nurse Doran caught me up in the corridor. She was carrying a hot drink in a polystyrene cup that I thought, for one wildly fanciful moment, might be for me. "Is he all right now?" she demanded taking a noisy sip. Her full upper lip exposed and then re-covered the bright, bathroom shine of her overbite. "The next of kin?"

She's pink and plump and from County Kerry and the brogue takes the needle out of many of her remarks. Undeservedly. I always *hope* for the beautiful Hayley Ford, Princess of High Dependency. I get The Doran.

"*All right?* Well he can move again now. He was able to stand up."

"That's all I meant," she said.

Unnoticed, because so small and masked by the Mountain of Mourne, when Doran moved off, I found Bernie Rosco standing in front of me. Bernie is ward-manager on Cardiology so brings me plenty of business. But if it were my last week on earth I'd choose Bernie to be overseeing my end (as opposed to The Doran, say).

"She died, then. The journalist lady."

"Calwen Brinkley?"

"Yeah. Came in last week – fever and productive cough but I thought, what with her history, it might be a red light – "

"Calwen Brinkley? A journalist? I don't think so – that was her father just went out. He –"

Bernie laughed. "Yeah, I know. But she was. We had her in Cardiology for her valve replacement last year. Congenital, I guess. It looked as though she might make it, but there's no guarantee, is there?

69

She was a lovely woman. Sharp as a very sharp thing, but funny with it. What a mouth on her. She worked on *The Guardian* not all that long ago. How about that, huh? Started on the *Chester Chronicle* and made it all the way to Wapping. She came back up here when things started to go pear-shaped 'cos her dad was her only family. Crease you up, she could. What a mouth she had!" he said again, nodding as though in retrospective admiration.

"But her father —"

A hand went up to stroke his own completely shaven skull as though there were Byronic locks to be smoothed into position. "Tell you what, Martin, I'll stop you looking and feeling a complete arse-hole. Let me put you right. Calwen Brinkley was Cal Brinkley. Ask that wife of yours, she'll know. The columnist, right? And off the Saltney council estate — just like me. I didn't remember her at first, because she was that much older and went off to college, but I remember her mum and her dad when I was growing up. We had a good old chin-wag about the Saltney days when she came in before. It was a touch rough even back then." He laughed again but I realised it wasn't something I was meant to join in with. In fact right from the start there'd been an edge to him. Someone else having tweaked his toggle, was my bet, before I'd walked up. "I'm sorry I missed her dad. Just gone, has he?"

He looked around as if even this piece of information, considering the source, might be unreliable. "Nice old bloke, couldn't keep out the bookie's." The eyes sparkled and filled and he waved aside my attempt to answer him. "Gotta go." A blue-clothed streak, emotion-charged, he dodged with a dancer's ease through the on-coming traffic of the forlorn.

v

As if in reward for the successful reanimation of Mr Brinkley there was a note on my desk. It said *From: Nancy Read, To: Martin Kent. Mr Congreve will join you for lunch at 2.10. Please be punctual as he has 20 minutes only.*

I could see her lips, smiling over the mock-formality as she'd written it and again as she'd laid it carefully in the exact centre of my closed lap-top.

The hospital refectory is where – it's an old joke – food goes to die. But I ate there usually because to drive into town seemed like an indulgence too far – as though I was doing a real job and therefore entitled to a meal called lunch in a wine bar or that little Italian place in Lower Bridge Street. Elly thinks I'm living the lie of being a professional man, earning a proper salary, paying his way. I'm not. But if I explained this to her, d'you think I'd ever get it up again?

When Richard sat down beside me there were no overt signs of either of the moods I'd prepared for: belligerence or contrition. On his tray the juice and sandwiches were a dietary swipe at my egg and chips but that was all.

"How're things?" I asked him. The eyes, which far from avoiding mine stared at me frankly, were less inflamed. Even that new blotchiness about them seemed to have faded.

"Strictly speaking that's my line. They're less kind-hearted, the ones I ask. They tell me."

All those characters that Richard could play; today we were *Mr Richard Congreve of The Donns' House, River Walk, Chester – Kings School and Imperial College, Consultant in vascular surgery at The Deva Hospital Trust since 2001, m. Pippa nee Hartley in 1996, 3s. Interests: squash, tennis, opera and theatre.*

(This is the man couldn't stay awake through *Cats*).

A lightweight suit and everything else good-looking, expensive, completed the image – no soiled white coat, no dangling stethoscope for our hero. I could always see how he had risen so quickly and so far. Nature had provided the perfect form for the alpha-male: height, strong facial bones, deep-set but widely spaced eyes. My God, the boy had been a baritone while the rest of us were still waiting for them to drop!

"You're chock-a-block, Nancy said," I offered.

"Mm." He knocked back the juice in one go and refilled the glass from my water bottle. "You don't mind? They'll keep upstairs like a bloody furnace up to the end of the month. Then it's 'to the pole with Captain Scott' till summer kicks in. Sorry I had to dash on Friday. Pip's into some new, fuck-all-use exercise regime. I'd promised to take the boys to the pool. You ever been to the Northgate Arena?"

71

"No."

"Complete bloody nightmare. The boys love it. I won't take them to the health club. They're too badly behaved." Richard always spoke about his children in the detached tone of an uncle or guardian. I suspect he cared about them as deeply as any other parent but would have found the expression of it to someone other than their mother ill-mannered. "So. You OK?"

"Fine."

"How is Elly?"

"Good – she's good. She –"

Nodding wisely, as though confirming his own diagnosis, "One of a kind, Elly," he pronounced. He picked up his glass again and drank the contents. The sandwich, face-down in its plastic pyramid, remained untouched.

"Richard, mate, what's going on?"

"Meaning?"

I leaned back, thinking I might enjoy the moment – after all, I'd been *that close* to winning, hadn't I? "You know in *Guys and Dolls* where Frank Sinatra – he's Nathan Detroit – and he's trying to get Marlon Brando to take his bet? But Marlon Brando says to him, 'What colour tie you wearing?'"

"Polka dot."

"Not him."

He stared me straight in the eye. "Green stripe."

"Too easy. Nathan's wearing a dickie. Normal tie's long enough to appear in peripheral vision."

He shrugged.

"What sort of sandwich is that?"

"Cheese." He turned it over with a grin, another game of black-jack ending in the house bust. "Always have just cheese. Never cheese with. Onion – breath problem. Tomato or cucumber – wind. Salad – soggy bread. Always have cheese – fat and carb to keep me going till late on."

"What's up, Richard?"

"*Nowt.*" He unpeeled his lunch, could have got a laugh out of his first failure to unwrap it but distained to, and started chewing as demonstration. "On a roll, as it happens. You try not to keep score – because, of course, it can easily go the other way. But I can't do a thing wrong at present. Four in a row that *definitely* shouldn't be here. Two safely tucked in upstairs and two more in Another Place –" this is how Richard alluded to the clinic where he performed privately – "all happy as sandboys with their new set of pipes. All of 'em pushing eighty. Howszat? Mike was suggesting if I carry on like this the pensions industry'll be taking out a contract. To off me, you know? We've got to be looking at another twenty-to-thirty years distributed between the four of them. Imagine *Granada Reports!*" he dropped into what he imagined was Northern-ish reporter-speak, "The Chancellor made a statement to The House today on the gunning down of respected vascular surgeon, Richard Congreve, on the doorstep of his Chester home. 'Whilst, of course, we must sympathise with the family and friends of this fine physician and deplore the mindless violence that seems to have taken hold in even the most affluent and civilized of our provincial towns, we have a duty also to consider the bigger picture. Mr Congreve's death will come as a huge relief to those of us entrusted with this nation's economic welfare –' "

I was about to chip in with something like "The pound is up, while in the City –" but he saw it coming. "You going anywhere?" he demanded. "You and Elly, I mean. Summer's on the way."

"We've only just had Easter, haven't we? And no. You?"

"Conference in Milan that falls nicely. There's a possibility of taking Pip with me. She seems to want to go. Old Grendel," this was Pippa's cousin, a meek and wry little woman who worshipped him and his sons, "will have the boys. I thought we'd do one of the lakes. Maggiore's favourite, apparently, at the moment. Como, if not."

"Very nice... for Pip. Are things all right on that score?"

There was always something to tell 'on that score.' Richard had tired of his wife somewhere between the arrival of Adam, their first born and Thomas, their second. It was as mundane as that – so common as to be commonplace. The fragile blonde wife becomes that bit more substantial in motherhood... not just in poundage but in the new, psychic roundness that motherhood imparts: *no, no, let me – I know, it's awful isn't it? And I'm the only one can pacify him!* For a while, joy and

73

pride in paternity will shore up the fractured edifice – all that *he's a really strong personality for such a small thing, grip like a Scottish pawnbroker, just like me at that age, apparently.* But the next child brings no novel nor deeper sensations, though added practical difficulties. Finally came Aaron: sired, according to Elly, in a fit of absent-mindedness.

Richard loved his children in whatever way it was put in him to love. One property of this love was that he wouldn't punish them for his having stopped loving their mother. (Although Richard might have phrased it as *in straining them out into the world their mother had become someone that no man could want,* which in his, Richard's, case, meant could love either). But even Elly had to agree it was estimable that he managed to keep this from them all. It was an interpretation of fatherhood that was becoming rarer. But in Richard's case it had needed the supporting acts of Siân, Gill and Veronique over the years. And now – who?

"As you say," fastidiously he wiped his mouth, then those big, blunt finger-ends with the two paper napkins he'd provided himself with, "very nice for Pip."

"What I said –"

"Oh, yes, what was that?" He was looking around the refectory as he murmured this as though for a colleague he needed to catch a word with – a real colleague such as Clausen or Prof MacFee, both of whom he detested. I could never be accounted one of Richard's co-workers. Everyone around who witnessed us eating together, every hospital employee at every table knew what I was. An old friend of the great man – a friend who'd done something stupid and had to be found a lowly job.

A scrap of gristle off Dr Fantastic's chateaubriand.

"About – you know? Whoever she is. None of my business." If all this was in the genuine spirit of friendship, here was the place to stop – but you can never be sure, even when it's yourself you're listening to. It seems it wasn't. "Heat of battle," I said. "Nothing to do with me, whoever...."

He grinned unconvincingly – no involvement in the upper face – as Staff Nurse Doran passed by with what looked like a couple of new Oriental nurses in tow. I watched Richard as he watched their slim adolescent backs... their sleek honey-coloured legs, tiny feet. Both beautiful. *Two girls in silk kimonos.* Polyester, anyway. But two of them, when one was enough to wrack you with aches.

Grow up, for Chrissake, I told myself – and then, if you were Richard, *how much* would you expect to get away with? "These agency nurses come and go, eh?" I said. "You'd need to be a fast worker. That'd be the problem. I'm just getting on nodding terms by the time they disappear."

He crumpled the plastic sandwich wrapping and seemed surprised to find it crawl along the shiny table-top to reshape itself. His manner was impossible to read. "It's all in the foot size," he said, "did you know that?"

"What?"

"Pelvic width. Small shoe-size," – ah, of course, it was that old, smutty, schoolboy challenge – "difficult childbirth. Pip, now, you'd think on the slight-side – or was, five three, but," he held up an index finger, "size six feet. So, three boys, easy as pie. Like shelling peas, she always says. You remember Aaron was nearly ten pounds? Took her half an hour. In fact, I almost had to do the honours in the morning room."

I tried to join in. "She'd have been better off with the vet."

"Too bloody true. I was scared witless. It's just as well Pippa's an old hand at it."

The Chinese girls settled close by, twittering like songbirds before The Doran's sour expression.

"When Irish eyes are smiling, eh? It'll rain pig-shit."

"Richard, if there is anything –"

"*What?*" Condescension, always his strong suit, I found the cruellest shot: "I think you must have me confused with one of your punters." Abruptly he jumped to his feet. "Be a sport, Martin. Fuck off." He began to walk away – a circuitous route that would have taken him past the ill-matched threesome; instead he turned back. "It worked though, didn't it?"

"Did it?"

"Well, you tell me. I thought I might be coming a cropper. That would be for the first time this year. Not that I keep count, of course."

"Course not."

"I'll tell you what – I can do something for you. How would this be? Why don't you and Elly have the cottage for a week? You've never been. You'll like it. It has all mod cons. Very cosy. It's bang on the coast – Aberhiw. And not a caravan in sight."

Strangely the little nurses had also risen as though in answer to Richard's latent, unquenchable masculine energy. Whatever purpose or errand they believed themselves engaged in, I knew better. It made me ungracious. "I could ask Elly if she fancies it..."

"That's up to you, dull-boy. I'm only providing the venue."

"If you're sure –"

"I wouldn't have offered otherwise. Take a week in summer. Put it in your diary. You'll need to get leave booked. Don't forget."

I began with the problem of recall. It seems that in the laying down of memories, an independent and completely separate set of variables is brought into play from what runs your conscious mind. And not all the bloody willpower in the universe can get them to change. Once, one broiling afternoon in a land far away, there was me and a well-nourished, insolent sixteen-year-old kid. The heat was extreme and I *think* it was insolence. I can repeat the exact words spoken by us both. His were the more pungent.

This vision of Richard, this tableau, was all set to be a sticker; I knew it even as I watched. And I was bang on.

He's distributed his morsel of *delice*, is leaving alone – and yet at the swing doors he turns in my direction again. Is he about to shout above the hubbub of the room, a final word regarding the arrangements, a good-bud tip? But no, Doran's charges have caught him up. Two girls in pale green polyester – both beautiful, one a gazelle.

They make eye-contact, all right: with him, with each other.

The other Richard, the decent-bloke – the one with little wifey Pippa nestled into his side – should get down out of that picture frame at this point. Should confront the bastard. Except I haven't seen the photo yet. It's a couple of months forward at the cottage. I've no idea what's in store him, for Pippa.

Richard holds open the double doors. His reach extends in both directions. It's spread wide in exaggerated courtesy, so that the child-like pair pass beneath his arms. And of course, all this whilst he's whispering some remark, private to the threesome, that sends the nurses out of sight, raucous with laughter.

A shocking response from the demure.

PART 3

A single beachcomber today.

If any window overlooked the curve of shingle it would reveal the shore's least compelling aspect on show. Waves slapping high up on the largest aggregate. High tide. Recent wild weather has procured useful pickings for the land, but it's passed over now. In the dirty-grey foam, nothing of value is offered: a fibre-glass splinter of hull from an ex-pleasure craft, a red and white ball, dented from the round. .

The walker makes painful progress along this edge, sliding, stumbling like an inebriate, brought to a sudden halt by the turning of a foot as it plunges between the loose stones. However often a fall seems certain, he will not look. Instead he searches the perfect calmness that is Aberhiw Bay this morning, filled with an exhausted sea. But even a calm surface is in continuing motion. A dip of slack water suggests a shape that grabs his gaze – until it is caulked from below and is replaced, always at the limit of vision, by another more promising illusion. This too fizzles to nothing even as the eyes focus.

Miles out, a smudge of deeper grey is an island or a huge vessel. To be certain he would need to watch, to check its changing position or lack of it. His head flicks north, west, south and then, from a fumbling at his own chest, a pair of binoculars are brought up to his face. Now, surely, he will examine that dark silhouette, the only feature between an empty sea and a birdless sky? But he sweeps the lenses over the water, up the chink in the low cliff wall where a brown stream breaks through, back to the far point, to the spur of rock that in weeks to come the porpoise-pod will use as its waymark. Closer and closer to the beach he scans – so near himself, so near his own feet, that it's almost comical to watch.

i

It began the night of the storm. Well no. Not true. It *really* began when my Great Aunt Dulcie went mad.

I had this Great Aunt Dulcie who everyone said I was the image of, being blue-eyed and blonde. I was even christened Pippa Dulcie for her. Dreadful, I know. By the time I was taking notice, her hair (still down to her shoulder blades) was grey-mouse. But I never minded the comparison. Not a tall woman but she was always impressive somehow. 'Held herself well' was how old people, like my parents, would've described it. Not beautiful, barely pretty. I like to think she was attractive in that way I've tried to follow on with, making the best of what you've got.

When I was around eight or maybe nine (not at boarding school yet, so less than eleven) she went mad. I can picture the onset – that first show of madness – as clearly as if it were yesterday. Here's Great Aunt Dulcie walking into our dining room. I think Daddy must have just picked her up from the station because he was with her. There was a suitcase somewhere in the background, somewhere in this picture, I have, I mean. Great Aunt Dulcie came striding into the dining room in our Knutsford house, where Mummy and I were playing *Find the Lady*. The coal-fire was spitting and bubbling tar – and there's good old Daddy probably still in the hall at this point but trying to jolly things along. He'd be saying, "Are you winning, Pippa?" and, "Dulcie's train was bang on time – wonders never cease! – but the whole world's driving to Alderley Edge today."

There wasn't any response to our greeting. Mine would've been genuine because I really liked the old lady and we were a bit short on relations. I think Mummy will've tried something like, "Well, what d'you think of her, Aunt Dulcie? Hasn't Pippa grown?" I hadn't of course but everyone Mummy tried it on used to agree for form's sake.

Not Great Aunt Dulcie.

Instead she looked carefully at each of us, paying especial attention to my mother and the least to me. Mummy reached out her hand. I think it was a first step to drawing her forward for a peck on the cheek. That's all it would've been because we didn't go in for hugs and kisses. But the touch seemed to have an amazing effect – well, not just amazing, an absolutely extraordinary effect.

First a series of shivers ran through my aunt's body although these could've been just the normal sort that old ladies produce at will. (Usually they're a warning of a complaint about drafts). But when this was over and done with she fell to her knees, right there in the bit of clear space between the Ercol carver and the oak dresser. No one else in the room moved, which was reasonable enough. There was no question of this being a fainting fit. She'd smoothed the fawn pleats of her jersey skirt as she dropped and gave them a little flick at the back as she landed. It spread a neat, corrugated semi-circle of jersey over her calves. Only when the skirt was taken good care of did she raise her arms to heaven and, in an absolutely deafening bellow, demand, "Oh Lord, why must evil descend upon the righteous?"

You never really know, do you? Not when you're eight or maybe nine.

Mummy and Daddy were turned to stone. Great Aunt Dulcie now screwed up her eyes – in fact her whole face – into a kind of ecstatic wince and began to sway from side to side, bending into the rhythm stiffly from the waist. I stood there with them. I just wasn't sure.

What if this was a real thing going on between Aunt Dulcie and God?

It could be that this sort of behaviour was if not common, then not uncommon.

A child's knowledge is so patchy. It might be the done thing amongst a whole host of different people suddenly to break off what they were about – for a tête à tête with Our Father. It might happen to farmers, say, or women who made Christmas crackers or West Indians – or hairdressers. For all I knew, while snipping away at a fringe, one of them might suddenly become the chosen one and then have to drop everything for a chat.

Perhaps He got lonely.

In our dining room still nobody spoke or moved.

"Oh Lord, *why?*" Dulcie demanded. It sounded actually as though she might be getting a tad cross with the Almighty now.

The moment seemed to spread out and yet stay the same piece of time. The only way I can describe it is as though a single second had been pulled like plasticine, longer and longer, thinner and thinner, rather than just being a tick of the clock that gave way to the next. After a bit more of this, the swaying and the grimacing I mean, I was certain of one thing. God wasn't going to reply. That took the zest out of it for me, I'm afraid. The zing. Because just for a while I really did think it was a possibility. I really did believe a deep, thrilling voice from somewhere (say, just above the plaster rose in the dining room ceiling) might pronounce, "No evil shall descend upon the righteous in this house, Dulcie. And by the way, there's no need to shout. It's rude." But the hope died. It became just another of my dried-up wishes – like being able to talk to the sparrows and train them not to fly off when I was putting out seed.

Daddy dropped Aunt Dulcie's suitcase and came properly into the room. He and my mother exchanged looks and then he put his arm around my shoulders and said something like, "Come on sweetheart, let's take the luggage upstairs." Mummy seemed released from the same spell and went and knelt down on the carpet next to poor old Dulcie. She whispered, "Oh dear, you must be tired. Why don't I get you settled here by the fire and then –" I can remember her throwing one last imploring look in my father's direction as I was hustled out, "get you some tea."

What with trying to remove a child from the room and pick up the suitcase he'd dropped, Daddy wasn't able to get the door closed in time – not in time to prevent my hearing Aunt Dulcie give a terrible shriek and start again on her interrogation of the Lord. "Why," she wanted to know now, "was this good woman to be destined for torment? Why must grief be heaped upon her –"

The rest was cut off.

We carried the cases up to the guest room. I could picture it as I climbed, just as I'd left it that morning. It had pale grey walls and a maroon quilt-cover and a vase of freshly-cut, ginger chrysanthemums – cut by me from the garden. Daddy made a great, put-on fuss about the weight of the big old monstrosity of a bag that had fallen to him. He rested on the half-landing, panting and wiping his forehead. I followed with my aunt's smaller vanity case (which I inherited and treasure still).

My father was shaken, I could tell. I, I'm sorry to admit, was absolutely delighted and hoping for more of the same. A lot more. You quickly forget, once grown-up, the thrill of seeing adults (but not your parents) behaving badly. It seemed a real possibility that before bedtime Aunt Dulcie would have another go at God. She might demand to know why He'd ever bothered to invent porridge. Or those useless hair-grips – although, come to think of it they *were* good for sticking in your ears and seeing if you could get wax out.

Aunt Dulcie was got to bed somehow while I was sent to "play those records of yours". *The Bay City Rollers* – to this day anything tartan reminds me of mental problems. A doctor must've been called while I was leaping about to *You Made Me Believe In Magic*. In the morning she came down, quiet, but not apologetic. It would certainly have been expected from me post *scene*. Her hands shook. She had difficulty buttering her toast – but the only bit of strangeness (which I gobbled up like one of those hungry sparrows) was her saying to my mother, "Pass the marzipan, Anne, will you?" and when my mother handed her the jar of Robertson's Silver Shred, spooning it out without comment.

In the afternoon I found her fast asleep on the sitting room sofa. Her mottled hands were folded neatly across her wool skirt and holding her teeth.

Two people, I remember, called late the next day. It was going dark when she drove away with them. We turned out, the three of us, to wave her off at the front door just as if it had been a normal good-bye. "Bye-bye." "Yes!" "Have a safe trip."

Great Aunt Dulcie (she was settled in the back with a woman in a navy coat) yawned and closed her eyes. The man in the driving seat – some sort of warder or just a tough-looking nurse? – had a badly shaved neck. It fascinated me, that neck. Poor Dulcie was nearly a supporting act by the time they left, on account of that neck. It was thick and red and had one huge pimple, just breaking out, like a rosy toadstool pushing up through turf.

You'll wonder why it was all so important – why I'm able to report this sort of detail. Obviously because I recalled it so often. Still do. It seems my old aunt – for no reason anyone could explain, at least not to me – had developed religious mania. Praying and talking about Good and Evil as though they were real things was fine in morning assembly, I now found. Fine when slotted between "Jesus Loves Me, This I Know" and an announcement about having your money in before Friday for the trip to Beatrix Potter's Cottage. *Not fine* at any other time – in fact downright bad manners.

Poor Dulcie.

Poor everyone else.

She had a spell in an institution near Manchester, was released, cured – was re-admitted. Out on the loose a second time she became an absolute pest to the poor priest in the Cheshire town where she lived. It must've been specially annoying for him because she'd never shown any interest in the church in all her previous sixty-something years. Before the end she'd be arrested for walking along the hard shoulder of the M6 singing excerpts from the Saint Matthew Passion. She still had most of the soprano part from her musical youth with the Congleton and Macclesfield Choral Society. She died – it'd be only about eighteen months ago – in a nursing home, aged ninety-one. Crazy as a loon, everyone agreed.

But she was so right, so justified, in her complaint to God, as it turned out. My mother, "this good woman", must have already been touched then by breast cancer. It would eat her up and kill her in *less* than eighteen months. I was only eight, or maybe nine, that afternoon. Probably not even Adam's (my eldest's) age. But in two more years I'd be off to boarding school with my mother's photograph in a little ebony frame.

Although people don't say it, now that I'm in my thirties, I'm looking more and more like Great Aunt Dulcie, what with the blonde hair right the way down my back, the blue eyes.

Certainly the way my life's shaping up, I think I may go mad.

ii

I can never work out how they do Easter, can you? Richard, my husband, who makes a point of knowing nothing that he's labelled UNIMPORTANT gave a kind of snort when I asked him. So in answer to, "How do they manage to get Easter at the end of March this year? I mean how do they decide that's when it will be?" he says, "There's a formula." And when I ask, "What is it?" he says, "Why on earth would anyone want to clutter up their brain with that one?"

Easter was early, anyway. Which meant it happened just after Easter.

Because Richard is so IMPORTANT – and skilled at what he does – he seems to spend less time at the hospital now. He spends less time doing what has made him so important and which he is so skilled at. That weekend he'd been speaking at a conference in Edinburgh – or he may have been just attending it, because I don't remember that tense build-up, when 'I am trying to produce a paper, here' would ring through the house. But handsome Edinburgh is stuck in my mind. It was where we began our honeymoon, just less than ten years ago, in the Osborne, a lovely old hotel. The Osborne had all those things I bet Great Aunt Dulcie would've adored, like spotless damask table cloths, heavy old silver cutlery, ancient waiters. But he wouldn't be back there, not Richard, not in *our* room with the giant Edwardian wardrobe that had gargoyles. Even if it still existed. The Steiner-Holtz Corporation had taken over a new country-club outside the city – he said.

Three days away, back on Sunday, but overnight.

At one-thirty Monday morning he woke me with a call: delays, confusion, no sure arrival time in Chester. There was not a sound in the background and I could visualise the train in some dark siding with its sleeping passengers – or more likely its cross, not-sleeping passengers. Just fighting my way out of a bad dream, I managed to irritate him with hardly any effort at all.

"Where are you, then?" I said.

"What do you me-an?" That's how it came out – two syllables.

"What?"

"I said, what do you mean? What does it matter where I am – where *we* are?"

That's when I imagined the dark railway backwater.

"Well, it doesn't – I just wondered how far away you were. From home. What time –?"

"I'll probably go straight to the hospital, have a shower and get cracking there."

His very precise voice seemed to be coming from much further away than the Scottish borders – the Shetlands perhaps – and was *especially* clipped. And then, in the silence that was left at the end of *there,* I caught a hint, the merest whisper of – what was it now? A hiss. A shu–sh–sh. Like escaping steam. Steam, as in steam-train.

I realised I must be falling back into the dream again. I sat up properly, tried to shake the sleepiness out of my head.

"But you'll be exhausted. Come back home first – can't you?"

"It's only clinic," he snapped. "I'm not going to doze off with somebody on the table."

So he – Richard – was due home on a drizzling Monday evening. The weekend had been true to the forecast. All the promised, early sunshine had arrived and with it the boys' first trip of the year to the zoo. Another missed Sunday, a new week started and he'd not set foot in his own house. Now it was a vile night which, to be honest, I think can add as much again to the misery of any sort of upset. The rain had been beating on the front face of the house since mid-afternoon and rattling every one of its original casements till I thought I'd start screaming. I went from one to the next, ramming in bits of tissue paper. It was as though a giant was playing a percussion piece on the building – and a pretty mean one at that. Perhaps it was 'his 'Orrible Symphony' I told Tom and Adam (my boys).

"Whack, whack, whack on the windows, rap, rap, rap on the letter-box!"

A bit not-clever that turned out, because it wound them up still tighter. That giant had them whizzing round the house hammering on anything that'd make a noise. It wasn't all percussion either. The woodwind joined in and blew syncopated puffs of soot down the morning room chimney. This had never happened before – and we've been in the place three years last Christmas. I got so sick of it I taped two copies of *The Lancet* across the opening, having thoughtlessly recycled *The Sunday Times.* Later Richard would explain how the soot-fall was because the storm came in from very nearly due west, instead of north-west as usual. It's why that family were killed in their car near Llangollen – *and* that mother and child in County Wexford, was it? He said you could have drawn one single line through our house in Chester *straight through the fatalities*. But that was next day, the geography lesson. Till then, he was too angry. I'd used this month's *Lancet* which he hadn't had a chance to read. That was his excuse.

Anyway the typhoon or whatever it was just kept on coming and when it died down, it was only to come bursting back. Here's another movement in the giant's symphony and not adagio. It drove the boys wild – I've said that, haven't I? Well wilder then. Having managed to get back from school with a car-full of shrieking banshees – every time some bit of rubbish hit the windscreen they cheered and whooped – there was no way they'd settle for tea and homework. They were up in the playroom in the attic one moment, down two flights and raiding the kitchen for ice-cream and canned drinks the next. "Whatever you're living on these days, don't slop it up the stairs," I threatened, "or Daddy'll have us all on sparkling water for the next month." Even Aaron, who to be honest, *is* the World's Perfectest Baby, even Aaron had been running a temperature – it had come on with the storm – and he was now alternatively moping and grizzling. His eyes had grown enormous, just like a little wild animal's, scared of the weather.

But I felt it too – unless the baby was picking it up from me. There was this scratchiness about the air, as though something stinging was being carried along in it – and no amount of raining could wash it out.

Richard was so late.

I actually got scared and had a neurotic-type flash which always brought Great Aunt Dulcie to mind. In it I saw his new shiny Jaguar crumpled under one of the big old lime trees down the hospital drive and that gritty rain washing over the wreckage and flowing in a river to the road, all bloody. *Pull yourself together, Pippa,* I thought, *and get yourself a drink* – which I did. But I still shivered as I sat at the kitchen table and downed it. When I rinsed the glass under the tap I realised it had been Richard's Oloroso, which we only keep for guests and I dislike. I had to have a piece of Galaxy for the taste.

Eight came and went. I bribed Adam and Tom to bathe and get ready for bed by the promise of the first episode of the new *Celebrity Shootout* – which was *the* thing amongst Adam's age group last year –

before lights out. They lay under their quilts, only two blond heads and two noses on show staring up at the far corner, instantly lost to anything I might say to them now. The unmistakable Barry Braddock, dressed in white from head to foot, was puffing around some derelict buildings with an impressive gun held out ahead of his stomach. Off camera what sounded like an old-fashioned metal dustbin being kicked over (who had metal dustbins these days?) made him freeze. The screen filled with a close-up of his face before blanking out as the credits rolled. I settled onto a corner of Tom's bed, ignored. They lay there chanting "Barry Braddick, Barry Brad*dick!*" and giggling.

"Don't be rude," I told them. He is though. I can't stand the little squirt, either.

"So what's it all about?"

Joyful, pitying looks were exchanged. Only your own children can do this without causing you any real harm. Adam is the older but, as usual, he let Tom start, let him have a stab at it before he felt the need to take over. "We-ell," Tom said, "it's all going to-o keep being in this really spooky old place. With houses that nobody lives in."

"It's a village," Adam corrected. "A village that died."

"A deserted village?"

They agreed.

A whole deserted village? Were there still such places in the current property market? More likely they'd had to build it specially.

"And all these boys and girls —"

"Famous boys and girls," Adam said.

"Get a load of chocolate and drinks —"

"And other food."

"And they have to live there and do things they're told to do until somebody shoots them. Every time somebody gets shot — and then they have to leave and go out."

"But," Adam seemed to feel this so important he leaned forward (just as I remember Daddy doing, grasping the essential point with a closed hand), "but they can shoot people too. So they don't *have* to get shot. Not if they shoot the other person first. Splat!" Most of him had to come back out from under the covers to go with this noise. "Splat! Splat!" His rosy face flushed to the roots of his hair — and for the very first time I noticed how his face had lengthened. It was a *boy*'s face, not a round pink child's face, like Tom's — who, of course, was up in an instant to join in.

"That's enough of that, thank you very much!"

"Spu-ul-at!" Tom shrieked.

I stared. "*Thank-you.*"

"And you can ring up and bet on who's next to get shot."

"Well you two *certainly* won't be ringing up."

"It's only pretend shooting," Adam said to maintain dignity. "With paint." And then as they wriggled back down and I turned off the overhead light, "It's kill or be killed. Those are the rules. Kill or be killed."

Nine o'clock came. *You can ring up.* I thought: I'm going to ring him, now. I'm going to commit the ultimate misdemeanour and open the door a crack. I'm going to stick my head over the threshold into that other world. The real and important world of Richard's work.

Determined, I stood in the morning room, the phone in hand — you see, being the only child of elderly parents I wasn't trained in being left out. There were never evenings when I was sent early to bed, listening to party noises filter up through the bedroom floor. Not me. I was down there with a place set at the table, listening to Ray Wakefield's stories of the stamp dealing business — or Mr and Mrs Ferguson bickering over whether Knutsford was now impossible to live in thanks to the growth of Manchester airport. The cheese was cleared away and the cards brought out and still I'd be allowed to linger at my father's side and practise my poker face when he drew a really fine hand. "What d'you think, Pippa?" he'd stage-whisper. I never answered, waiting instead with mounting excitement and pride for his "Six no-trumps" in that deep, confident voice that I could hear *and feel,* my shoulder pressed up against his chest.

Years later it came as a shock that the man I married intended to teach me how to be excluded. How to be invisible.

"I'd rather you never rang me at work but if you absolutely *have to,* ring Nancy. And — and," he could forecast objections, "if Nancy's not there and I am, then it's probably so bloody pressing, the last thing I need is a personal call."

Perhaps I'd be lucky. Perhaps Richard would be in HDU and that lovely boy, Bernie would pick up. Say something funny or sweet. When he was leaving our house after a party once, he stopped and said, "Never forget, Pippa – you're on the side of light." Nice, whatever it meant.

I dialled 0, which after all commits you to nothing, and then one which is almost nothing and two, and then double four – twice lucky, my lucky numbers. My finger hovered over the eight, the slightest of pressure and somehow, electronically (to be honest I've not an inkling how) I'd be a step closer to my missing husband – and then I caught my reflection in the mirror over fireplace. And – oh, God, why did she have to choose this moment to put in an appearance? – there, looking back at me, stood Dulcie.

Not a ghost. The figure that stared back – that small fair woman, the white phone clasped in one hand as though it were a weapon, one finger still hovering over the eight button – that was me *and* it was Dulcie.

Tired, that's what I was – and all cramped up around the neck and shoulders with worry. Very ageing, everybody knows that. But out of the corner of my eye I watched Dulcie replace the receiver and Great Aunt Dulcie shake her long colourless hair.

The morning room chimney gave one last *scherzando* toot of black.

The Storm Giant's breath was settling on a pale carpet that I'd known from the moment it was laid wouldn't prove very practical. Richard's key probed the lock and I checked on the sleeping Aaron before running out into the hall. There must've been guilt written all over me.

A tall man was wiping his feet on the coconut matting, one foot, change and then back to the first. It was done mechanically, if very thoroughly, all the time looking not at his shoes but at some point near the foot of the staircase – where there was nothing. As he turned towards me I saw his face was streaming with raindrops and very red and stiff with the cold. "Oh, am I glad to see you!" I said.

I meant to go straight and put my arms around him but I found, somehow, they just stayed down there at my sides.

He brought the outside in with him in a gust, a by-blow. High up in the house a door slammed, loud as a thunder clap and Richard jumped, dropping his keys.

Aaron, only just quiet, started up again.

"Sorry," Richard said, "How many times have I told them about that play-room door?" and then, locating the downstairs origin of the wailing, "Where is he?"

"I put him down on the sofa in the morning room –"

"What on earth for?" Over his suit, he had on a raincoat, darkened and drenched right through to the lining. He struggled out of it and handed it me. "Thanks."

I carried it off to hang in the cloakroom saying, "Because he's not well – been running a temperature all day." I expected him to go to Aaron but when I came back his Louis Vuitton bag lay where he'd thrown it. Beyond it there he was, framed in the sitting room doorway, just adding a splash of tonic to something else colourless.

"We're out of gin."

"What's that then?"

"Vodka – I can't stand the bloody stuff."

I burst out laughing. "Well nobody's forcing you to drink it!"

He threw himself down in a chair.

Aaron's cry changed from disappointed to desperate and I turned to go to him. But by some trick – his lungs were starting to become congested by this time with whatever bug would torment him for the whole of the next week – anyway, he drew breath and there was one of those pauses that you get with babies. They're the prelude to a really heart-felt wail. And (though I was out in the hall and the Storm Giant was still fumbling about with the roof, getting his fingernails under the slates now) and there were all those other sounds around me like the faraway mumble of the boys TV and the hum of the extractor fan as it tried to whisk away the evidence of our desiccating meal and even the heavy cotton of my trousers as the legs rubbed together, all this and yet I still heard it.

"Just fuck-off Pip," Richard muttered. Then there was the chink of his glass, not ice but a mistimed contact of his teeth on the rim.

What would you do?

I hesitated. By the time I'd run and snatched up Aaron and curled back down with him on the sofa, his body along my thighs and his burning little head against my collar bone, I could believe I hadn't heard it. I must've made a mistake.

He, Richard, wandered in after a while having waited (I was sure) until Aaron's whimpering subsided. Then he came and knelt down and put a hand on his forehead. "Has he had plenty of fluids?"

"He's had just drinks all day," I said, nettled by that *fluids* as though this wasn't his own child.

Aaron was going to be sandy. That was well-established already, whereas the first two are blond. The fine down on his baby cheeks with its forward nap, in Aaron's case, was gold. Adam's and Tom's had been pure silver. How could Richard be inches apart from that child (a child that was wearing his Congreve colours like a little page-boy wearing livery) and say *fluids* in that just-fact-gathering, medical way? I know I've read it's all imaginary, this parent in the face of the child thing. But I could make out in miniature under Aaron's flushed face Richard's bones. Couldn't he? We watched together as he slid back down into a troubled sleep, his eyes rolling and a bubble forming and bursting, forming and collapsing under his blocked-up nose.

"He snores like a pig," Richard said.

When I had him, when I came home with him from the hospital and Martin and Elly were in for a first look (as though they cared!) I heard Richard say to Elly. "Yes, he is, isn't he? A bit like a Tamworth piglet, I thought." Just to make Elly laugh. And it did.

At least he took a clenched baby-fist in his own. Far from the long delicate-fingered job people think of as a surgeon's hand, it's big and thick and ruddy as a navvy's. It's manual labour, fixing folk.

But *Fuck off, Pip,* I heard him say over and over in my head until it had lost any chance of being misheard. My pulse raced like little Aaron's to its rapid double-beat.

…Fuck off, fuck off, fuck off, fuck off.
Fuck off, fuck off, fuck off, Pip.

iii

I suppose we must've eaten. I suppose we prepared for and went to bed.

And the storm followed us up.

The warmth I could feel in the trapped air along my right side was coming off a stranger. This was someone I didn't know at all and he'd got into the house where I and my children lived....

The moment passed. His stomach rumbled in an acid-throwing contest with the dry, four-hour baked lasagne. Good, I thought. Richard's stomach, Richard's total lack of concern at forking down a ruined meal as fuel. The rain beating on the oh so quaint rippled window panes and the boys, disappointed and dismissed to sleep and the blackened curls of cheese and pasta welded to the dish-sides, none of it mattered to him. It had all stopped mattering on one particular day. There would have been a day on the calendar if anyone had thought to record it, when I was doing – something. A date – just some date, like Easter, that I couldn't ever have predicted. Even if Richard could've brought himself to explain it. Because squatting down before his son (I realised now) his mind had been elsewhere. He'd come home all right – but not, not really.

It was the early hours before the storm finally moved on to some other lucky householders. When it took off from Chester it knocked down tree after tree in Delamere forest out on the Cheshire plain and killed its final victim in Derby next morning. It was, according to the experts, "related to Hurricane Irma, in that it was a minor part of the same weather system". While Irma's little sister still hung around, Richard and I lay side by side beneath the quilt, not sleeping and not touching. We were both alert to every rolling bit of rubbish outside, flinching at each bang, crash and scrape. Those ornamental, olde worlde bins (considered suitable by the council for the Victorian walks along the river bank) had proved themselves not up to it. They hadn't been able to meet the challenge of a twenty-first century hurricanette.

"He'll be fine now," Richard whispered. "For God's sake don't go staying awake, listening to every snuffle. It's just a cold." Aaron's cot was in a box-room off our bedroom. Its existence was about the only convenient oddity in the whole damn house.

"D'you want me to push his door to?"

"Of course not."

He shifted further away, stretched until he touched the footboard in that familiar ritual of relaxation.

"Was it worth it?"

"*What?*"

"Going to the conference."

"Oh." Long pause. "Yes. It seems –" a yawn cut in and he mumbled a few words that ended, "more than a day ago, now."

"You never said why you were so late."

"Work. For Christ's sake Pip, what d'you think I'm doing?"

"It's just that – that you usually say if you'll be late," I realised now that Aaron's wasn't the only door ajar. I found I hadn't got the nerve to push against another door, one that had half-opened with that *Fuck off, Pip*.

If that's what I'd heard.

"A woman was stabbed in the chest – if you want to know. I was just leaving. Mike was on but he's got this bug and looked like death. I asked him if he wanted me to hang on and he actually said he did, so you can tell how bad he must've been feeling." I could sense him grinning in the dark, or thought I could. "Think what that must've cost him."

"Did it go well?"

"Not for her. There was just too much to do when I got in… and – complete mess, anyhow. Bloody miracle she made it into theatre really."

"Was she young?"

"No! Late fifties – there was that as well… Husband *didn't do it*, amazingly."

Where was I to go from here?

Nothing is ever just itself. Richard's last bit of information wasn't only filling me in because I'd shown an interest, just as the row we were cooking up between us wasn't just about this night or this long weekend that had spread itself out into Monday.

Like the bed we were lying apart in wasn't just a bed. It wasn't any old inlaid mahogany headboard and footboard with boxwood lining.

Not any old slatted base supporting its specially sprung mattress for a tall man who spent his working life bent over a table and suffered lower back pain – and which I'd found out about and had made specially to help with. Twenty-four hours in the past, it was the bed I'd smoothed clean linen over, expecting my husband home.

It was the bed I'd conceived Aaron in two years and a bit ago.

In the close darkness Richard sighed and I hoped it was nothing apart from being worn out because if it were anything else –

I could feel the misery of that else like a stitch, same place as last time.

Gill, her name was. I never saw her. I never talked to anyone who had seen her. I heard her say just six words on the extension. They were "See you there, then", and "Be good".

She told my husband to be good. She said words that were meant to imply something special to my husband, something more than they meant to anyone else. Her and my husband, either end of this short word-chain. Each of them pulling it tight. Just a short chain, just a few words.

Husband didn't do it, amazingly.

It amazed the hell out of me.

What can soothe a pain when nothing can soothe the pain? Another, bigger pain, of course! If you have an aching tooth you can always prod it into absolute agony with your tongue.

"Aaron's been poorly, and just got worse as the day's gone on," I said. "I'm not being neurotic. When you've got a child sick and your husband's a doctor, you really look forward to having him home – sharing the grief, you know?"

"Yes."

As if by telepathy a whimpery sort of cough filtered through from the box room. Against the two grey rectangles of the windows I had this vision (very close-up) of Aaron's big blue eyes. They had just flicked open and were staring hard at whatever sort of demon babies watched when you abandoned them, all alone and vulnerable in the back of the cave. All those terrified babies – thousands, millions of babies whimpering away, never able to say what it was frightening them. Just that it was slithering over the floor across to them and threatening to stop their little hearts. What was after Aaron? I guessed for him. It'd be khaki-coloured, stinking, poison-fanged, long-nosed. It crept in to snaffle the infants of absent parents. As an almost-orphan in my school dorm, it had come for me. Or rather come back for me and I had remembered it and wet myself with fear. And *I* was big enough to get up, run away (not that I could really, of course) scream out, tell somebody (not that I ever did).

"D'you remember Great Aunt Dulcie?"

Richard groaned and pulled the quilt up over one shoulder – it was an old tennis injury and could give him gyp if chilled. Our accumulated heat was lost to me in the movement and new, chill air replaced it. My pyjamas felt thin – just one more item not up to the job.

"Pip, of course I remember your Great Aunt Dulcie. Because although I was never lucky enough to meet dear old Dulcie – I *believe* I have. No, I know I have." His voice was normal in volume – not whispering, just conversational – but wrong, also. Some wrong tone was being used – and it was fast, much too fast. The sentences were fired off one after another. I guessed I was hearing the dregs of whatever he'd taken to stay awake today, or yesterday – wherever we were with days. One quick in-breath and then: "You tell stories about her so bloody often, I must recognise all the key events in her life now. I could sit a bloody exam. Running away from home, a spell on the stage, then that chap – Grainger, wasn't it? – who owned the Crewe Variety Theatre. You could tell me now she came to our wedding and I'd expect to find her on the photographs even though, *as we both know*, they'd locked her up again by that time."

This could have sounded moderately funny. It didn't.

"No, listen. It's that thing about – you know, her knowing about Mummy and the cancer."

"How many times, for Christ's sake? *She didn't know.* She was just getting into her mania and your mother just happened along. As a stimulus to a bit of acting out. Cases like that – all the time, all the bloody time – you find they'll be doing trial runs of nuttiness on family or friends. And that's ages before they present with symptoms. It's the sense of security gives them license. A case of I'm-home-they'll-put-up-with-it. We've been through all this –"

"No, please," I said. I had to stop him. Just as with the boys, I knew without working it out that it was bad for him, to go bowling along with his own anger. Him and this huge snowball of fury at so many things, gathering speed. Some of it was at me – plainly. And I had my own anger but if the two joined forces there'd be no stopping us. The avalanche hits the valley – and then there are the after-effects. People never understand about Richard and his temper. What you have to do is stand in its way. I bet Gill never knew how to do it – not Gill with that cocky little *Be good*. "Please! Richard. It's a real fear I have," I said. "What if one day I touch Adam or Tom or... or Aaron and whatever it was, that thing Great Aunt Dulcie felt, what if I feel it about one of the boys? A blinding flash or electric shock or something worse. I don't know what she felt. So what if one day I experience this something – and I just *know*. All afternoon I've been feeling worse and worse about Aaron and then about you being so late – and then about everything together. As though – I can't explain – it was terrible."

"Pip!" It's an odd thing when a couple are lying together in the blackness staring at the invisible ceiling and one of them shouts at the other – but just keeps looking straight upward. "You're being morbid. A day spent looking after a small child –"

"He's not a small child – *he's our baby*."

"Hardly a baby anymore. Eighteen months. Don't try to keep him a baby, will you? Just because he's the last."

You learn something new every night, don't you?

"Be sensible. You've gone from a... from a –" the tiredness was weighing down every syllable now – which was better than the other. The search for a hardly-used describing word was almost beyond him. There was a wait long enough for it to suggest, *Why are you doing this to me? Why now?* which was a huge improvement.

A pity it was also long enough for me to recall *Fuck off, fuck off, fuck off Pip.* "You've gone from an old woman's non-existent gift of second sight to – to thinking one day you'll start having visions yourself. Every mother worries over her children."

The statement, the words themselves, came across as patronising. But the tone – that was at odds with the verbal brush-off. The tone was barely controlled – pleading almost. What could he want? Of me? I was always the one who had to ask.

But of course. He wanted me to disappear – to *fuck off, Pip*.

"Mothers worry about their children. I'd never have guessed."

"I've had it, OK? Sleep. Before dawn, preferably."

I think the mention of it must have given us a jolt, a reminder of the outside world. In the quiet we realised the storm had passed over. There was a wind still, rattling a window, but only above us, only a playroom window, now, right at the top of the house. The exciting, wonder-what-it'll-go-for-next sort of storm, had gone on its way. I felt his weariness, greater than his own weight, pulling him down into the bed.

Perhaps it was the mention of dawn. *Never let the sun go down on a quarrel,* my mother had so often said. She'd draw me to her as I lay, martyred and sullen, all stiff with some kiddy-resentment. *Let's kiss and make up, now.*

Richard had always possessed the knack of clutching at sleep, quickly and greedily. It was, he claimed, a "defining ability". Those that didn't have it could never hope to survive a medical apprenticeship with its end-to-end shifts. Now his breathing become slower and deeper although at the low point of each breath there was a slight catch, reminding me of a child that had cried itself to sleep.

Had I ever seen him so exhausted? Carefully, so as not to interrupt his downward slide into those first dreams – the ones that you always forget – I slid my hand across the space between us, laid my palm gently on his upper arm. I touched him for the first time since he'd come home.

And then it happened.

I found out what had dropped an old lady to her knees.

iv

Elly Kent wouldn't have been my first choice as confidant. Elly was the sort of friend you have for years (in this case since Richard and I got engaged) but you never know any better. For well over a decade it had been Elly and Martin, Richard and Pippa – but it was a foursome that always left me dangling out the side. In the first place, the two husbands had been to the same school – had been classmates, for goodness' sake. At King's, *the* Chester school, of course. Elly had been to Queens, the girls' counterpart. Then when Richard went to Imperial, Elly and Martin had gone off to Oxford together, married, stayed married. But as loyal Chester children they'd all ended up back here, linked up again.

What is it about the past? Every time you find it in competition with the present, it wins, hands down.

No, I wouldn't have chosen Elly, but apart from Viv, the nicest mother from Toddler Group, who was there left? I couldn't talk to Viv and have those pitying eyes turned on me ever after, or at least three times a week until it was time for Aaron to start Infants. My cousin Greta (known in our house as The Only Living Relative – just guess who made that one up!) well, she might've been a possible, but there were two arguments against. She was genuinely fond of Richard and it isn't something you want to spoil without a cast-iron reason for doing it. And she'd caught Aaron's bug after coming to the zoo with us, that awful Edinburgh weekend. Currently Greta was coughing away what was left of the month in her bungalow over at Congleton. But, good for Greta, she was not being a nuisance. She was being tended with superhuman kindness by her next door neighbour, Howard. He ran *Sugar and Spice*, a wonderful delicatessen, down in the town and had catered our housewarming. A long time ago, that seemed now. It was back when our house could be warmed by a few cases of wine and some individual smoked salmon tartlets.

"And d'you know what?" I said to Elly when she came back with the drinks, "This is all in his lunch hour. I hope he doesn't catch it."

"I suppose he can feed her out of the shop."

"Well yes, but that's not the point, is it? I mean could you imagine

Martin doing all that?"

"Or Richard?" she added helpfully.

I could've pointed out that Richard would've been far too busy, being fully employed.

"This Howard chap's –?"

"A widower, I think."

"Good arrangement for them both," she smiled. "If only my mother-in-law could hook up with some nice – Na." My concerns were never going to hold her interest for long. "I've been thinking about calling her just *Marj*... What d'you reckon? How much would she hate that?" Then she said out of nowhere, "What would you like your name to have been if you hadn't been a Pippa? Any idea?" And she beamed at me as though she really expected an answer and only looked for her drink when it was obvious I didn't have one.

Going to pick up her orange juice, she straightened the cuff of her toffee-coloured blazer, instead – and took a crafty peek at her watch. Considering they were meant to have no money, Elly managed to look pretty well-turned out. If she relied on charity shops, there was a good eye at work. The jacket was teamed with jeans and old brown boots but also that string of turquoise beads I've always liked. I'm not desperate about jewellery but these aren't showy.

Between us in his buggy, Aaron, now almost recovered, dozed away the happy hour between five and six. We were squeezed into a corner of the café under Browns department store. Once called *The Crypt,* because it's a basement and all arches and stone, it had been genteel. I could imagine Greta down here, say, being treated by Great Aunt Dulcie, before her run-in with God. At the till an old lady asked, "How long have you been self-service?"

A couple of years, I could've told her.

Now it was *Café Venue,* a cyber-café and this meant long gleaming counter, aluminium strip lighting. Black Gaggia machines the size of water tanks threatened Aaron's nap with every customer served. Nothing gets better, does it?

Perhaps I was turning into Great Aunt Dulcie.

I was having a proper drink even though it wasn't even lighting-up time. The crypt had been Elly's suggestion. Elly had never had to bounce a sleeping child in a buggy, with great care, down those stone steps from the street. Elly never would have to, in all likelihood. Lucky Elly, was probably how Elly saw it. But at least half of the girls and women who passed the baby, either on their way in or out or both, smiled at Aaron and then, as a sort of acknowledgement, at me. His cheeks were the colour of cranberry juice where the warm air had hit, two round fruity circles that I kept wanting to put my finger on. Elly hadn't looked at him once since she's arrived.

" – and you've got this cottage," she was saying. "In Wales, isn't it? That must be lovely."

"Yes. I mean yes, of course – but the boys get bored, you know? And then Richard... and I've never really liked the sea." I took a long gulp at my Chardonnay. "We're having an awful time, Richard and I – I may as well say," I said.

"Ah."

"Don't really know what to do about it."

Elly focused somewhere beyond the rough sandstone of the café's arches. It came to me that she disliked my husband these days. She must be trying to find an expression that hid it. Instead she surprised me. "He never strikes me as someone who's happy at all. I don't think he ever was. When we were all kids he always had – enthusiasms. It was, oh, I don't know – America, once. We were all going to go and live in California – all three of us – and just be rich. No-o. Successful and pleased with what he's got, that's Richard – but not happy." All this could have been said in the sort of tone that offered sympathy – and maybe an opening of a subject I could pick up and carry on with. But it wasn't. It was just Elly, noting down what she's seen.

"Happy?" I could've countered. *Who is?* But I wouldn't give her the satisfaction. "We've got the boys," I said. "That's got to count for something, hasn't it? No one could want better boys."

How could I have made such a stupid mistake, thinking someone like Elly – thinking *Elly* – had the background, the *nous,* to understand normal family life? It was about as sensible as expecting God to take questions. *Elly* – who'd known her husband Martin since school days, who'd bummed around the world with him, like a pair of retarded teenagers, never planning for what the next day might bring.

And when it had caught up with them who was it was who'd bailed them out? The grown-ups, that's who – Marjorie, Martin's much-despised mother. And Richard to some extent.

"Men are different."

She said it very confidently and sipped her juice. You can't help but wonder, can you? Elly wasn't beautiful but there was that thing about her, something that attracted men's eyes. She was pretty and thin and had a way of moving, directing her attention or just turning her head on that long slim neck of hers. It gave men ideas.

Everything went quiet inside my chest, as though even my heart was waiting. Just as once I thought *Will He speak now?* and had looked up at the ceiling for God's response to Great Aunt Dulcie, now I thought *Is it Elly?*

"Richard's forty," he was only thirty-nine but she didn't correct me. Wouldn't she be bound to correct me, if –? Of course it couldn't be Elly. Richard called Elly the Queen of Darkness, behind Elly's back, and I guessed Elly, who was always the clever one with words, I bet Elly had something nastier, funnier, for Richard. "He's got more than most men ever have. Are you saying you can understand him?"

"No."

"Can you understand him when he can't keep his mind on what I'm saying – not even until I get to the end of my sentence? When his little boy's ill – really ill, as Aaron was the other week – and he doesn't seem to care?" As you have to at times like this, the more heated up I became, the lower I had to drop my voice because we were still in the basement of a Chester store. Elly had to lean her sleek head in to catch it all. Above us, at street level, the city was emptying now, all those well-shod feet hurrying home to lives that seemed less at risk than my own. "When I make a single joke, a very mild bit of a joke at his expense, can you understand him when he says *Fuck off, Pip?*"

Elly reached out and took the hand I was counting off my points with and gave it a squeeze. Her hand was very cold – from her glass, I guess – but the squeeze felt like the real thing. If it *was* Elly, she was even meaner than I'd ever thought.

"Shu-sh, no. I'm not saying any of that. I'm just saying – I don't know what I'm saying." She let go my hand and ran hers through her hair. "D'you think he's seeing someone else?" At least she had the good manners not to add 'again'.

"Absolutely."

"Shit, huh?"

"It's not the same though, as last time."

"Mm-m. There was that, um... from the drug company."

"Gill," I said, "her name was Gill. It was before Aaron."

Did Elly know the drug company bit because Richard had told Martin? (how? how would he have told Martin – sadly, angrily, shame-facedly? *boastfully*?) and Martin had told Elly. But I had a sudden surge of pride even through the misery. Aaron: tiny, fragile Aaron had seen off smart, glossy Gill.

Watch them in the pre-match warm up, examine their form. "Let's see if the handicapper's been a good chap," as I can remember Daddy saying. Get up early and go down to the rail – whisper your questions about their training times, what sort of exercise plan they're following. Gill, who I'd never seen but I pictured as dark-haired and fit-looking, would look like a clear favourite. All bright and hard. And then there's this pink scrap, clinging on to your thumb. Who'd have put their shirt on my little Aaron? I would, actually.

"Gill, mm-mm." Elly murmured as though it wouldn't have been polite to bring her to mind without an effort. "So how's it not the same?"

"Last time – all that year, he was kinder, nicer, you know? I think what it was, he was really happy, really pleased with what was going on – with her, I suppose and it was as if he wanted everyone else to – get a share of it. He was better than he's ever been with the boys. We all went to Euro-Disney, remember? Could you ever imagine Richard going to a place like that normally?"

"Maybe if Mickey Mouse had an aneurysm."

"And he enjoyed it! He made sure we all did."

"Ah well, Richard giveth and Richard taketh away, blessed be the name of Richard, isn't it?"

I couldn't help myself. My eyes just filled up and I felt a sob in my chest, a bubble of grief that was going to rise to the surface come what may. Elly looked at me aghast and then looked around to check if we were being watched. All I could do was knock back half a glass of wine in one go and pray for an authentic-sounding fit of coughing. Elly passed across the tissues from her bag. "I'm sorry to be such a heap," I said, "every time I think about – about him *caring* if some other bloody woman's got a headache or – " (*Don't mention the message!* a warning voice said, *the message from Boodles for him to pick up 'the item' – the one you're still waiting for – tell Elly that and she'll make something even more terrifying out of it*).

I told her of course. She was fascinated. "And it's never materialised? And you can't really ask... no, no. Mm-mm. Oh well, perhaps it's for an occasion. An anniversary, something like that. It'll turn up." She started fingering those lovely beads of hers. You could tell she didn't believe it would.

"I know it just hurts so bloody much. *Really* hurts, like you've been – stabbed in the chest or something. And that's before you even get to thinking of the going to bed bit, you know?" She at least had the good grace to nod. "And then, there's this feeling I have – this thing I've been getting since – oh Christmas really... it started at Christmas. As though something bad will happen and I'm going to know. A couple of weeks ago, when Richard went to Edinburgh, it was at its *absolute worst*. He was late and I got scared, I suppose. But it hasn't gone away – not really. Not since then. You don't play, do you?" She blinked, confused. "Play the piano, I mean. It's a note. That's what it's like. You're hearing this note with the sustaining pedal. On and on. It's a torment some days. I'm almost too afraid to touch Tom or Adam, in case it'll be one of them... or even –" But I couldn't say it. I just had to look down at the little sleeping creature in his buggy, his head on one side, fingers flapping across the zipper of his yellow fleece jerkin, learning all about zip-up fleeces and how to get out of them in his baby dreams.

I realised I'd eaten the chocolate muffin I'd bought him.

"What do you mean, *going to know*? Like clairvoyance?" The word coming out of Elly's mouth was full of mockery.

"Well yes, if you like. The night Richard came back from Edinburgh and I touched him. But – but it can't be what it seems to be –" She looked at me as though I had mush for brains. "Anyway,

I got this feeling."

"I'll bet you did!" Ah, embarrassment. She was going to try and laugh it off.

I said, "It's to do with knowing there's something waiting to get you. It's like a dam that's going to burst – and it'll sweep up everything you have and want to hold onto – it'll sweep it away."

By the time I got to the end of that one there was another bigger sob that was agonising to keep down. Forget knives and nice clean, merciful stabbings. This was that *Alien* monstrosity, from the film, you know? I was about to rip apart like a ripe seed pod. I had to screw my eyes tight shut and hold my breath. When I opened them all I could see was withdrawal in Elly's expression – she'd actually sat back in her small uncomfortable chair.

"Yes, well, I can imagine what it must sound like –" I said.

"It sounds like it's coming from someone who's scared – very anxious anyway. About their marriage and the future. And if what you think's going on – with Richard, yeah? – if it's true, then you've got every right to be hurt and depressed and absolutely furious."

I could see where this was headed. I was about to get the brush off. She was going to point me in the direction of someone who could pretend to give-a-damn. Any minute now, we'd get round to whether they had a female GP at our practice.

It *could* be Elly – even now. I wouldn't have put it past the two of them.

"I am hurt," I said, "and bloody angry – as you'd be, if it were Martin. Has he ever, you know, had anyone else?"

She smiled and shook her head. It was one of those moments when all it takes is for two things to start up at the same time and you miss one of them. Aaron opened his eyes, though still asleep, and had a half-hearted grumble. Elly drank her orange juice and said a few words over the top of the glass, finishing with " – unless you count brandy."

All these years and I'd never guessed Martin had a drink problem. But of course, it made sense. Afterwards it made sense. Mooching round the world from job to job, then the business with that boy in the school – whatever that was all about. It had meant months in jail and back to Mummy's place, grounded. I didn't react – and then it was too late to react.

At the next table a tall, brunette twenty-ish girl was being helped into a coat by a friend. " – and then only if I feel like it," the girl was saying, "and if I don't, he knows what he can do." Their laughter was close enough and loud enough to wake the baby properly. I was aware of a sudden loathing for them both, the dark girl who had managed to become even more eye-catching simply by putting on a long black coat, and the friend or sister – she could have been either – who'd helped. I wished with all my strength for the taller to stumble on one of those hard stones edges in her high-heeled boots. Fall. Try laughing that off.

No wonder something bad was in store for me when I was filled with this much hate.

"I'm not depressed," I said. "This is different. I *am* miserable a lot of the time. It's – hard to explain. But this is *worse* than miserable. *We're all under threat.*"

I could see I was getting nowhere. Apart from Martin, Elly didn't care for a soul. *Don't go trying to make a bosom-buddy of Elly,* Richard had once warned me. *It can't be done.* And I thought it was because she'd been making fun – of him.

I could almost wish it was Elly because if it was, then Richard might find he'd met his match.

"And all this began when he came back from Edinburgh?"

"Yes, sort of. It started then. I just touched him, that's all."

What I really saw the night I laid my hand on my husband – well, I'd never dared to say it out loud. I'd stowed it away, as you can do with things that happen in the early hours, when you're frazzled and sleepless. They're not from the real world, are they?

You might be wrong, after all.

I couldn't share it with Richard but it had to be with someone. And quickly. The huge shop above us had gone quiet. No more passing trade. *Café Venue* had emptied without me noticing. Now, at the street end, the lights over those impossible, steep steps were all being turned off – to stop new customers being lured down to the wonderful creepiness.

Imagine being locked in here.

The pretty little girl who'd served our drinks was hovering, damp cloth at the ready. "Look," I said to Elly, just taking a sip from my almost empty glass to buy us a moment or two extra. "Look – do you ever remember me telling you about my Great Aunt Dulcie?"

PART 4

PART 4

The tide rarely touches even the mouth of Twll Beda — Bede's Hole. Those who know this coast from long experience will say that it never enters the cave. These two running along the shore-line, they believe this. They have their kindling, their blanket, their provisions.

On the far arm of the bay, they notice clouds are building. A better eye for this small, complex portion of coast would be needed to notice also how the waves, though of reasonable size, are striking the beach very frequently and at an angle to the shoreline. Sets of waves are throwing their stored energy at the northern wrist of Aberhiw.

From the cliff, if anyone were there to see it, something unusual is happening. A fifty-foot, dirty brown snake appears on the surface, complete within a few seconds, all of a piece. Foam the colour of dead skin breaks over its back. It races across the bay, shunning the shore, untroubled by the incoming press of water and darts out to sea in what should be an impossible manoeuvre. No living thing, surely, can resist this tide. And yet, as the creature seems to dive or swim out to deep water in the south-west, its litter-mate is delivered in the north and begins its mad journey across the lanes of the wave-traffic.

And by the time this one has reached its destination, a third rip-current had been born.

None of this can be assessed from the beach. The wind, strong but not so cold, competes with the surf-rattle to fill the whole sky with noise, so that the runners, when they do turn to each other, converse in raised voices, almost a shout. One gives up the attempt to be understood, grimaces and points to the cave's mouth. The other nods and follows.

Soon there's the brilliance of a fire to counteract the chill of what had started out as a promising April afternoon (their day not having really begun until around twelve o'clock). The warmth is welcome. Smoke is an annoyance though, because it refuses to do the decent thing and just rise. One second it's on its way blamelessly to the roof, the next thrown back in their faces, only to change its mind again. Having reduced them both to coughing ancients, it exits via the slit of an entrance.

There's bad air in here, too; a fistula, far back in the darkness, is feeding a dank rot-gas from the piled-up earth and today, like smoke, its only vent is seaward.

"Can you smell that? There it is again! Something in here reeks. I mean minging!"

"It's the fire."

"It's not the fire! I know what smoke smells like. This is – I dunno. Not burning – something going off, more like."

There's the flash of polished steel and the heavy chink of glass on glass.

"Come over here and drink this – I've started the steaks now. Some picnic on the beach! If you don't want, we don't have to stay when we've eaten."

"But it's come on to rain. I can see from here. It's meant to be the spring. It's meant to be better than this. What a shitty day this has turned out!"

"It can improve. After this we could –"

"No, it's a crap day! It's done for. And don't give me that look. It's how I am. Take it or leave it."

This is what I do. It's not everything I do. I live a normal life, much like the next man – but it's the best.

First of all Fate or Chance chooses my mark for me. Once I'm sure he or she (but usually he) is suitably subdued, I eviscerate the victim. I use a mid-line incision which exposes the major abdominal organs. I try not to waste time about it. Much depends, of course, on the level of obesity. Not many people understand how physically tiring it can be carving your way through an outcrop of yellow fat. Ask yourself this. Why were butchers, the proper ones you saw in childhood with gory aprons, why were they always such brawny brutes?

The body is designed in such a way as to stop the inside getting out and vice versa. Opening it up can be hard work because it's not meant to happen. And then there are the taboos. There's the locked door, the magic casket. Consider the significance of these and there's only one outcome. A fit of trembling on the threshold. A failure of nerve. Me, I make sure I've had a good breakfast and a half-decent night's sleep. That's the way to be sure that when it is *you*, it'll be the full, Richard Congreve Special that you are getting.

So, I push on in there and have a quick look round. My main concern are the kidneys. Small, huffy organs. Any excuse to go shutting down. Deprive them of circulation (an hour will do it) and they don't want to know. I need to be careful while I'm having my rummage, and that's one of the first rules. Don't fall out with the neighbours. Livers, they'll take a bit of punishment (and most of them do in this life), the spleen you can get by without. Gallbladder, ditto. Intestines, well, you've excess capacity there. But the kidneys, they're little bastards if you really want to know.

What I'm looking for is none of the above, though.

It's infrarenal, usually, saccular (round-ish like a balloon) or fusiform (like an inflated pygmy condom) and varies in size. 5cm is about the smallest I do but they can be *big*. I've had some whoppers. Those are the ones a medical student with a blinding hangover can find by touch in a darkened room. A blood-filled, anti-personnel mine waiting for that extra-energetic bowel movement or that first hypertensive sentence at the daughter's wedding reception.

"Now as everyone that's here today knows, this happy occasion —"

Pop.

The satisfied gourmand, the proud father becomes the soft suicide.

A ruptured aneurysm. It's the third commonest cause of sudden death. Tell that to the layman or even some in the profession and they won't believe you. Absolutely gospel, though. Aneurysms. They sit inside doing no harm to anybody until they decide to detonate. They're in necks, legs but most often the abdomen. Just a bit of a bulge where the wall of the vessel weakens. You've seen the cartoons, where the pipe swells and swells before it bursts, and then the force of it sweeps both cat and mouse off their feet? The principle's the same with your common or garden aneurysm. Pressure and release.

Occasionally they present at casualty. Feeling peaky that morning, usually with lower back pain. They thought of trying the GP but couldn't get in. "And then I said to meself, you know, you did the lawns yesterday. Not surprising you've got a twinge or two." Surprising how stoical the Northern British, particularly the elderly, can be. They fall to their knees in front of some mildly interested third party. The sweat breaks out. Then the nausea boils up as the blood pressure dives. Already grey as a granite headstone, they whisper, "Sorry, doctor, not feeling too goo —"

If they're very lucky as to venue, you might get them onto the table. Less than one in ten survive. Choose the wrong day, the wrong time, the wrong place (and that's in the unlikely event they make it to the hospital at all) and what do we have? Some eager young registrar decides on taking heroic measures, opens them up there and then. And finds? We call it brisk bleeding.

In this budding TV medic goes. No thought of the locked door. Forget the magic casket.

The following scene? The same but now he (or she, but it's usually he) is up to his ankles in the poor sod's entire blood supply. The patient's almost always a pensioner, usually smokes. Vascular health? Don't make me laugh. It's an oxymoron, especially in these northerly climes. Patients, typically, will've been employed in weird heaving and cramping jobs for years on end. There's Merseyside with its docks, ship building, heavy industry, Ellesmere Port and all the way up to Runcorn, with more industry, oil-refineries, chemicals, assembly lines, take your pick. It's surprising how many of them choose to come and die within referral distance of an historic walled city. Of course they'll have worked bloody hard in many respects but never done all those things their bodies were *really* designed for. No walking and jogging twenty miles through the forest, eating a load of stuff just picked or just picked up and then sleeping it off for ten hours. Without a care in the world.

You can't blame this poor bright-eyed registrar, this young Turk with the barely run-in stethoscope and, now, his or her newly splattered Calvin Klein casuals. You couldn't take offence if he or she slapped the just-deceased right there on the trolley and shouted, "What d'you expect? You never gave me a chance. You got old. You drove the vehicle into the ground and then you turn up here with it, expecting me to fix it, expecting to be allowed back onto the road. I don't think so!"

Christ, how you long for a bit of variety sometimes. Something with all its own teeth, something not completely and totally clapped out. The young – ah, the young now, you can bring them back to life. Got a chap in once, nineteen maybe twenty, mistaken, he said, for a drug dealer. He was walking along a Birkenhead street and was shot five times. *Five times.*

We're not talking about a hit man here, just another teenager who kept shooting till his nerve and bladder control broke and he had to run away. But five times. When you're shot that often something has got to break. Here's the best bit. His friends brought him in by car. Not knowing what it was all about they drove a young man bleeding to death from five separate holes all the way to the Deva, past at least one other major accident and emergency facility. Because? So he could be treated 'somewhere he weren't known.'

He was called Patrick. The target.

He was dead when we first met. It took us hours (me and *my* posse) revealing, clamping, sucking out and suturing. And the next one please!

For eight weeks we had him in High Dependency where they

worked in shifts on his ABC – Airway, Breathing, Circulation. Eight weeks. Really, not bad going. That's less than a fortnight per bullet-hole.

For eight weeks he was like a bunny in the headlights, too scared to move.

Even after that, and we had the pleasure of his company for a couple of months, I think, he was careful, shall we say? He'd been to the Pearly Gates. He'd a word through the bars with St Peter and exchanged contact numbers. But he was nineteen pushing twenty, a candidate for resurrection.

ii

I hate birthdays and Christmas. They're like coffee, giving off this ester, this promise of physical pleasure they never make good. They can be better or more accurately, less bad than you expect. Never really worth the effort. But one morning when you're alone and the sun's streaming in and you're all set for the day, just stop. Let yourself really breathe in what lifts off that surface of a freshly brewed cup of Jamaican Blue Mountain medium roast. Close your eyes and hold it in to the depth of your diaphragm. Then you'll understand. Nothing can be *that* wonderful. Nothing can deliver that promise of total gratification.

Now you can drink it.

And it doesn't.

Last Christmas was mild, which began it. Bitter weather might have saved me. But this was an almost balmy Christmas Day with a suggestion of sunshine on the soupy old River Dee. The boys were restless, roaming the house. Aaron, our youngest, through excitement, over-stimulation and E-numbers in the surfeit of sweets, had turned into a miniature Dervish. Across the hall he staggered, letting out his near ultra-sonic siren noise, into the drawing room, through the gaudy wreckage still everywhere after a six am start. He was making sure, of course, he pulped anything soft and edible well down into the pile of the pale grey Aubusson. If it's your own child and your own rug, you're not supposed to mind. So I'm told.

"Why don't I get rid of some of this stuff?" Greta suggested. Greta's my wife's cousin. Much older than either of us, she's taken it upon herself to fill out into an entire catalogue of relations. She can be big sister, aunt, godmother. Just occasionally she oversteps the line into surrogate parenthood. But she's neat and small. Sometimes you can enter a room and not see her straightaway.

"Don't bother," Pippa said, drugged with food and drink like the rest of us but relaxed, not caring, "they'll only get it out again. Or most of it."

Above our heads a stampede that surely involved more than four feet was being transmitted through the entire house by way of its slim, cheap timbers.

The Georgians lived in, no – they bloody revelled in a world of sensations. A high level of background noise was probably one of the less important ones. So they built the Donns' House to keep out the rain but not much beside. The idea that you might want a rest from endless conversation, the rattle of carriages and the pack of mongrels fighting over a corpse on the eighteenth century river bank never seems to have occurred.

"That sounds," I pointed out in what I hoped was an even tone, "as if they're in our bedroom."

"Does it?"

I walked to the bottom of the stairs hobbled by Aaron who'd attached himself to one of my legs bellowing "Dancy Daddy, dancy Aar-run."

"Adam! Tom! What are you doing?"

A few seconds silence was followed by a crash. I swept Aaron up, much to his delight, approval signalled by a sort of soprano-sax riff which was completely unfamiliar and must've been only just added to his repertoire. He smelled, of course, of chocolate. Dickensian pudding was a no-no in our household. Greta's Light-and-Dark Chocolate Mouse had finished an immense feast, its remains congealing next door. Beneath the sickly-sweet odour was something else, though. Organic, not unpleasant but not quite fresh: it was Aaron. Had the other two boys, either of them, such distinctive olfactory signatures? Certainly I couldn't bring to mind any time when I'd noticed it. Coffee, yes, but children, no.

Our eyes met as he attained the level of my face. He grinned, the completely happy little animal, fed, watered, safe. Already he was losing that rounded, little-Buddha, infant structure. The femur and carpel bones were lengthening, the hand that fastened stickily onto my shirt collar was less doll-like, more little boy's (or girl's) than baby's. The cherub was morphing into toddler as I looked. But I wouldn't dream of mentioning any of this to Pip. In a few more months, a year at most, she'd start lingering in front of anonymous prams for a top-up of what she craved. No need to start that off before we had to. "Here," I said putting him down into his mother's lap. "I'll go and see what's going on."

"I'll tell you what," Greta offered, "Why don't I round them up and get out down the river for an hour? I'll take his nibs there as well. Pop him in the pushchair and he'll be asleep."

I didn't know about Aaron. When I returned from the ten-minute-process of getting Greta and the boys through the door Pip was breathing softly and rhythmically in front of the fire. Strands of fair hair had come free from some sort of black-velvet restraint at the back of her head. A wisp of it moved across her parted lips with each exhalation. One flat, soft-leather shoe had fallen from her outstretched foot. I noticed that the patterned tights I'd half-watched her struggle into early this morning were inside out, a tuft of thread sticking up from the final stitch at each big toe.

Depressed and grouchy was how I'd felt seeing them off. But the process had an unexpected effect. It woke something energetic and hopeful where there'd been nothing before, and that with just a brief lungful of the fresh air. Our house opens almost onto the road, if you don't count five feet of decorative limestone sets and topiary in pots. It came as a surprise, after the over-heated privacy of a family Christmas, to find the world still turning away out there. Doing ordinary stuff. A giant Volvo was being manoeuvred along the cobbles, slowly, in the vain hope of a parking spot with a river-view. Couples were out with their pedigree retrievers and spaniels, striding over the suspension bridge to the Earl's Eye meadows.

To the fire, almost settled into ash, I added a log. I replaced the guard and turned back to the room. In the foreground there was the guaranteed-non-shedding spruce with its tartan ribbons and trinkets that spun in the rising air. Beyond the curtains and the French windows, laurel and holly bushes marked out the intervals of brick and gravel to the lichened birdbath. Scrawl *We Wish You A Merry Christmas* across the bit of grey sky and the picture could easily have made it onto any one of the hundred cards strung up throughout the house.

Pip's gentle snoring seemed to grow in the new peace of the room, of the house. But then I could catch the dishwasher's hum and just an occasional raised voice seeping through the tiny gaps around door and window sashes from the public space at the front.

Why can this house never be totally silent?

My face still tingled with the cool, damp atmosphere of the outside. Something in me fastened on the doings of complete strangers beyond the glass. A young woman was walking briskly past, citywards. When her arms came up in a Gallic gesture, the husband or partner was startled, backing off.

The suddenness of the challenge conjured up a friend's wife. And then the friend. *Poor sod.*

From the burr-elm bowl I picked up my keys, threw a raincoat over my arm. I let myself out as quietly as I could through a door too heavy for its hinges since the day of installation. As the lock clicked I braced myself for that other noise, the one there was no controlling, the one that would rouse my sleeping wife. I heard it as I turned to sprint out onto the road. Way up in the attics, snatched by the ascending draft, the playroom door slammed.

But I was gone.

Only usage spoils this city. I resent bitterly having to share it with the tourist hoards that, year on year, increase to the extent they're wearing it away. Queens Park, on the far bank from the Donns House, was where I was born and grew up. I went away to train and then to work but I always knew this was the place I'd spend my adult life, if I could. It was always *the* town for me, *the* city.

"I'll take you into town for one," I can hear my mother's voice promising. Chester was the town. And then came shock after shock, over the years, of the trips away, of the shows, the shopping expeditions, the museums in Liverpool and Manchester. So, I discovered, there are other towns, other cities. But what poor imitations! Rivers you could hardly see or get at. No magic rows with nooks and crannies for hiding in, and long passages from which to look down (and drop things!) onto the lower, and inferior, pavement. No sudden flights of steps between levels. No shop piled onto shop. The retail-pairings were important, mystically significant. Here would be a shoe-shop... groan. But above it, toys. At street level chocolates, with a useless jewellers sitting on its back. Lower and Upper Bridge Street, Watergate and Eastgate, they were a continuous beam and brick and stuccoed display of a child's want and hate.

These other towns, these non-Chester towns, had straight, shabby streets, either meaninglessly huge or suddenly constricted. What was the point of these places, I wondered? What stopped the inhabitants getting out?

Even London came as an anti-climax. Its monuments and pleasure domes were scattered too sparsely amongst all that other grimy sameness.

On Christmas afternoon Chester (the Roman *Deva* and all those layers of historical stone, timber and brick that had piled on top of it since) looked faultless. People were out walking the pavements in groups of two, three or five, but all well-spaced and well-dressed with hardly a car cruising around the semi-circular obstruction that was the excavated half of a Roman amphitheatre.

If I'd admitted to a destination my quickest route would've had me keeping to the river bank, into Dee Lane and up to The Barrs before making for –

Instead, after a brisk circuit of the park, here I was in St John's Street. For the first and only time I've ever seen it, it was completely devoid of pedestrians or traffic. This uninterrupted vista alone was enough to up my adrenalin, quicken my step. I'd have run the length of it if I hadn't been afraid I'd draw attention to myself from anyone joining me from the far end, a tall man, dark chinos, dark open-necked shirt, expensive raincoat and running, through not pursued.

Not pursued but in pursuit. I turned right. I was heading away from the centre, to where the white-only Christmas lights ended and the listed buildings failed. I was heading, strictly speaking up-town. It had taken several visits to other types of cities before I grasped the Mobius strip quality to my own pocket-urbs. Strictly speaking, I live downtown, in that the river runs virtually through the city centre. If I step outside, as those Georgian generations will have done, five minutes places me amongst shops, offices, banks and restaurants. Out in the suburbs there's social as well as architectural decline. Handbridge, across the ancient bridge is fine enough, although the horrors of Lache and Saltney lie beyond. To the east and south Upton, Newton, Hoole are places where the aspirational are involved in DIY. You see the soil-and-rubble-filled skips everywhere. They're all plotting their collective great escape.

Boughton, straddling the Shropshire Union Canal, just about hangs on to its city status. But it's outside the walls. It's busy, Ritzy these days, everything being redeveloped into new apartments behind any old façade. But in Chester there must be something preservative in the air. On the very edge of Boughton-cum-Hoole, guarding a dual carriageway that (like every other bit of the city) has been shrubbed and treed to bursting point, stand three Sixties tower blocks. *Not exactly* the Cestrian answer to the Trellick Tower. But even these half-hearted attempts at Modernism have been tenderly maintained. In an hypnotically black and white city they are painted in shocking colours. Green and cream. I was making for the tower that's called St Annes. Around half-way up it to be precise.

At the lower end of Frodsham Street just beyond where the Kaleyards pierces the mediaeval wall I stopped, alone again as far as I could see in both directions. Over the canal bridge, partly obscured by an assortment of phoney half-timbered low-rises, St Anne's stood square and ugly in the sun. And from somewhere (bizarrely it seemed to come from under my feet) I heard singing.

Little child-ren wake and list-en
Songs are breaking o'er the earth.
While the stars in heaven glist-en
Hear the news of Jesus' birth.

123

Of course it was just a boat passing directly below me on the canal. I leaned over to look just as its stern with its pair of grey-headed singers appeared from beneath Cow Lane Bridge. They were well-wrapped up but still clinging together, his arm around her dumpy little body, her woolly-gloved hand on the tiller. Neither of them looked at me but I saw him nod to her and she began again. He joined her in an old man's wavering baritone.

Long ago in lonely mea-dow
Angels brought the message down.
Now each year in midnight shad-ow
It is heard in every town.

All I had to do was turn away now, walk up onto the walls and they'd decant me at home after one of the finest urban walks in Europe. I leaned against the rail of the bridge and texted RU THR? and cancelled it again.

Because the city had displayed itself in all its mock-mediaeval best and because the discomfort of excess stomach contents was relieved by exercise and because I wanted it to be so, up until the moment I pressed the intercom button, it never occurred to me that I might be disappointed.

There was a long wait. A longer wait. A too-long wait. I pressed again, turned away.

"Yes?" she said.

"It's me."

"*Hello* me."

Crackly laughter.

"Are you letting me come up? Or what?"

"Depends on the what," she said and freed the door.

The lift smelt of theatre-scrub. When it opened there was no sign of her but the door to her flat, directly opposite, stood back against the wall. Beyond the hall, music coupled with shouting told me the television was on rather than a wild afternoon party. I walked through from the cramped little hall to the cramped little living space. An oak table with one raised leaf still held the remains of a meal. Even from across the room I could see it was newly decorated with a series of glass-sized water marks. I had paid for the table one hot afternoon in a plush Watergate Street antique dealer's, the day after being served a micro-waved curry in here on a tray. It was still the only decent piece in the room. The cheap sofa's padding had an unhealthy, nodular quality over the arms and was covered in a crumpled throw. The metal shelving held unsorted CDs, a player, a plastic travel clock, a new DVD player and a stack of magazines. The single book was the latest Harry Potter. In the far corner, next to the doors to the balcony, was the portable television I'd heard. This was perched on another bit of frail metal piping and topped with a dying plant.

The owner of this miserable collection of stuff wasn't visible. The TV screen held the only bit of animation. A black man and a white man chased another black man along a filthy deserted street. All three looked distinctly lacking in Christmas spirit.

She popped her head around the corner then from the kitchen alcove.

"Good God! What have you done to your hair?"

Her thick dark hair, cut in a sort of feathery effect around her perfect face, was now streaked with various shades of red. She ran her fingers through it to display the full colour-chart effect. "I had it done yesterday, when I got off – girls' night out last night. D'you like?"

"No. I think it's horrible."

"That's all right then. Wan-a-drink?" Without waiting for a response she disappeared again. She came in with an opened bottle of Jacob's Creek and a single glass. She put them down on the floor in front of me, and came back with her own half-consumed drink. "You see," she said, settling with plenty of squirming beside me on the sofa and leaving me to pour or not pour for myself, "I could've pretended I wasn't drinking on my own – too sad, too cheesy, don't let on, don't give him the satisfaction! – but I haven't been."

I hardly caught her meaning. One of the things, one of several things, that had drawn me across the city was the sound of her voice. It was light and highly expressive of mood or suggestion as though it had been trained. But completely natural. There wasn't a trace of anything that could tie it to region or class. The voice had travelled with its owner and that owner's army family.

"You say," I said, "you *haven't* been drinking?"

"Been drinking *alone*. Drink I had to have. I got up with this head – you wouldn't believe it. But I've had company – as it happens."

"Oh, yes?"

"Oo-oo, old poker face! It was Bernie from next door. He was going to go to his sister's, but they had a row last minute, so he came round here and did us both pizza and chips, ice-cream and black cherries out of a jar. Delish. Beats turkey any day."

Grinning, egging me on to say something derogatory, about Bernie Rosco, about the choice of food and her enjoyment of it, how can I describe Hayley? Twenty-five. But that won't do it. The world's full of stupid, plain, surplus-to-requirements twenty five-year-olds. Tall and brunette? But so is the Tories' new spokesperson on health.

Hayley was lying back against a heap of multi-coloured cushions, ethnic designs, abstract as a Persian carpet, brown, red, orange, ultramarine. Behind her head there were brilliant blue flowers. She was wearing striped silk pyjamas (my gift) in some of the same tones and now her newly-dyed hair picked up the crimson and every other shade of red from both.

I'm not practised at this. The need to describe one thing with reference to another doesn't come easily or often. But if you've ever seen anything painted by Klimt, and the only one I know for sure is The Kiss, you can get a hint of what I was – bombarded with, I'd have to say. Think of the pale, exceptionally clear skin in a sea of gold curves and black oblongs. Think of the scarlet swirls that end in a fold of white elbow, that are cut off from view by another arrangement of lines or splodges, another hint of continuing jazziness beyond the edge of the frame, the scope of vision.

Her face, because of the dark brows, dark fringe of hair, dark eyes, strongly coloured lips was the vivid centre of all this. And then there's the matter of its beauty, that mere accident of millimetric composition, of eye-lids of sufficient but no greater heaviness, chin just lightly defined by a master technician, cheek bones' rise and hollows beneath delicate as the South Downs, the exact and proper width to the bridge of the nose....

126

When I kissed her she tasted of wine and cherries but mainly of the newly applied lipstick.

"I've walked," I said when she pulled away.

Her eyes widened but of course she's clowning. "That's a bit of a mission."

"Fifteen minutes. And that's the pretty way. You're the laziest creature I've ever met."

"How long?" she asked.

"What sort of question is that to ask a —"

Terrible, terrible blunder. What phrase was I going fit in here now? There was the one that hung between us, or I thought it did. "What? A respectably married man?" she said. "But you're not are you? You're an unrespectably married man."

A joke, that's all it was to her. She ran one red-nailed foot along my calf but that was it. She'd be kissed and wasn't intending to kiss me back. She'd offer the wine and the bottle and let me pour.

"I've brought you a present." Sometimes you have to question your own intentions. What I had for Hayley was in my pocket, wedged down in the dark, there, nestling next to my balls. It had lain there since early this morning. Some time between showering and breakfast, while Adam and Thomas gave the two flights of stairs and three storeys of the Donns' House a thorough workout and Aaron could be heard trailing them good-naturedly, I'd taken it from my briefcase. I'd thrust it quickly into my trouser pocket. There it'd been throughout Christmas morning, when I'd simulated delight at the complete Gershwin boxed set from Pip. It's a miracle I didn't feel it as I explained how Browns would change the Italian bag for another if Pip cared to, listened to how much she didn't care to, had welcomed Greta. Now I had to lean sideways to get a hand in that pocket, almost having to lean over Hayley. Another opportunity for her to give something back, anything, my face inches from hers, my chest against the amazing silk-heat of her arm. Not taken. "Here." I passed across a small gold-papered box. Unwrapped.

"I thought I'd had my big present?" She didn't open the box but tapped it, speculatively.

"That? I —" Did she mean the perfume I'd picked up, dashing for

Euston last week, and having her suddenly appear in my head? Or those pyjamas, surely ages ago? "Those weren't Christmas presents. I told you. Open it."

"Is it something nice?"

"I think so."

She rattled the box until the contents moved.

"It's tiny."

"Open it."

"Will I like it, d'you think?"

"I bought it with that intention, obviously."

"Oh, you *bought* it."

Now I knew what she meant. "Just open it and see."

The television, suddenly intrusive, displayed one of those never-ending, saloon-bar fights, except that these were suit-and-tie participants instead of cowboys. A punch was thrown that sent a well-muscled man reeling twenty-feet across a room, but left him otherwise unharmed. Another character was hit across the throat with a chair-leg, the force used being certainly sufficient to crush the larynx.

A minute from now he'd be walking along the filthy street we'd been introduced to in a previous scene. He'd be brushing himself down, massaging his throat and suggesting they try somewhere else for a beer. I rummaged for the remote, flicked to some fat and vaguely familiar comic got up in drag as the Queen. Barry Somebody – I flicked back. Just as I'd thought. Our hero had escaped without so much as minor lacerations. "Are you watching this?"

"I was. I was waiting for Barry's Christmas Message 'cos –"

"Open your present."

"I've nothing for you."

"Good."

"How can I when –"

"I know."

She could be so still. Long and lean, longer and leaner in the striped pyjamas that were also my gift, not moving, not lifting a finger, which is all it would've taken to flick the little golden lid off the little golden box. When a single shot rang out in a new, quieter scene, she blinked. I got to my feet, took her by the hand and pulled her up.

"D'you have the time?" she mocked.

"No."

"We could stay here – I could keep up with the plot," she nodded at the screen, "over your shoulder." I kissed her mouth again with all of her pressed against me. The surge of feelings that shot through my body were a still-novel mix for me, about three-fifths lust, two parts childish yearning. Even so, my brain asked a perfectly reasonable question. It was this. Did evolution come up with kissing to fill in all those gaps made when women said things to which you didn't dare let yourself reply?

When we got into her unmade bed the sheets were cool enough to make me shiver. But that was the last sensation that wasn't totally connected with, inspired by and originating in Hayley. If it wasn't Hayley's body, it was Hayley's scent. Then there were those few words in Hayley's voice that were whispered very clearly and deliberately as to when and how.

"*Richard*," she said twice or maybe three times. From her mouth, somehow in the short journey from out of that mouth, it became infinitely sexual. Because she never otherwise used my name. I was *Mr Congreve*. Occasionally I was *Doctor,* this usually when we were at work but managing a brief moment alone. She laughed over it: "So what can doctors and nurses play when everyone else wants to play doctors and nurses?"

Out of bed and out of the hospital she called me *you* or, in bed, *Big Beast*. She had picked the phrase up from somewhere, believing it meant any important man rather than a player in the political world.

Sometimes she called me *Babes*.

No woman had ever used it to me or in front of me. Martin, a chap who works at the hospital where I do my stuff, said the usage is called an idiolect. This was in response to my enquiry, one of those generalised fool-nobody type enquiries along the lines of "Have you ever noticed how some people seem to have words that only they use – no I can't think of a good example now, it's just something I came across the other day."

"It's an idiolect," he said. "Like a dialect, but in this case a language of one. Some individuals use a word or a phrase in a way that's unique to that person alone."

When Hayley said *Babes* it was explosively intimate. What I needed to remind myself of is this, they were both terms from her language of one. *Babes*. That one syllable could cause satiation to evaporate instantly. *Babes*. The perfect solute in the perfect solvent. And Hayley, herself, she was the salt-water. The more you gulped down, the more you craved.

I could specify what we did. But where would be the point? I've got every detail here, clear. The first twinges, the adjacent, subsidiary effects, the moments of remission and the inevitable progress of the condition. Desire is a malady like any other. Sex is just treating the symptoms. One thing I can tell you about fucking Hayley, and it'll do a lot more to explain how it was than all that "I forced my fingers into the warm tightness of her". As a boy in the wintertime I'd arrive home from school and our housekeeper would have the tea made, the chocolate fingers all rowed up, the grill already hot. She'd cook potato cakes for me, off the steel rack, onto the plate, the butter vanishing as it hit them. I like them. I loved them. *But they tasted best when they were too hot to eat.*

When it was over I lay and saw how the dark shape of the wardrobe grew until its shadow engulfed it and then merged, second by second, into the greyness of the bedroom wall. Nothing was in my mind at first. I assumed I'd drift off to sleep and was doing what I learned years ago whilst training, which involved telling an obedient subconscious *ten minutes, then wake,* when a fleur de lys, the new tattoo on the inside of her thigh, formed itself behind my eyes. And then in front of my eyes. Fully conscious and aware of sounds beyond the room yet *I could make it happen.* I found I could bring it up the way you bring up the brightness on a TV screen. The image hung, mid-air, about three feet in front of my face. There and yet, obviously, not there. Persisting. In the past, I've only done uppers out of necessity and never the hallucinogens. But this state I was in, it was more than a light-trance. It was a degree or two less connected with Self. And there was a mirage....

There the tattoo floated, its three petals welded at the base. Three leaves, the *un*lucky clover. Three feathers. The sign of cowardice? A logo for my adulterer's uniform, anyway. Persisting. There and not there. I watched it for a while longer and then I let it go. I must have fallen asleep.

iii

Afterwards, hours afterwards, I guess, I swung my legs down out of bed and felt broken glass beneath one bare sole. In fact a sliver of broken glass had pierced it and would need excavating out later that night. What I was standing on had been a photograph. Hayley and two other less beautiful young nurses, taken outside a building I'd never seen, were doubled up with laughter at a remark I'd never shared. The living subject of the picture had turned away from me. On the pillow the outrageous red and brown hair was an out-sized dahlia, though its Mexican handicraft colours were faded by the dusk. The quilt was pulled up for warmth. The flat's eccentric heating system left any supposedly unused room to chill, in this case the bedroom during the day. Used to comfort, I'd complained only a few weeks ago. This would be back in the autumn when my visits became established and frequent. "You should get together with the other residents," I'd instructed her, "get the management company to have the system modernised. It's ridiculous not to have heat."

"Why would I bother? I'm just a tenant."

"That's not the point."

"Anyway I don't know the other tenants – only Bernie. And he could be doing a flit soon. He thinks he might move in with Phil. Did I say the three of us were all gonna book for Blackpool for New Year? Now – he's just said it today, he might be somewhere else. Proper tease, that Bernie – don't you think?"

"You shouldn't have to put up with being cold," I said.

"What?... I'll really miss Bernie, you know?" She had laughed and stretched herself out like an ivory panther along the full length of the sofa. I was sitting on the floor, but half-turned to rest my face on the concavity formed by her soft, hairless pubis and sharp hip-bones. "And I'm not the one who's cold," she said. In one quick movement she's curled around my head, her thighs coming up against my hair, flat breasts against my eyes and mouth. The heat of her flesh is mockery

131

enough but Hayley's not one for delicate detail. "Poor thing," she jeers, "getting old, feeling the cold."

I remember the rhyme now, feeling especially tender toward that panic-stricken self, that past me, lying in the vice of her body. In the grip of something I never expected. A failure of nerve. The sharp scent, laid down on her so recently and still as recognisably mine as my cast-off clothing, brought no comfort. How rapidly I could be and would be showered away. I might have pulled back, extricated myself easily enough. But what would have been the point, when I had nothing to say, no counter-barb, no bogey-man of loss to frighten her with?

I left it late to discover all those traveller's tales of love were based on a real thing. Power is something I could map out for you. "I'm your consultant. If I tell you you're going to survive, don't bother the undertaker." But never love.

Hayley stirred, rolled onto her back and smiled. Her lids remained shut tight in the sexiest, painfullest demonstration of one-upmanship. "Had a sleep," she boasted.

"I know." Beyond the window it was fully dark and the headlights down on the dual carriageway were regular as any normal post-rush hour evening. But, I need reminding because it's outlandish, this is Christmas Night. Respectably partnered-up men are making or escaping from duty visits. A wife or girlfriend is sulking in the passenger seat of whatever vehicle fate has entitled them to, and the only evidence of their existence is the child or children in the back.

And every one of those men would choose, if it could be done secretly, to change places with me.

I should be concerned, I tell myself. You stepped out leaving another sleeping woman, how long ago? Stepped out in the pretence that this was a blameless amble. That if it had an admitted object then achieving it would add just a few minutes to your jaunt. And the small defection could somehow be made to vanish the instant you opened the door to the Donns' House.

'*Daddy* is back.'

'You were out like a light,' I'd tell Pippa. 'Oh, cool, you know, but good for walking. Sherry Greta? Did they behave themselves?'

You shouldn't be concerned. You should be appalled. Because

132

that's gone by. The point when it could've happened is a long way in the past. You've committed that fatal error. You've lost track.

I hadn't meant to let it slip away, but then you never intend to. You run out of time and the heart turns into a wet paper bag. What I want is what I know I'm going to do. *Never go back.*

There's nothing complex or frightening about the revelation. Instead, what I feel is the new future. It's suffusing me like morphine. One minute there's pain and just the rest of things around its edges. The next, the pain's draining away. Even better, the world that seeps back is superior in every detail. My existence has decided to unclench. For months I've been doubled up with agony, fearing the complaint and the treatment pretty well equally. Now it's done. Relief comes over me in the form of inertia. I register the crumpled heap of sheet beneath my hip and do nothing to ease the discomfort. And the suction-clamminess of her sharp shoulder on my chest, it isn't pleasant as an isolated sensation but it's one I won't bring myself to break.

Outside there's the half-dark of a city's glow. I'm not even on my feet, getting dressed. I'm not saying any of the things I'd need to say before I could walk through the door. And it's as though I've said this out loud, all of it, the way she's looking at me now. She must know because she's getting up without a word, insinuating her thin legs over the same side of the bed I'm sitting on so all of her touches along all of me for an instant. "Put the lamp on, will you, or I'll fall over your stuff." By the time I flick it on she's at the door, her body glowing. She could be marble or metal, even, from where I lie. Except her eyes, which are everywhere. "Hey, my picture's smashed!" Miraculously she has walked through the scattered shards and missed each one.

She's gone what seems like only a short while, which I waste in doing nothing. The television plays on next door. The film must have ended, other more Christmassy fare replaced it because I hear drunken singing that ends with coarse laughter. She returns with two glasses, her own filled up and mine in which the cross-section of lemon sways, the ice cube sparkles. I can smell the gin and the tonic as separate parties, so alive have my rested senses become. But something's wrong. One finger is pressed to her lips and a spot of blood from it has already lengthened and pulled down one side of her mouth.

"Let me see," I offer.

"Not likely." She tenses the muscles in her forearm so I can't prize the hand away, sucks harder on the cut. From a brief glimpse I get of the gash it seems long but shallow, just caught on the fringe of the same stroke that's cut the lemon in half.

"Does it hurt?"

"Of course it fucking hurts. It's got acid in it." She grimaces, letting me see the red, liquid blood on her lower teeth. "I'll live."

The freezing air has puckered her nipples into bronze stars. They are quite small, much smaller than Pip's, and much less authentic-looking. Like cinnamon berries, these are, and the juice from them soaking out circles in the surrounding flesh.

"Here," she says, "you've got ten minutes. You're too wrecked to walk it." The instant she utters the words I am exhausted. "Don't worry. I'll call you a taxi."

"On Christmas Day?"

"Yeah, on Christmas Day!"

We are sparring over what the day is when it's virtually used up and what we should be doing is mapping out tomorrow. And the next one, please.

I could tell her now. But belief in her understanding has deserted me since she left the bed. How could she share what I feel, what I know is going to happen? I'll need to explain everything, step by step, point by point, as though it were a new and untried regime. Our future. A method of getting through the next twenty-four hours, and then the one after that.

Instead of passing over my drink, she puts it down beside her own and sits across me, pushing until I lie back with her astride. In the place on my chest where she rests her hands I can feel the bloody print forming. "Now, you know what you're always telling us girls, down in High Dependency."

"There's an empty bed in Harper Ward. Go in first and pull round the curtains?"

"Not that!"

"What then?"

She leans forward, kisses me and forces in her tongue, where it flicks around the inside of one cheek, the other cheek, the roof of my mouth (which is a touch sore, I note) and on to my back teeth. "ABC," she sighs deeply, "Airway." Her tongue is long and lithe, probing. "Breathing." Now soft, it moves over my face and into my ear and despite myself, despite the determination not to play after that *ten minutes* gibe, I catch my breath. "*And,*" she sits up again and her good hand disappears behind her back. Such a simple childlike gesture you could guess she was about to perform some new trick, learned that day at school. I feel her fingers at work between my closed legs, "Circulation." Her eyes are wide, her pupils so huge, the hazel irises are all but gone. It's just the poor light, of course. And there are a myriad reasons for dilation. I need to stamp on this one straightaway before it can fire up a host of other niggles and familiar mental stitches.

Like, *What, if anything, is she not on?*

I take hold of her face to pull her back to me. When I press the earlobes against her head I find beneath the hair, the little gold, dagger–shaped studs are neatly embedded. "I see you opened your present."

But she won't answer.

PART 5

"I thought we were going for a swim?"

"Sea won't be warm enough. Rather be in here. Anyway I'm not made of floating stuff."

"Of course you are – everyone is."

"I'm not. That's why baths can give me the creeps, sometimes. If I let myself think about it. If I let my hands come up and I watch them there. They sort of pop up just from the elbow and I know the rest of me'd just sink to the bottom if there was a bottom... somebody famous drowned in the bath. It wasn't Marilyn Monroe was it? No – it was somebody else. Who was it?"

If there's an answer it's lost. Or the question is lost.

"Just as well there's no bathtub in this place, then."

Beyond the window, rain starts up with such force someone might be showering up on the roof – with such force that, although only liquid, it wrings from the glass the occasional Ping! as though hail or gravel were intermixed. The voice from within the misted cubicle competes with both the genteel white noise that surrounds the showerer and the fierce outside hiss.

"Is that rain?"

"'Fraid so. Beach tomorrow."

"You may as well just go out and stand in it now."

"Be cold."

"We could both do it. Then we'd both be cold."

"Where's the fun in that?"

"I'd have to show you."

"And then there's the neighbours –"

"There aren't any neighbours."

"No, that's right."

Suddenly the shower is quenched and an outside lull coincides with its cessation.

"Now I'm too hot – had it too hot, I think."

"Perhaps you should go out. I'd love to see you out there. All pink on the wet grass. Rolling around. All pink and –"

"No way."

"Why not?"

"I don't do tricks."

The window flung wide admits a cold, saturated dollop of air that falls instantly to the floor and sends steam out in its place; ragged coils of white last

139

until the touch of the slate sends them to nothingness. The showerer retreats.

"Have you noticed — don't look like that! I'm being serious now. And you can just forget that rolling about on the lawn stuff — it'll never happen. I've made this resolution — well I made lots, but this is one of them. You're not asking? Oh-oh. Well it's to stop being so obliging. What I was saying was — Pay attention! Have you ever noticed how —"

"I notice everything. You've been told."

A Gorgeous Young Nurse Called Hayley

I'm a Scorpio. The Scorpion? I can't say I'm fussed about it. There's an even more horrible sign than mine though. I mean I'd hate to be Cancer the Crab.

Scorpios don't like to show weakness to others. That's probably why I never sent that letter to Kat. I'd made a mistake I'd be admitting. And a big one. It was called Chester. *Follow The Romans And Come To Chester* I saw on a bus. And I'm sure it was a hot and happening place when the Romans had it. Just not anymore and not for me. That's what kept popping into my mind nearly every day for the first few weeks. What am I doing here?

No! I mean really *what am I doing here?*

How am I going to stand it? The hospital, the Deva (I asked – its Roman for Chester) *and* the city – I've never hated anywhere worse and I've been around.

And the way they talked about the place.

--There can be rough stuff now and again I remember The Doran putting me right. --Just occasionally. It's the drink you know.

Oh yeah. Thanks for the word. I've had three years at Newcastle General. *She*'s about as well-travelled as you'd expect of someone straight out the Kerry badlands. Obviously I wanted telling.

They drink in Newcastle – in case you didn't know Doran. Like Vikings. I've never been at an A and E in Denmark or Norway and I don't need to. I've been to a hen party on the Floating Tuxedo. Me and Kat – who was my best mate back then – had to take the nearly-bride in to work with us (we were on earlies) and get her straight onto a saline drip without going through triage. Then she went and vomited and stopped breathing and we had to own up to her as a real punter. God that caused more trouble than if we'd just let her die! A verbal warning for us both and that made two for Kat. And all this with not a squeak out of the patient herself – no complaint nothing. Well she couldn't could she? She was grateful when she came round and we helped her get the puke out of her hair. All she wanted was a minicab and her knickers back. But it wasn't all good for her either. The happy couple had to put off the wedding a week and that lost them their booking at Hetton Manor. And their deposit. But the flight to Miami and the villa were all booked so they had the honeymoon first.

Now *that*'s what I call a mistake. But if you can't make them at our age when?

And I've known worse. Friend of a friend's fiancé actually died on the stag-night. They were going to that new place opened on Castle Hill – when I say going I mean going on to – and he just fell out of the taxi there in the centre of Durham. Hit his head on the curb. Kat's take on it?

--At least she didn't have time to get too fond of him.

I missed Kat like mad at first. When I got this new flat and all the new stuff I was having a clearout. I found the letter in a drawer.

Sunday (I think)

Dear Kat

Don't know about this. Could be a case of Hayley a gorgeous young nurse whose relationship with Scott Freemantle the handsome but arrogant physiotherapist has ended badly moves to an exciting new job in another town to rebuild her life. But she finds dot dot dot.

Don't know do I? Don't know what I'll find. The Deva's much what I reckoned after the interview. Rhonda the Kiwi I met – the one I told you about in High Dep? a real laugh she was – she's gone! Worked her notice out the day I walked onto the unit. Can you beat it? Had some sort of real bust-up with one of the Masters of the Universe – this absolute bastard Richard Congreve. Mr Congreve to family and friends. I don't need to send you a photo do I? Tall thin – Armani suit. Just can't wait to get started on how much his shoes cost. I had him down as gay! He ponced in and – oh could I not have done with you there. You'd of looked him up and down looked at me. I can see it on your face. Well you just know, don't you? That's what you'd of said.

Not gay as it turns out. Worse! Thinks he's a total fanny-magnet – what a laugh.

On the A-side there's a gorgeous baby doctor just loose on the wards. Bit like Rio Ferdinand but funny with it. Bit more mature than the pebble-dash skin gang. Twenty-two I'd guess. That's years to you not cm dirty girl!

Chester's OK. Lynn this house share-woman took me for a night

142

out. You start at this big hotel bar (doorman wears a top hat – I thought there was a fancy-dress on!) and there's a lot of seriously loaded drinkers about. I tell you there's more money round here – am definitely considering the sugar granddad scene! There's the scuzzy bits too – where I'm going to have to start flat hunting. I'm not going to stick it with Lynn. Every sodding night its her ex did this her ex did that and how if only he hadn't done the other they'd still be together. And I'm like Hello? did someone in this room ask to hear the story of your bloody boring existence again? I don't think so.

There's no sign-off. None of that love-Hayley meet-up talk-soon rubbish. That's as far as it got. But I kept it anyway – ?

And that medical student that I was getting all eager over? What a fully signed up creep he turned out to be. The delightful Shaun.

--Sorry, he says --it doesn't usually happen. I mean its never happened. Its just 'cos you're so beautiful.

Sorry! Sorry? I mean what's that old saying? Once its an accident twice its just plain careless?

Still owes me thirty quid for an Indian.

I'm not big on letter writing. The only other one I wrote since I was a kid was to Mum at Christmas – had to send it care of Her Maj's forces. I don't know where she and her new bloke went after they left Germany. And of course I got a oh-Hayley-how-lovely-to-hear-from-you-at-this-time-of-year straight back didn't I?

Yeah right.

Didn't hear from either of them on my birthday.

Not that I believe in it but I'm a Scorpio which means as I tell people – well men – my bark is definitely not worse than my bite. I only read the horoscopes for a laugh and I remember picking up Cosmo when I was on the train over here for the interview. It said how I was feeling in need of more fun in my life and less friction. How offers in the near future should be taken up as they might not come again. That's the sort of thing a Cosmo girl likes to hear isn't it? That'd make a believer out of her. And then I get to Chester. Its OK. I've seen a lot worse. The Deva's big and modern just out of town but not the back of beyond either. It doesn't look as if its short on friction – but then there's Rhonda saying --Come on girl! Give us a go. I've been to the North East. It was freezing. The beach was made of coal dust and the men all had no necks. What is there to think about?

Maybe Cosmo was right. Maybe here was the fun.

So what the hell? I thought.

--Yes, I said. I'll work my notice in Newcastle and I'll take it. High Dependency Unit here I come. They didn't even have to hit me with the promise of all those Friday lunchtime multi-disciplinary ethics meetings and the *almost certain* secondment to the Psychological Effects of HDU on Next of Kin research team. (Piece of cake I could've told them. They're bad the effects – really bad).

Yes I said. I'll take it.

I was easy.

Why Men Duck and Dive

I'm glad I never sent that letter to Kat. I can imagine her standing in the hallway of the Shield Street flat. The bare red tiles will be making her hop from foot to foot and she's shivering in one of those that not-even-decent T-shirts she sleeps in winter months. Saturday morning but only just. Coffee's in last night's rinsed mug – put down on the windowsill so she could pick up the post – or a half-made spliff the post has interrupted.

Me telling her all that about Richard – *poncing in – thought he was gay – fanny-magnet.*

He won't say now what he first thought about me.

I was walking down the drive – late it was definitely late going dark and suddenly there's the Jaguar cruising up behind me and that voice. I knew who without turning round.

--I can give you a left into town, if that's your direction. The window was down and the car was leaking some old-fashioned music off the CD. When I got in he killed it and I *just knew* as our Kat would say.

You see here was I twenty-five and not looking bad – a whole lot better than not bad even after nine hours on. Here was him. Nearer forty. Wife – kids – big expensive car that sadly for him says middle-aged bloke but still hoping. And all he thinks is wrong is his choice of music. He thinks OK the bands have changed but everything else is the same. See me – I always was a player. And now there's all this cash – that's got to even things out a bit.

I'm a bitch sometimes. --Don't turn it off on my account I tell him. --What was it, anyway?

He looks well pleased. --Eva Cassidy, she's –

--Yeah, I know it, I say. --I got it for my Auntie Vicky for Christmas.

Do I have an Auntie Vicky? What do you think?

The traffic has stopped streaming out of Chester and started slopping back in. For a while all there is is the clicking of the indicator and the silence that was Eva Cassidy. He is so pissed off I want to give myself a hug.

--So where are you going? he asks when we make it out onto the Saughall Road. I know where *he* is going. The whole hospital's heard of Congreve Towers on the river bank. To get to it he'll need to cross the city on one of those duck and dive routes that must have something to do with the bloody Romans. Everything else has.

--Into town. Its not far – just past the college and before you get to the – you know fountain thingy.

--The roundabout? he says.

--Yeah, the roundabout with the fountains on it.

Why the big deal? Everybody knows the fountains roundabout for God's sake. Its so *Chester*. Shiny shrubs – all neat edges. Five jets of white water about two storeys high. You wouldn't get one of those in Newcastle. Not likely. By the end of the first week it would've filled up with Geordies floating in a lager-sick mix.

The car is all leather and wood inside just reeking of cash. I can look at Mr Congreve because he's not going to look at me. I can see the profile of his face which is – but hang on. Let's get this in the right order.

That first time there in the car with Richard (who wasn't *Richard* to me back then) it wasn't the face or the voice or the big hands with the big fingers and the one gold ring. It was his smell. Geordie boys can be clean when its called for. They can splash on the Aramis good as the next man. I didn't even know what it was Richard wore. And I caught just a touch of it – but it was – wow. He smelled expensive – like his car.

--Its just here, I said.

I'm peering ahead I can't help but notice they've switched the fountains off. An omen or what?

--You're almost on the doorstep.

--I don't like to walk, I said.

You know what men can't resist? Its extremes. Be always up and always on the go – Iliketoswim, Ilovetodance – they can't get enough of that. On the other hand I'm not walking all that way or I'm not climbing to the top of that or I think I'll just lie here and watch you – all this sort of stuff drives them off their heads.

He looked me straight in the eye. Held it.

--Like a drink? I said. --You've saved me a hike.

He came in. We finished off Lynn's bottle of red (she only opens one when I say --I'm knackered, gotta go up).

He sniffed it when he thought I wasn't noticing and downed a big full glass in one. Loosened up you could see him taking a look at the room. Bowled over I don't think.

--Is this your house?

I could see what he meant. It was all typical good-enough-for-tenants type gear.

--Not what you're used to?

He smiled. Nice that. A smile in a big thin looking-down-my-nose-at-the-world sort of face. And with the smile taking over the cautious look had to give way to a nicer one. It must be something to do with the cheek muscles and how they can't crinkle up the sides and keep that heavy-lidded thing going at the same time. I hadn't seen him smile – oh no not never! Not when he came into HDU. Or anywhere else. He managed to make it seem like a prize. Yum. His line in chat wasn't too cheesy either even though it came across like he was taking a history. Which he was.

Not only had I not seen him smile before I can't have ever really looked at him properly. What had The Mirror said that morning? *You are open to new ideas today – just watch out who comes up with them!*

Well this was my idea. Richard Congreve wasn't the dark blot on the horizon I had him down for.

So when I said --Not what your used to? And he said, --Of course I didn't mean that! I could tell exactly what he meant. He meant --I did and I didn't.

--Coffee, I say, for two drinks on an empty stomach. I wander into the kitchen all casual. I hear him (can see him in my head) stretched out shoulders back and making a call. Confident sod.

But I find its a turn-on this being up for a change of direction – to put something or someone else off. I know I should've felt guilty – the wife – the kids – but I know this about blokes like our Mr Congreve here. If he's not picking the phone up for you – if he's not spinning some yarn about the father of four they're just prepping for theatre – he's doing it for somebody else. Maybe its the job makes you hard. You see them go on their way – old – young – good – bad. In the last year in Newcastle I nursed Joan Sergeant (she was on the news and because of all her work in Africa you know with the baby elephants and other animals and stuff) and Derek McHugh. You won't have heard of him – or not so much. He killed his wife and then drank everything he could find in the cleaning cupboard. Prat. We were chock-a-block that weekend too – an eight-bed unit (counting Intensive Care) and every one of them occupied. We had to turf an old man out into the general ward. He'd been on Assist Mode Ventilation for the previous three days – its where the patient takes some breaths themselves and has the machine to make up the rest. (--Just think of it as the lung-fairy, Kat said when I was first new on the unit --doing the business while you sleep). But they whipped the old guy off it and into Men's Medical. All they could do for him in Men's Medical was continuous positive airway pressure. No more lung-fairy for him. Chucked into the wind-tunnel more like.

What am I saying about Joan and Derek? I'm saying we lost them both. *And* the old man we moved. The night he died I dreamt he and me were waltzing (as if!) round and round HDU somehow missing the monitors and missing the stand for Joan Sergeant's plasma (A negative – we were low already and nearly ran out she had that many units) and only just missing the fat detective by Derek McHugh's bed –

Anyway back I come from the kitchen with a couple of mugs that don't match but at least are both white and very nearly go flying over the feet in those famous shoes that probably cost more than the carpet. He catches the tray and then catches hold of me to steady me even though by this time I've got it covered. Those big hands that always look so cold – you see the patients flinch from them – they're hot.

An hour comes and goes with me praying to the Yoga-god not to let Lynn out from her class too early.

I say this. He says that. Eyes never leaving your face while you're answering a question and explaining how you got to be here. Its a cheap trick but that's how the trick got to be cheap isn't it? Mass production on account of how it works.

Just under my belly-button. That's where it worked on me.

There's Lynn's big blue-poppy throw over the landlord's old sofa – and we move about so much on our separate ends it gradually comes down into a ruck behind our backs. *Mucho uncomfortablo.*

--Get up, I say. --I'll sort this.

I'm leaning forward and flicking the thing into the air as you'd do with a bed-sheet when there he is behind me with his hands on my hips. I let it go. Turn around.

I'm not a big fan of mouth to mouth but its a good one this is holding my lower lip between his. No tongue. None of that I'm going to smother you in kisses stuff. Slobber more like. I prefer to breathe at my own pace and no waiting for the lung-fairy for me thank-you very much. Anyway he must catch on quick. He takes a break. Then does my forehead with those big hands holding my head.

Another break. Tells me all the usual.

--Too tired, I say. --Way too tired.

To be honest I could almost have – but then I reckon na. You've had your clutch. Why set yourself up girl as the cabaret? You know what I mean – the tasty bit of gossip for him and that skanky Clausen bloke to have a snigger over while they're scrubbing up.

A married man I think. So he'll be well-used to rejection.

He laughs. The bastard *laughs.*

--Hayley, he says, -- so am I.

Why You Just Can't Beat Stolen Goods

Fast forward — it'll be about six or seven months — no it has to be six because its the end of my deal with Lynn over the house.

Obviously I didn't keep him waiting that long. We're in my bed in the front room Richard and me. From it you get the full effect of the ambulances on their way to the Deva blaring along Liverpool Road and up Saughall. It never sounds fast enough that building up of the sound and then it falling off again. Always makes you want to run to the window and shout --Get out of its road you stupid buggers! They don't want to be unloading a corpse at the other end do they?

I have one knee crooked over his hip. He's staring straight into my face and moving very slowly with his hand in the small of my back. There's no rush. I know he's looking only because I've just taken a quick peek. I close my eyes again and arch the rest of me away from where we're joined. I can feel my spine stretching out the pleasure before it sort of snaps in on itself —

I never ever want to look. I've seen too much. Too much. flesh. Too many bodies. I mean don't get me wrong *his* is good straight out of the shower — its all a raindrops on the muscles of his chest and his thighs sort of deal. All really good — but now I'd rather have the dark. In my head you see he's there but he's not that important. Not so much as the blue waves I'm floating on and the blue island all soft and round that's rising out of this lovely warm sea. Every wave bigger than the one that's come before it. Getting further and further up all those shiny black rocks. I love this world. The water's thick and warm like syrup. The waves are pushing and pushing all the time and at the crest of each one — just as it makes the next new line on the rocks — there's a pinch or a nip. Its just there at the very end. A twisted little pain that comes up right to the back of your mouth and you have to swallow hard to make it go down.

But everything's twisted isn't it? Everything's that any good.

On the navy blue island everything's just plain wrong. But I mean wrong in a really good way — some of it. Words you can just about make out in your ear. Bad words.

Really bad words from someone who doesn't even say fuck when I spill coffee on him.

And there's that sticky heat where you're pressed down. I've never liked that — always too concerned about breathing before. But its different with him.

And there's the really dark blue of the sky rushing under my lids and —

The blue poppies they just break open.

And then that's it.

--Very nice Mr Congreve I say.

He's got blue irises flecked with grey — and in the left one there's a single black speck like one of those microdots in a spy film. He's sandy not blond but the hair on his body's brown (thank Christ!) and a lot more of it than you'd expect. He's at least six inches taller than me but lying face to face it only shows where the tips of my toes rub his ankle. Finally he shuts his eyes.

--I'm in love with you Hayley, he says.

--Its all right, I said. --Quality control's already passed this batch of product. You can stop trying now.

--I mean it.

Lying face to face — like we were — you can still be wrong-footed. This wasn't what I expected. But I won't pretend I didn't enjoy hearing it. If only because of the stooping thing.

The Great Man my mate Bernie from Cardiology calls him. He stoops to conquer — that's what they say about him round the hospital and you don't even have to know what it means really to see its about right. So what has Bernie and the rest of them got against him? Not that much.

Just everything that you hear him mutter in that mean-sod way he's got with the word ends — so its never quite caught by whoever's on the receiving end but its definitely a complaint no mistake.

Just every question that some poor bugger can't answer.

Just every silent-bastard stare when just a couple of words would've made you feel easy.

Just this constant acting that you're never sure is an act but you can't believe is the real thing — just like the voice.

I don't think I'll ever get used to it — that bloody voice so posh and precise no one can credit it comes out naturally like your own does without thinking. It must take a real effort. It's got to be like a telephone voice you can only keep up for a bit. But it isn't.

And after all that? He's not stooping anymore. He's kneeling.

--I love you, he says again. In that poshest of the posh voices.

But it might mean nothing. Hold that thought. And – though its sort of exciting – you've no idea what you really want it to mean. Its good. But it might also be bad.

I'm a different girl to the one with the scent of Jaguar's best leather seats in her nostrils.

Suddenly its like I've got these X-ray eyes. I can see into the wallet even though its hanging in a grey wool jacket on the back of a kitchen chair. I can see a faded snapshot of a blonde in it. This blonde's wearing a pearly choker and a bit of a strained smile. (I'm nothing psychic – the pic just popped out one day when he was looking for some plastic and I grabbed it off the floor and handed it back. He said nothing – me neither).

But its like I can do magic. Now the blonde's joined by three little boys. I don't know their names but I have a pretty good idea how old they all are.

From here its easy to find Crazy Street.

Its the only form of defence I've got. I've pulled away from him and I'm even madder to see he still has his eyes shut fast. It doesn't matter how I take it I realise. Its just a fact to him.

He says --We have to decide what to do. There's the immediate future. You can't stay in this place. Its not the place you should be in. We need to get you something else, something of your own I mean. Then there's the longer term.

--Just let the after-effects wear off, I say because I'm stalling for time. --You'll have, er – I wasn't quite sure where I was going with this one. He just lies there. Then he gets a hand free and rubs it across his forehead where there's a trickle of sweat threatening to run. Then he puts the same hand on my bare shoulder feels its getting a bit cool I suppose and pulls the cover up over it – as though it was his own shoulder that's aching from that old tennis-injury.

--Richard, I say.

--What?

I don't know what.

--Don't worry about it, Babes, I say, --it'll all look different with your trousers on.

--I'm not worried, he says.

Something else – and I don't know if I like it or I hate it – is that he never bothers overmuch about the condom. I mean he's really good about having one and using one (being a nice public-school boy I've decided and it makes all the difference from that creep Freewanker). But afterwards most blokes can't wait to be rid – that's if they manage not to actually misplace the bloody thing and then have to practically give you a D and C to get it back – but our Mr Congreve nothing phases him. He'll fall asleep as though there was nothing there forget it completely take care of it when he comes to – or lose it in the bed its all the same to him. He's drifting off now. --Why would I worry? he mumbles – and he's gone.

Why would he be worried? You can do anything with money.

By the end of the week he'd got a one-year lease on a flat in Boughton, which just happens to be along his way home to Congreve Towers. This is a fourth floor with a balcony – mine looked out over the courtyard, not the other direction at the dual carriageway – though afterwards I thought I wouldn't have minded the traffic side of the building because I found out that from four up that side you can see the fountains at that bloody roundabout (when they're on) and that would've given me a nice feeling remembering him bringing me home that first night.

--You're almost on the doorstep, him saying.

I furnished it myself from MFI on the Sealand Road. His face was a picture when he walked in.

--Its absolute rubbish. I've never seen furniture like it.

Its a good job I know how to take him.

--It won't last five minutes, he has to point out.

--Who wants it to last?

Seriously – who in their right mind wants the same furniture to be with you year after year? Not when you could get new that nobody's spilt a drink on? He gives the shelves that I haven't even put anything up on yet a poke with his toe. What does he expect? They move.

Then he homes in on the throw – the blue poppy throw I've got over the rubbishy flimsy little cream sofa. Its got memories that throw. All tangled up one afternoon the blue poppies turned navy with sweat. Me picking it up after and saying --Well now we find out if it goes in the wash – and him turning away like an embarrassed kid.

He fiddles with one of the tassels at its corner. --I didn't know this was yours.

--It isn't.

--Whose then?

--Its Lynn's.

I was grinning now – you don't often see him stuck for words.

--No! Its not a house-warming present, I told him. --We couldn't stand each other Lynn and me. But I really liked it. And it goes in the wash! Haven't seen one anywhere else – in fact I think it might've come from abroad. So I took it. Fair exchange for all those hours listening to her droning on. John did this, John said that –

--*You stole it?*

--Yeah.

--But she'll notice, surely? She'll know you stole it.

--I guess.

He ran his hand through his hair forgetting he'd just had it cut that morning – forgetting that that's what he's still meant to be doing now. Getting his hair cut not dropping in on me for a quick grope.

--But –

--Oh she knows. She asked me about it yesterday. I said I hadn't seen it.

--But she knows you took it?

Why was he having so much trouble with it? --Of course she knows I took it. We both know I took it. I just wanted it. What's she going to do – send the FBI round?

He shook his head and sat down on the stolen blue poppies. Just for a second I caught the strangest look on his face. A lot stranger than blue poppies if you thought about who and what and where. It was fear. Then he grabbed my wrist and pulled me down with him and the look had changed into the more familiar. --Jesus wept, Hayley, he sort of croaks.

I liked him being so big and not *all that* heavy. I hate that pressed and pinned-down feeling. Close up you could see a fine scattering of sandy hair-ends across one cheek bone left there by the barber. I kissed the other side so as not to disturb the evidence.

Stolen goods. You can't beat em.

Hayley Forest Gateau

There's no right and wrong, I reckon, just better or worse. Joan died, Derek died, the old bloke died that I danced with. Bernie's looking after this famous writer-woman off the papers he knows with a dicky valve. Wicked she is. Could go either way with her.

Scorpios are meant to be always up for a good time but can turn nasty as quick as they can see a joke.

Maybe a bit on the close side for me that without being exactly bang-on.

Everything was fine. No everything was more than fine till my birthday. Scorpios are October 23rd to November 21st which if you think about it is the last time you can pretend its the Autumn. After November 21st its winter all the way. You notice these things if you've lived in the North East but you're not local – and you wait for a lot of taxis. The local girls have a special layer of subcutaneous fibre-glass. Legs – arses – backs. Oh and the arms. (I've seen Kat go out Christmas Eve in the blouse she bought for Eilat. Nothing on top).

November 11th 1977 I was born.

I looked it up once but nothing much happened that year.

November 11th this year. By now we've settled into a life. Mr Congreve has cut back on his private practice. He's shifted the supervision of the SHO to a Miss Gann the new consultant. In practical terms this means we have seven hours a week to spend together on average. Plus a caz half hour in passing. If I'm in which I don't guarantee to be.

Everything was fine until my birthday and most of that was pretty good until we got to the eating part. My twenty-sixth birthday but it wasn't as if I was counting. I was top of the world.

First of all its Monday so by a three-way switch I can get it off. For reasons that are just too boring to go over it only works with Mondays this swopping thing.

Second Monday afternoon isn't one of the six sessions Richard gives to the Deva, so from two o'clock say he can be away. *But* he'll often be doing a private clinic on the other side of the City. Not today.

And the result of all this whatdymacallit is we get five hours together.

I've never been a mistress before. That's what I am. We're not having a bit of a fling we're certainly not having an affair if only because it sounds so dead old-fashioned. And anyway he should know. He's upfront about it. He's done both. That's something else I've got on poor Pippa (that's her name). I know all about the others. So there's just me knows about them – and that Martin bloke he used to be at school with.

--Mistress, I said to him a couple of weeks back --So this is a new position you've created in your department is it?

I don't know why – perhaps its two esses at the end – that word mistress it always makes me think of curly things. Lace – frills – flounces – whatever flounces are. Doesn't seem to go with someone working forty-hour weeks in HDU washing her hands so often the skin round the nails dries to rough ridges does it?

Quarter to two he's buzzing to come up.

I have a bottle of Mumm in the fridge because its what he brings. The first one I've ever bought though. Christ that man can spend.

--Why don't you open that for us?

He's wearing the dark trousers from one of those all-identical suits he has and a fawn striped cotton shirt the cuffs loosened. He looks like a bank-manager on his lunch-hour. I tell him

--What do you expect? I've come straight from Medical Audit. I'll have just half a glass.

He hands me the bottle back. He's not going to risk those Austin Reeds. --I thought we'd go out? There's a good Italian in Parkgate. Martin mentioned it again the other day. I've booked for two-ish. Therefore – I know – he must know to the last second and to the last inch where and when Pippa is out and about today. --Happy

Birthday, by the way!

He kisses me light on the mouth and hard on the side of my neck.

--Its good to be out of the bloody place. Good to be here. I thought I wasn't going to get away. Happy Birthday! He drops onto my much-mocked sofa. But when I come back with two glasses of bubbly his hand isn't steady.

--Are you OK? I ask him.

--Of course. Here. I bought you something.

The something is a soft shop-wrapped parcel. An Agent Provocateur short black kimono edged with red. Inside its all pure scarlet. **AP** embroidered on the belt. --Big thanks. I hold it up. --You should look around – I mean when you're looking to replace me you should go in for an Angie Price or an Anna Pringle or something. There must be a half-decent one around. Just think how impressive that'd be.

I expect him to say something about not wanting to replace me just yet.

He doesn't. He knocks back the wine.

Oh shit!

--There's something else in there. I bought them as well.

--So you did.

The red and dark red pyjamas slither from the box onto the floor. We both look at them. They're beautiful. But I'm thinking, Is he thinking what I'm thinking? That the way they move its like something he's just cut out dropping into a dish – a dish that's being held out by another of his adoring women. I've seen the way Zoe and Becky and the rest move it up a gear when he's around. Even Bernie does.

--Shall we get going? We don't want to lose the table.

Just to break the silence in the car – and not because I give a stuff – I say --Didn't you say Martin lives in Parkgate? Are you sure this is such a good idea?

--Yes he does, he almost snaps at me. --It doesn't matter though.

In what way doesn't this matter?

Doesn't matter because Martin's a Good Bud?

Doesn't matter because at the hospital (which we've just driven past for the second time for him and the first for me that day) Martin

156

is certainly nose to the grindstone? So it doesn't matter because... ?

Then he says --It's his wife you have to watch. That sort of woman never lets anything go.

--Like what?

Pretends he hasn't heard.

Parkgate's about twenty minutes out of town. I've been before. Weird stuff for weird places I think. Basically Parkgate's this spooky little one-horse town that looks like it should be the seaside. But its right on the edge of a marsh. They call it the Dee Estuary but I'm talking grass and mud and pools. If it was somewhere warm you'd call it a swamp. And this goes on for miles and only ends with Wales – which today is a nice pale blue with green hills. According to Lynn the sea *used* to come right the way up here and there was sand and donkey rides – but that must've been back in the days when the Queen was a size 10. No-o. Parkgate's a swampside resort now. It's got a front where people even in November are queuing for ice-cream from a shop with a blue and white stripy canopy flapping in the breeze (freezing of course). And they walk along like its Ibiza only with their grandchildren and their dogs in tow. From our table at Paulo's – the best one – you can look over the marsh where the sand and the donkeys used to be and straight along the river. You can get just a glimpse of the tops of a few waves so you know its really sea out there. When the sun makes it through the clouds it brings up the white of the lighthouse over on the Welsh side and the new windmills that Richard has been going on about while we were driving here. These are so far out they look like toy windmills and none of them are going round.

Like I said a bit on the weird side but it beats South Shields.

--What is it about you and the wet stuff? I ask when we sit down. --live by it, eat by it?

--Don't you like it?

Apart from ourselves there's four old bids just finishing their coffee chatting away in such low voices you'd think they were doing espionage.

Paulo's is small and smart with a polished wood floor and sunshine yellow walls – and soon its going to feel really empty.

--Yeah, its fine.

--If you don't like it –

--I love it. I'm a Scorpio. That's a water sign.

His face puckers – its all *garbage* to him of course. --They're staying open specially.

There's a pause while what I take to be Paulo glides over with an ice bucket.

--That's a waste, I tell him. --The bottle back at the flat's open and you can only have the one.

Drink I meant.

--You have some.

He pours leaving Paulo nothing to do but grin at us and vanish.

Today our Mr Congreve looks blindingly handsome as though I've never noticed it before. And – *pel-ease* – don't tell me anyone is going to get away underimpressed with that they're-staying-open-specially line. I watch the bubbles pop into life in the bottom of the champagne glass and bolt to the surface all at different speeds and then burst as I get them to my lips. I love the feeling.

I love that cow of an SHO having to be *careful* how she asks me for a bit of extra effort --I'm sure you should have been long gone by now Hayley. Sorr-e-ee. Because, well, she doesn't *know*. She might suspect. Just a word to the wise as The Doran would say. Probably was The Doran told her to watch her back.

But nobody *knows* not even Martin knows. As for looking out for Martin's wife why would I?

There's no choice of eats. When the soup comes its cold. I don't mean not very hot. This is freezing. I put the spoon down and – a bit lame this – consider. Try nibbling a bit of bread. What's going on? Richard's already half-through his bowlful. He gets it, of course the mean bastard. --Its meant to be chilled. This is "Vichyssoise". Try it again. It'll grow on you.

I put another spoonful into my mouth. There's a taste is there somewhere – it just keeps getting away from you. The texture is – strange. Nice – really nice on your tongue. And stays nice all the way down or at least I think it does. Just so long as you don't let yourself think the word *slimy*. But once you've done the swallowing its not something you want to repeat.

--Is it Italian?

--French. I asked for it.

--Why?

He gave this more thought than you'd think it needed and managed to finish his last spoonful while he did it. Lucky bugger. --Because, he said, --I like it very much. Because its pale and smooth and cool. It grows on you. There are days when nothing else will do.

I almost ask him to say it again – and then I think about laughing (--You what?) but instead just let it go. My stomach's a knot.

Once the soup's cleared I have another go at the champagne to get it out of my system. Richard I know from past experience is more than happy to sit and look at me or watch something away out at sea or passing the window – then turn back and smile and fill my glass. All without bothering to speak. I can't do it myself. If this is a brush-off brunch –

--Look, what's up? I say.

--Nothing. Is there? I was hoping we were having a good lunch.

On cue Paulo arrives with a trolley affair. There's a deep bowl of spaghetti which he tosses in its red sauce in a pretty professional sort of way and divides between us. There's a lighted burner as well with something cooking on it. He flicks once – twice – and arranges the things he's tipped out the dish around the pasta.

--Enjoy, he says. The accent's more Bootle than Bologna. Perhaps he isn't Paulo after all.

I wait for him to hurry off to the four oldies who are making another meal out of dividing up the bill. --What's this then?

--What do they look like?

--Mini lobsters.

--Close. They're crayfish.

I start to eat out of the middle. --I warn you, its not a pretty sight me and spaghetti – um – wow!

The chilli had just hit my taste buds.

--A sting in the tail.

--I see. Oh, don't tell me, you ordered it all specially? The soup is –

--Exactly what I said it was. And then crayfish were the closest I could get.

I prodded one strawberry-coloured shell with a fork, wondering how you were meant to eat it.

He says --Paulo doesn't do Spaghetti Scorpion.

--Yeah, yeah.

One of the things you need to be able to do as a nurse (aside from all that mopping up and prodding back in) is think quick. An acute condition can alter in an instant. As can what's required. Richard, the same Richard but a different Richard, sat across from me eating now – choosing and winding up strands of red-flecked pasta with surgical niftiness.

This was all for me.

Are you getting this Hayley? I had to ask myself. Are you sure you're getting the full absolutely full-frontal buzz? *This is all for you.*

No one had ever done anything for me – well that's not true. People – Mum and Dad – had done things for me of course when I was still little and sweet. Kat had been a brilliant mate. But no one like Richard (in fact no man) had ever done anything so homed-in on and tailored especially for me.

As a sort of failsafe I couldn't help wondering if it wasn't – well a bit mimsy or naff in a way. The whole meal wasn't just for me. It was about me.

--D'you want to hear what I thought was going on? I asked him.

--Where?

--Here! I thought we were going to finish. I was aiming to sound completely cool and I-could-care-less about it. After that soup I reckoned he had it coming. To demonstrate the not-bothered effect even more I really got stuck into the spaghetti. Soon there'd be nothing left but five fake birth-signs holding pincers around the plate. They'd have to be faced.

I realised he'd put down his spoon and fork.

--I've got you another present, he said. --You'd better have it now.

There was a wave of something that was very like the kick of champagne on an empty stomach but a lot stronger. I thought of my Mum boogying around the little house in Aldershot that was my first

160

home with the sun shining through the slit of a window and the dust flying up into it. *I'm not in lo-ove*, she was singing, *Don't you forge-et it. Its just a silly thing I'm going through.* And then, --Daddy's home tonight, Hayley.

Happiness, just plain stupid old happiness.

God he was handsome – my Dad. When I was a kid. Even handsomer than old handsome-chops here.

--OK I said. --Gimme.

Richard got up and walked across the empty room (even Paulo had disappeared). I saw him struggle with the trenchcoat hanging on its own on the row of hooks. Wrong pocket – right pocket. Whatever it was it was small enough to get lost for a mo. When he came back he sat down and took my hand and placed a little leather jeweller's box in it. Only the fact that this thing looked ancient – and I mean really battered – stopped the whole production being *mucho cornyo*.

I got the one look – then he covered it over with his own hand.

--Before you open it I have something to explain, he says.

Jesus! I think why can nothing be easy with him? Why does even a prezzie have to come with a fucking instruction manual? I don't say it of course and after a second a few more of those bubbles just get around my bloodstream and start to burst.

--Shoot, I tell him.

He gives me the stare. No one can be as full-on as Richard can be when it suits him.

--I want us to be together Hayley, he says. --I can't get much out of life I now find if it doesn't involve you. So that's it. There's no question as far as I'm concerned. Whatever it takes. In the long term I can't see anything else. I *won't have* anything else.

Wow.

I mean – first off – eat your heart out Bridget Jones!

So the thing was – the thing was this. The Richard that'd stood up and walked across to get me the expensive gift (though I'd rather have had a sparkling *new* expensive gift it was – you could bet on it – at least a quality prez) that Richard was a different Richard to the one sitting here now. Because this Richard had changed. If you think of all the him/her stuff as a battle – which it is – you keep hoping that one day the him you're with'll change sides. Be on your side instead of almost everybody's side but yours. Fat chance?

The word is – *it can happen.* You keep hearing about it happening – never to the poor cow that's telling you of course but to someone they know. And it's always really true.

He's moved five hundred miles.

He's blanking all his horrible mates.

He's sold his Harley Davidson.

He's left the band.

It's not that I've ever wanted anyone to do all of the above for me. It's just I've never met anyone who would. Till now.

I stuck my nails in my own knee under the table where he couldn't see me do it. So this was it. I couldn't give a stuff what was in the box now. This was my moment. My Bridget Jones moment.

Except she didn't live in the real world did she? – where Pippa and Richard's boys ate and slept and liked some things and not others? Got colds and scraped their little knees falling over. Were just normal. Who'd only done one bad thing and that was to be there.

--The only question is, Richard said breaking into what I was thinking, is *when.*

--Right.

--I know what this sounds like! Sweet Jesus, if you'd told me a year ago! He looked disbelieving. --This sounds as if I'm one more bastard on the make and spinning you a story. That's the point about what's in the box.

He took it back off me and opened it up and presented me with what was inside like we were in a shop.

The *look* on him – poker-faced – pained – just as though he was the one doing the asking not the giving. And I really didn't want to be bothered with the bloody thing – you know? I just liked that look so much.

I took a peek.

To be honest I was well-disappointed. At first.

It was big – but obviously very old. A big old ring that's all it was – what I remember my Nana Pat calling "costume jewellery". Flashy – the sort of thing that's meant to look like Prince Charles buys Camilla.

Goes with long dresses and cloaks.

Obviously – touching really – it had just been cleaned. Everything was nice and polished up and no dark greasy bits of its previous owner lurking in the crevices. There were two white stones which were just about small enough to be realistic. Think 100mg of Ibuprofen. But the middle one – the pink – was a real monster. Have that on your finger and you'd never get on a pair of gloves. And without gloves you'd be catching everything. Hit someone with it on and you'd leave a bruise on them the size of a plum.

You could always suggest they bowed and kissed it though – like in the mafia.

--Wow, I said out loud this time.

He picked the thing out of its box which to be honest was even scruffier close-to. (When he'd got it done up why hadn't he at least got them to do him another box?) He took hold of my right hand and pushed the ring up over the knuckle of my ring finger. A perfect fit.

--That's lucky!

His expression was pitying but with a bit of a smile to take the worst out. --I made an impression of that silver thing you wear, he said.

--Its very – I don't know. Very different, I suppose – from anything else I've had.

--It will be, he said.

I felt the pressing on my hand get harder till it was nearly pain. He wasn't looking at me anymore. Way out to sea he was looking now. Then even further out than the lighthouse and the windmills something seemed to catch his eye – but when I turned to find out what there was nothing there or I mean nothing extra there. Just the waves getting *latte*-ed by the wind. --Its been in my family a good long time. Its The Rose Ring, he said.

Nobody likes to look a complete dim-bulb.

OK. So –

I could actually feel my brain twittering on – engagement ring dress ring eternity ring friendship ring signet ring navel ring nipple ring *nose* ring no rose ring fuck.

--My great-grandparents were married out in India. (I loved that 'out' thing)

--This is over a century ago. They lived in Chandrapore. Sounds exotic... really very... stuffy and English. I nearly went to India once. Didn't... in the end. Anyway my great-grandfather was.... But his wife... an extraordinary woman by all accounts. Her name was Rose – Rose you see? He, my great-grandfather... absolutely besotted with her....

OK. So its boring right? I'm not exactly hanging on his every word.

--Celebrate their tenth anniversary, he goes, and on and on. --Ring made. He put the word out... gem dealers all over India... a pink diamond... to Amsterdam to be cut and polished. Its six and a half carats now – it would've been bigger when rough because... in the cutting. I've just had it in for appraisal. And then it needed – adjustment. I think its come up pretty well – don't you?

What do you say? I just nodded – and hoped my mouth hadn't been hanging open.

--Do you know they had an old chap working for them whose *father* still remembered it? The father... knew the man who'd done the setting. But it seems to have made an impression even back then. The story as well as the ring I'd say. He thinks Country Life did a piece on it but I haven't been able to... you'd need the exact date –

His voice trailed off, almost nervous? Na.

He said --I suppose the other two diamonds were just because of the style of the times. You can't imagine the Victorians as solitaire types.

Whatever this last bit was on about the story was meant to give the ring a touch of more-than. I gave it a turn so if he was looking he could see me admiring etc. Ni-i-ce. Even if it was still so flash it was embarrassing. And he was giving it me. I couldn't have got that wrong – could I? I was warm – all warm inside – *and* I'd managed not to say --You mean its real?

Another good thing. Now time to make a real effort, girl.

--Anyway, he goes on, --as often happened in those days, poor Rose died while she was still a young woman. The ring went into the bank and didn't come out again till my grandfather volunteered for the Second World War. I think the idea was to give it to my grandmother on her tenth wedding anniversary. But she got it a year early... old man... afraid... son... come back – and of course... a little boy by this time my father to carry on.... He knew the ring wouldn't have just gone out of the family... it was important.

He stopped talking. I'm stupid I know. I thought I was keeping up but you don't do you? He'd said that was important. And before that he'd been saying stuff about the family – but it was his family for Chrissake. Who really listens when people start going on about their sister in Canada or Grandad Somebody who was in the war? Nobody. If it had been about Richard himself of course I'd have been right on in there –

--But he did come back. His wife gave it to my mother on – I'm sure you're getting the hang of this now – *her* and my father's –

--Tenth anniversary, I filled in. Was I pleased or what?

--Exactly.

There was another pause while he sort of stroked the ring but only for a second and then laid the same hand on my bare arm. It certainly helped with the concentration. --When she died it went back into the bank. And when the old man himself died –

I'd known he'd lost both his parents but –

--So when did your Dad die?

--Last March. Eight months ago.

--But – ohmygod Richard that was when we first –

--Met. He smiled like there was nothing painful at all attached to it.

--So it could only have been – a week or so? I'm trying to ask but –

--Ah thank you!

A little dumpy woman had popped up out of nowhere and was trying to clear our plates.

--It was very nice, I felt I had to say even though the mini-lobster things were still in their daisy-chain whereas most of Richard's had been sort of post-mortemed. How had he managed that while also doing the whole Bollywood plot? And how had I not noticed?

--Would you like pudding?

--Is it Hayley Forest Gateau or something?

--Close.

--Can we have it in a few minutes? Are you all right for time?

--Of course. And yes.

He said --Pudding in a while and then coffee, to the woman – who now I bothered to have a proper look at her was a dead-ringer for Dame Judi Dench. She probably *was* Dame Judi Dench. Ordered specially. To me once she was out of earshot he said --My father was found dead that day I picked you up at the end of the drive.

--Bloody hell, Richard!

--To get back to the ring? I haven't finished what I wanted to tell you.

My father was found dead that day I picked you up.

He'd stopped and wound down the window and let Eva Cassidy come spilling out – and inside his head was this new future opening up – one where his Dad was gone for good. I'd seen it often enough in HDU. The gobsmacked expressions. The totally off-the-wall things they said.

Sometimes they howl like an animal and sometimes they just cave-in with misery.

Sometimes of course they're thinking of the quickest route home to check-up on the will. But Richard had made his move on the new nurse – the one he'd had his eye since she'd arrived.

--Right, I said.

--Pippa has never seen it. She knows there's my mother's jewellery but she's never shown any interest in it.

--But she must know the story!

--No. She doesn't.

--Why doesn't she?

--I don't know. I never told her. The old man – you have to understand he thought the world of Pippa. He bought her something – something new – when each of the boys was born. If he'd been alive he's the one that would've given it her. I imagine.

He was smart. You had to hand it to him. He knew it was time to stop mentioning Pippa that someone else thought the world of. --In six weeks' time I'll have been married for ten years.

--And –

Its not that I'm slow on the uptake its that you don't want to be caught out looking a complete idjut. How stupid would I feel if I was just meant to admire – say something along the lines of I'm-sure-she'll-love-that and hand it back?

--And you're giving it to *me*?

--Attempting to.

All we needed were for those bloody windmills to choose this moment to start spinning. But they stayed still. They stayed just a forest of little white sticks and crosses in the mist. It must have been the one thing Richard couldn't arrange.

Why Mistresses Never Have Beams

--He said it was worth *how much*?

Bernie Rosco, my mate Bernie, lives in the flat next door. The one with the fountains-view over four lanes of traffic. I want it. Well some days I want it. But then it was only down to Bernie I'd got my own place him knowing me from work and knowing I was on the look-out. (Richard was on the look-out).

If you saw Bernie first off you'd think *weirdo*. What a funny little bloke. He's so white he's pink (never goes in the sun – *says* he's allergic but he's terrified of wrinkles – which is why he's got half of Boots in his bathroom cupboard and when he does go out in the daylight its smothered in Factor 95). But then he's got this – well you'd have to say pretty face and it must be regular in a way that most faces aren't because – here's a creepy thing – when Bernie looks in a mirror he's exactly the same. Oh and he's got proper cheekbones. Now mine are good but his – God I'll wish I had those cheekbones in twenty years' time.

He's a lot smaller than your average – only comes up to my shoulder when he's in bare feet – and very quick. Everything he does is quick but not *hurried* – which is a no-no for a nurse anyway tending to scare the shit out the sick. But with him its like he's living at a faster pace than the rest of us. He sits down – he jumps up – he's putting on music – he's noticing your hair –

He's lovely anyway. Sometimes if you just stop thinking what people ought to look like he's beautiful. I've never met anyone who could grow on you like Bernie.

--Its worth about seventy-five thousand pounds, I said. --*At least* seventy-five thousand.

--One ring?

--Yeah – cheapskate! Where d'you get yours – out of a cracker?

--Oh! Get Zsa Zsa Gabor!

--Who?

Bernie hated it. --You know quite well who she is.

--I don't.

--You're just taking the piss.

--I'm not. Would I?

What a little madam he could be when rubbed up – or down – the wrong way.

--Of course, he said all nasty his eyes going wide as a little kid's that couldn't manage innocent. --Of course, he said, you only have his word for it, don't you? I mean its a great line but like so many other great lines it doesn't have to be true.

We were in his bathroom which was the image of my bathroom only cleaner and with more stuff in it. Even from across the steamy room (I was sitting on a carved wood affair that you can bet came from Bangkok) I could see the suds on his bathwater had started to settle. --Give your bubbles a whip up, will you? I don't want reminding of Men's Medical while I'm off.

He stared down before giving it a stir. --Don't tell me you get to see a body like this one every day. He pinched his own biceps but lovingly. --Not on Belgrave Ward, you don't.

This was one-nil to him to be honest. He may be all of five-foot in his loafers but hour after hour at the Northgate Arena (which was handily between us and those bloody fountains) kept everything that needed work on a twenty-seven year old in exactly the right place. Too tight that. Really.

Bernie's is a great little body. Makes you think of one of those athletes in the white leotards that do all that spinning round things with clenched buttocks and pointed toes. As you can imagine he has a bit of a following at the hospital – and they're not all grateful dischargees from Cardiology either. A few of them wouldn't mind the view I was getting from my Thai torture-seat. The dome of his head glittered with waterdrops being completely shiny – as was everything else I could see.

Egg smooth and pink. It was Bernie got me into waxing – you know the full Brazilian – but he had The Lot! Back. Crack. And sack. What a pain threshold. He reminded me of a plastic doll that was the only boy doll I ever had. Jonathan I called him. You could dress him as a sailor, a fireman or a doctor.

Bernie took the real sponge and squeezed it over his shiny scalp. Spluttered.

--I mean seventy-five thousand pounds. *At least.* I'm sorry love but really how likely is it? Trust me – its a guy-thing.

I nearly choked laughing.

--Oh well Miss Done-It-All – you'll see.

--You just don't get it! I told him.

Do you know how when you're writing a letter (which I don't) you only find out what you mean to say as you get it down? Bernie certainly didn't get it – but then neither did I till I opened my mouth to argue it out. It was as though Bernie was that blank sheet of paper and I was making up my plan for the future on him – but as I went along.

Dear Bernie – You know this Richard Congreve I've been mentioning off and on? The God's gift to femalekind? The old bloke thinks he's still front-of-the-chiller-fresh? Well I've got to tell you – he's fit!

--Run us some more hot in there's a love, Bernie said. --If I move from here you'll be getting the vapours again.

Funny isn't it? – how in lots of ways Bernie was so much easier to be with than Richard? – needed so much less effort that you didn't have to be on your guard a lot of the time thinking about the next move? Through the new steam straight from the tap his rosy little face was full of interest – and if it wasn't entirely friendly and just for the person he was looking at it wasn't neutral either. A good nurse's expression that.

You could see how he massaged hearts all right.

--Its like I told you about the moving-in thing.

--You think that'll be next?

--Oh yeah I do. We have some good times at the cottage. *Really* good times – but its just playing house isn't it? Its not real. You sit there at this dinky little table with your dinky little coffee mugs – its two o'clock in the afternoon and you're talking about whether you should go and see Portmeirion or just go back to bed. That's not real.

He surprised me by flashing me this tragic look. --Can be overrated real life. If you ask me.

I could've asked. I know now I should've asked. --So, I said, --I'm going to say no. When he wants to move in here. I know it sounds big-headed but I know its coming. These days he never wants to get going on his way. And – *and* its as though he's daring himself to do it. You see him at it leaving it later and later. But we've got the cottage so we can always have a weekend away – and yes I know I've said I'll take you sometime but I'm not taking Phil all right? Oh – and did I tell you the latest? He's given Nancy my number. This number – just in case? Its a bloody nuisance sometimes. And did you catch that? *I'm going to say no!*

He must have water in his ears.

--And if she's in on it – well obviously she's totally tight-lipped when it comes to her best boy but – come on! You don't think there's anybody else at the hospital? We've been so not careless. *I'm going to say no by the way to him moving in.* Apart from you and that SHO –

--The Doran, Bernie chipped in.

--So she does know! Not Chatroom Doran! You're sure about that are you?

He grinned.

--Because you told her. *Bernie!*

He said --Sweetheart it was a trade.

Well-miffed I stomped off next door and poured myself a glass of that flat champagne. It was still in the fridge from Monday. In my new silk pyjamas and with the tall new champagne glass in my hand I could sit and look out over the balcony if I wanted. Watch all those poor turkeys coming and going down in the courtyard. Yeah here was one. Fat squeezed into a too-tight jacket that I bet was no match for that wind. And she was dragging a baby-buggy towards the entrance to my block and being held back by shopping bags and a toddler. I could see by the look on his little face he was in mid-whinge and she – his mum – gave his arm a bit of a tug – not that hard but you could hear him howl from four floors up. Who'd want to be her eh? Still it was too cold and miserable to have the poor little thing out.

For a while everything went quiet. Where the circles from the lamps didn't quite meet it got properly black. I don't know why but just looking at that pattern of sicky artificial light and the black shadows really creeped me out. Keep your eyes on those shadows for long enough and they turned into holes – that was it. The pavement had come out in this rash of deep black holes and the paths were just a narrow way through them. How on earth that woman and her pushchair had made it to the lobby –

Of course blink and it wasn't there anymore. That old familiar courtyard clicked back into place. But tea-time it shouldn't be this empty. Not with most of the lights on in my block and the other low-rises round the square. There ought to be a lot more in the way of life going on down there. I had this urge to carry on watching and waiting until there was at least another sign of not being the last woman on the planet. At last *finally* this skinny kid well bloke but my age – I'd seen him around – rode up on a racing bike and tried to bolt it to an also-skinny tree. I could see it was a struggle.

I almost knew him. It was somebody came to visit Bernie now and again but – not being hospital – I didn't have a name. He was another part of Bernie – a part of Bernie not for sharing. (--I am a man of many parts and all of them scrumptious, he'd say).

Chaining the bike to a tree was what I'd seen this bloke do before. But for some reason this time he botched it. A bit wouldn't catch or wouldn't reach. He stepped away and turned to get the light on what he was fiddling with and dropped something – the lock or chain I guess – and you could watch him lose patience. The shoulders got all bunched up inside his Lycra suit and he rounded on the bike like he expected it was about to take a bite out of his arse. Suddenly some metal object got thrown down. Even from up here I thought I could hear the clang as it hit the paving – o-oh temper! I bet if I remember to look there'll be a hole in that slab. And you know the thing about people knowing when they're being watched? Its true. I swear he knew. He looked straight up at me. Stared. Didn't like it.

He gave up then. He must've left the lock. Just rode off really fast – pedalling out his anger.

I had to laugh. I didn't have a name still but I knew who this was.

A month ago I'd been sitting in Bernie's all-cream lounge waiting while he was getting ready. I was fed up (Richard had taken Pippa and the kids to the cottage) and I was off to the multiplex on the Greyhound Park to see some poncy new thriller Bernie said we had to see. It'd be so lame – I knew before we got there – but Bernie being Bernie he wouldn't let me fall asleep. Anyway the phone went and – well I could say without thinking I picked it up. But I thought about it all right. And then I picked it up.

--Hello.

--Is Ross there? I want to speak to Ross please.

The voice was a bit sharp. *And what I've got to tell him he's not going to like* it seemed to say. It reminded me of the voices around the army camp when I was little – not servicemen I mean. Not the blokes who'd call for Dad to go out on the piss because they came from all over and some you couldn't even understand. This was a civvie voice. A local. And local when I was a kid was anywhere around Aldershot.

--There's no one called Ross lives here.

I nearly put it down he waited so long to speak.

--Is that his sister?

--No! I've said. --There isn't any Ross here.

(A big, noisy sigh).

--Just put him on will you?

--Just piss off will you?

--Piss off yourself.

Bernie wandered in all sweet smelling and rosy as a cherub to see me slamming down. --What's going on?

--Somebody wanting Ross. I told them they'd got the wrong –

--What did he say?

--*He* told me to piss off – oh yeah and was I Ross's sister?

What made me really mad was how Bernie burst out laughing at this. He laughed so much he had to hold his ribs and then he lay on the cream carpet in his cream bathrobe and rolled and drummed his heels.

--Get up, you soft sod, I told him.

--Are you my sister? he nearly sobbed. --You didn't tell him you were, did you? Oh please – *purl-ease* – tell me you didn't tell him you were?

--Why would I do that?

I was getting in a strop not that Bernie ever cared about how mad he made you. Always knew he could talk you round. --I just told him this Ross bloke wasn't here. He wanted somebody called Ross, didn't he?

--Oh yes, of course he did. Just Ross. And not even Ross Ber*nard*.

He made it sound like a French hairdresser. Bernie had to get up now because he'd stopped laughing and lost his excuse for being down there on his back. One second he was flat on the carpet the next he was standing in front of the electric fire glass in hand. It was the slickest move ever like a video of him falling over had been rewound.

--And was he confused I'll bet! he said. Serve him right.

And if that wasn't Mr Aldershot down in the courtyard and now peddling along Black Diamond Street with a face that could make cheese I was Miss Chester.

OK I thought. OK I could exfoliate something or start on the box of Belgian brandy truffles that had been Bernie's present (I can eat anything me) – and all the time imagine a real mistress might do this sort of stuff of a late afternoon on a week day. I could –

The wine without its bubbles looked like a specimen waiting for a glucose-tolerance test. I chucked it down the sink and went for a rifle through the bedroom.

Richard was more in here than anywhere else. In here I could believe there was his smell and his shape in the mattress (although I'd slept in it on my own twice since then). On top of the white chest of drawers I suddenly noticed there was his stripy green silk tie sort of squirming around the Body Shop bottles and pots and letting its tail hang down to the first set of handles. Shit! What if it was missed? If it was a favourite. What if it was a special gift – like a tie bought on that trip him and her took to London something of that sort? – or worse, what if it was a Fathers' Day/Christmas/birthday present from 'The Boys'?

I was going to say no.

Its not that I'm mad-keen on boys – little boys that is. In the event of me getting pregnant I'll be doing my damnedest to pop out a girl even if it means a lemon and yoghurt dressing on you-know-what *and* hanging upside-down from the light-fitting, before and after sex. One. Yeah – just the one mini-me Hayley-Jane. I could manage that. Whereas I don't even like little boys – its all that pulling the legs off things and the shoes whiffing of wee. But –

And here's the But big as Staff Nurse Doran's.

Why do the dirty on them when you can avoid it? Its not as if –

But I don't know as if what.

Richard should understand. After all who is it made sure every single one of the kids' bits and bobs were stashed out of sight in the cottage? (And then leaves out the photos of them and their mother for me to see).

Things don't have to be one or the other that's all I'm saying. Being a mistress you have plenty of time to think it through weigh it up. Because you're the one. I mean in every film and mini-series and in all the soaps – you're the one. You're the bad girl. By the end of it the people watching want you to die in a road accident or slip in the shower – or better still turn out to be the next victim of that bonkers bloke that's killed ten girls already in really messy ways.

There you are with your modern flat

They never have beams mistresses.

Its always a modern flat – and a shiny car.

Richard's got the bronze Polo on order.

I don't want to be that one – the one that has the wife crying in close-up and filling the screen so you can see even her nose running – the snot of misery running down her nose.

In the background the kids are all wide-eyed and scared about what'll happen next.

When he asks? 'cos he will. --No I'll say – you can't move in here. Not for a good bit yet.

Stay at home sometimes and pretend because you can bet they'll pretend along with you.

I don't go a bundle on all this honesty business.

Look what it did for Charles and Di.

Let's give it a couple of years.

I might even wear the bloody thing now and again.

Let's just keep it to half-hours and half-days and the odd weekend away.

Its A Mad World

--Kiss and make-up? I texted you twice. Your phone's off.

I was just getting myself ready for an early night when there's Bernie at the door black trackie bottoms and black cashmere V-neck and bare feet with the nails new-varnished – more black. I stood back to let him in.

--Can we not do the kiss-bit? I said. I was still narked.

--Aw, Hayley. I'm only jealous. I'm still waiting for some rich stiff to sweep me off my feet – that's all it is. He glided past in a wave of Hugo Boss. The pink flush from the hot water was still showing on his neck and the waxed-smooth triangle of chest. What with the bright hall bulb picking out every pore he very nearly looked his age – which cheered me up no end. But then I wasn't the faithful Phil or whoever – no I was the girl who'd found the first grey hair in her fringe that morning. A dye job – that's what I was going to get.

--I'm not offering you anything, I said following him in. --I've cleaned my teeth.

--Oh and there's me thinking we'd go over to Baby Cream and have a bite. Its not what you'd call late, is it? (Baby Cream was our night out of choice at the moment). --Except I was there with well never mind and anyway we come out and somebody got bricked. Right in front of us. There's a zip-up goes on top of this – he pointed at the sweater --and Phil's got me new *snakeskin* loafers. I look so good in

175

the whole lot I'm dangerous.

His eyes flicked round and then stuck on something down on the courtyard – just the way it happens when somebody walks in and gets interested in your telly. Really bothers me that. When people do it you just have to have a look yourself don't you? In case its Posh and Becks on a bed of jelly.

--What is it? I asked him.

--Nothing, he goes. --I thought I saw something – no, nothing.

I nearly mentioned Mr Aldershot but came down on the side of him not deserving it.

--Are you here to see me or just for the view?

You can't quell Bernie. He curled up on the sofa and hugged his own knees and started admiring his toes – then had a test prod at the varnish and a grumble under his breath at whatever small not-right something he'd found. --You couldn't tempt me anyway, he said, I'm on the Atkins till the end of – ooh next month probably. Right up to the twenty-fifth. I've got my sights set on losing half a stone. See I'm going to our Hazel's for Christmas – its Yule-tide with Mother for poor old Phil. *But* Hazel's hubby can't stand me – naturally! – so I'm going as svelte. Just to put his *twenty-four-inch* (I swear to God!) neck to shame.

It wasn't in me to stay mad at him. Nobody could. Who else is going to get my intercom when he knows Richard is down there and shout No trainers! Home you go! --Diet? I say. --It was only the other week you were telling me how now you're perfect. Remember – how I said I was getting that stripy dress from Cheshire Oaks after all and you said to get away with stripes I'd need to be prefect *like you*? I remember you saying it. As you would if I'd said it to you. Anyway you're svelte already whatever svelte means – don't you need to be tall?

--You do not!

--Bernie?

--What?

--Can fat boys be gay?

--They are taken on, he said all serious --as probationers. We give them six months to get in shape and then they're reweighed. If they fail the floor opens up like on James Bond and sends them straight to

Fat Queen Hell – where everybody has to wear a T-shirt from Cecil Gee and a big black belt with studs to hold their gut up.

I nearly asked him about the bony biker.

I nearly gave in and suggested we hit Richard's gin except I don't really like it. In fact I need to be desperate. If pressed – if say you said this is your last drink on earth so what'llitbeHayley it wouldn't be Mumm that's for sure. I'd go for a peach schnapps half-and-half with lemonade. Lesbo's you call them. Kat and I used to make them on a slow night in.

--Why go to Hazel's if he hates you? I asked him. --You get enough invites I'll bet.

--Because – well be-e-cause-se he works for some load of boring sods that do things with pylons – don't ask me what sort of things I can't begin to explain. Its enough for you to know that Pete does things up them. He lives in a very rarefied atmosphere – up his pylons. I'm broadening his horizons. Bringing him into contact with the gay community – down here on the ground.

I yawned.

--Well, that's enough about me. What about this ring then? You know I can resist anything but a luxury gift. Bring it on. Let the dog see the rabbit. Let's see if old tit-face has got taste as well as a temper.

--I didn't say I took it did I? I pointed out.

--No. No you didn't.

He gave me one of his old-fashioned looks and winked. --And of course I can easily see how it might've gone. Bernie had this deep voice that he adopted when he was trying to imitate Richard. Needless to say nothing like. He slipped into it now.

--Oh Hayley I love you! Please take this really really expensive family heirloom off my hands (he does a falsetto – much more convincing) --Oh no Mr Congreve! What sort of girl d'you think I am? You can't buy me with a big diamond ring. *And* anyway you've already had me in every position bar dangling from the suspension bridge on a Sunday afternoon.

I went into the bedroom and found the little leather case where I'd put it to be safe with my Next store-card and my address book and my provisional driving license and my Dad's last ever card from

Kuwait. There they were all huddled together under my knickers like some saddo time-capsule. I came back wearing the ring. It actually looked more ridiculously oversized now than when Richard had put it on me.

--Just don't drool all over my sofa. I pulled it off again – handed it across.

Bernie's little pink paw was on it like a shot. It was pushed up his own ring finger and held out for what I guessed was intending to be snide admiration.

--Lord love a duck! Its fucking *massive*!

His normally I'm so knowing you don't get one over on me look completely deserted him. After *massive* his mouth just hung open.

--See!

--Its absolutely drop-dead humungous! Hayley its – Christ. Christ. I'm –

He had a fiddle with it and lined it up more neatly on his hand and stuck it out again to pick up the light. --Oh my God!

--Nice isn't it?

--You think?

--Well, I do now.

--Can I have a lend of it?

--No!

--Aw yes! Say yes. Go on you tight bitch. Look at it! He wiggled his finger in my face, --Just look at it. David Furnish – that's me.

--Who?

He was so excited he had to jump to his feet and parade around my living room –which didn't really offer the space for parading – and try and catch his reflection in my big long mirror and try to get the ring to flash on his hand.

And then I realized why it was I'd never bothered keeping in touch with Kat since I'd come to Chester. Why I hadn't really missed her.

Bernie was Kat.

Well-smitten with some different bloke every week but always going back to Phil his ever-attentive paramedic. Always ready to spill the complete tin of beans down to the last mouthful of tomato sauce. Always up for a laugh.

--Go on. You've got to. You've got to, he wheedled. --It looks better on me. You must see that. Anyone can see it does. Oh – and, oh, no!

He was whirling round. Then he jumped up and down with one hand gripping the other. --No-oo! Its stuck! See? Won't come off. Stuck fast. Its mine. Mine I say!

--Cut it out Gollum. I threw a cushion at him that bounced off his polished head and nearly hit some of the stuff that never quite balanced on the shelves. Since I was on my feet to rescue the cushion I held out my hand. He dropped the ring into it. --It must be love then, eh? he said, --You and him.

I put in on. Still a perfect fit. --Yeah. Its been sort-of quick, you know? But yeah it is. This is it. I really love him Bernie. How lame is that? Go on. How bloody lame is that – you tell me? It'll take a while sorting through the crapheap. But that'll be OK. That'll be an OK thing to do – you know not grabbing too much for yourself? You have to think of other people – like I've had a lot of practice at that! *And* sometimes he makes me want to scream.

--Oh sex still good then.

--Brilliant since you're asking. I mean excellent.

I could hardly even say it right there in cold blood to Bernie without a bit of a shiver. Now that was way out of Scott Freemantle's league. --There are times – oh Christ! – is he up for it Bernie. Even when I'm getting on his nerves – taking the piss you know?

--Oh I *know*!

He was nodding away sitting there like a pocket Buddha. With his old/young face and the shiny-head-thing and his shrewd little eyes he could easily have passed for the God of Something. Something a bit pervy.

We both go quiet at this thinking our separate things. And then he starts to sing Bernie does. He's got a real voice too not karaoke.

Little children waiting till they feel good,
Happy birthday, happy birthday.

--Ah, nice one! I said.

Have you noticed how when people *can* sing they always have to do it?

And I think its kinda funny
I think its kinda sad
That the dreams in which I'm dying
Are the best I ever had
Its a mad world

--Hey, d'you want to hear something really funny? he said. --I've got this friend right? And he's absolutely crazy about this song. Thinks its the best song ever written – well he tends to go over the top – *inn-ten-sse* you know? – always playing it. Thinks Donnie Darko's the greatest movie ever made. (It isn't). Sees it ten times anyway. Then it starts – he's singing it when he thinks no one's about. So I come in this day and he's – what was it? – yeah he's cooking us a meal. And he's there by the cooker – you need to picture this you really do – he's there frying away with his onions and peppers or whatever and he's singing, Bernie dropped his voice so I guessed the friend was lower than him, more *manly* I'll bet. --I promise to God he's singing, And I think its kinda funny/I think its kinda sad that the *jeans* in which I'm dying are the best I ever had. Its a mad world.

--What did you say?

--Well it cracked me up didn't it? I just had to tell him. The pillock! The jeans in which I'm dying – I ask you?

--Oh I bet he loved that.

He nodded and you could see the mood change – the fun go out of the fair as I remember Kat saying once. --Not so much David Furnish, am I? Fuck – that means I must be Elton John!

--I've got it if you want – *Mad World*. I could put it on?

--No, let's not shame poor Gary. I'm an impossible act to follow.

I flicked through and found something I liked just then.

Suddenly he leaps up and grabs me and we dance around the room – around the sofa that we can only get behind by Bernie pushing it with the top of his thigh but still dancing like it was part of it and back into the centre where he leans away from me and pumps up the Scissors Sisters and turns me hip to hip against the wall. *Out of the corner of my eye/ I turned to look and it was gone,* I think they're going. We sing along circling back again – sofa – shelves – back towards the open curtains and the black glass of the doors. Our reflections pop up as though they're shimmying on the balcony. Not too shabby at all.

What is going on with him tonight? He's sneaking another look outside when he thinks I'm not noticing – just a peek as we twirl. With everything bright and fun – and foxy me as well – he wants to gawp at the dark! But he seems to see – or not see – what he needs to and snuggles up again.

--D'you like Barry Braddock? he asks out of nowhere. --They say he's gonna be on the next *Celebrity Shootout*.

--Yeah, he's well-witty.

--Isn't he just? And yet I know somebody can't stand him.

I nearly whisper *What's his name then?*

--Takes all sorts I say.

He thinks about this a bit. --What you have to remember sweetie, he says his face pressed along my chin bone, --is this. Sex is more like feeding than its like friendship. You get it? That's why it can go all to hell in a big way.

--Maybe I say fending him off and I flop down. I give him one last flash of diamonds before I go to put the ring away. --But I've got this!

I flaunt it under his cute nose.

I say --I know what Cinder-elton! Some time if you're a really good boy and be my slave then you can borrow it. But just the once.

PART 6

The image for the postcard has been taken in another season. It shows a sky of un-mixed blue hung between the upper corners. Beneath, there's a wide arc of turquoise water. A tropical glare is laid across this still surface: a true mirror for the out-of-shot sun.

Even the empty sand dazzles.

"What's that? Just on the edge – poking through those bushy things. The thing there. A hat?"

"It's a chimney pot."

"Uh-huh."

"That's the cottage... This is the place – I thought you'd want to see it."

"Right. Why's there nobody on the beach?"

"I don't know. I suppose it just happened that way – perhaps whoever took the photo waited for it to clear."

"But there aren't any footprints."

The card is twisted though it resists tearing even at the point of holding, even as it becomes the focus of a silent struggle. But the faultless sky, the luminous sea, crack beneath their shiny coating.

"Aw! Now look!"

"It's only a postcard. But there aren't any footprints, are there? No sandcastles. Nobody's kids or dogs. No people. What does that tell you?"

"It tells me it's just a postcard. For tourists. Look. Look there. Says Morning, Aberhiw Bay, by Ian Southerin."

"Who sent it you?"

"Nobody sent it me, did they? It was for sending – to someone else. Somebody else bought it and then gave it me. I just wanted you to see where we're going."

i

"Elly! Elly, quick! They've found a body," Martin said.

"Good for them," I said. I'd hardly peeled my jacket off. I was all bitter through work, still, and responding on autopilot to Martin's voice. An angry exchange with my boss was on continuous loop in my head, though it had been over for hours.

Across the lawn Marjorie, immaculate in lilac linen, was pretending to dead-head Dorothy Perkins. But any moment she'd be over here. A timely coughing bout for attention, then: *I see you've nothing planned, Elly – come through in about an hour. I've made enough* (Fill in blank) *to feed....*

"No, listen," he said, pulling me with him into the next room. "It'll come on again at the end, with the headlines." We stared at a screen-full of stationary traffic which could be from the same batch I'd been sitting in. Martin had to raise his voice over the litany of travel misery. "Just give it a minute. They've found a body on the beach. You know – *the beach?* Washed up yesterday."

Shock: not at the finding of the body but at the sudden fear I had of having treated it with disrespect. *A real whole body – no, forget the whole bit. A real body.*

Just a human finger, its emblem, had accompanied me as I'd cleared the table, climbed the stairs, undressed. And then it had found its way back here... and followed me to the office, week after week. While I rattled away at a keyboard, my third eye watched over it. I visualised the thing, curled in the bottom of a Moorcroft pot and far from secure on a bathroom shelf. Out on the Aberhiw shingle, hadn't I thought it *so* funny? I'd told myself there was always going to be something comic about *parts*.

It's early evening on a Friday in Edens Drive: Martin's curtailed working day is still-lifed in an empty Peroni bottle up against a chair-leg, a plate full of crumbs on the hearth. Several new paperbacks are fanned like a hand of cards on the sofa.

"Tell me now. What they said."

"Not much. You know how they put these things. Police are – are trying to identify a badly decomposed body or remains... yes, remains found, um – didn't say who by. But they definitely said Aberhiw Bay.

186

Gave a shot of the beach. Empty though."

"Is that it?"

By now I'm feeling for a seat with the backs of my trembling legs. My whole frame seems to engage itself in guilt and fear, as though the muscles themselves have been used in some aberrant act and are about to be found out. Inevitably my chest tightens. Soon I'll *have* to sit... a real dead person was out there all the time, while Martin and I drank Chilean red and spit sand out from the rim of plastic beakers. Our backs against the warm cliff, we'd lazed an afternoon away with the *Hamlyn* guide to birdlife that we'd found in the cottage. Once, Martin had been convinced he'd seen a dolphin. A glimpse of a body wouldn't have been out of the question, then.

We'd sifted the flotsam and jetsam like a couple of totters.

And despite that second yellowing note in Pippa's hand: **All Visitors Please Take Care This Bay Can Be Dangerous – The Tide Comes In Very Fast And There Are Strong Currents**, we'd bathed.

I don't believe in ghosts but Christ am I scared of them. My blameless stomach is now trying to return the afternoon's espresso into my gullet. I say, "*Martin*, what else? Have they any idea who she is?"

"She?"

"She! The woman whose body you're supposed to be telling me about –"

"They didn't say she. She's a he. They said 'what are believed to be the remains of a man's body'. Yeah, that was it. I'm sure." He looked absurdly satisfied with this accomplishment of recall.

"Who is it?"

"No idea – I mean they've got no idea."

"A man?"

"Yes-s."

"*A man?*"

"Do you think they've got it wrong?"

I can feel my heart hammering on my ribcage. A minute comes and goes while I fail to muster the breath to respond to this typical Martin suggestion. *No, Martin I don't suppose there's any mistake.*

ii

I think it was just the detachment that did it. Say you find a single human finger at the highest margin of the Aberhiw tide-line. It's somebody's finger. Look closer… it's somebody's ring-finger. With just one finger so much is left to be resolved. A death, a kidnapping, a gruesome act of self-mutilation that'll be sure to get attention. Pretty-well nothing's unfeasible. Make of it what you like. It's your commission. Anywhere is the place of its origin, anyone its closest living relative. And yet at the same time it's a pointer to clarity. Because whatever else goes on, there is this single something that has to be – at some time, in whatever fashion – joined up.

Write me, the finger said. *Do it. You know who I belong to.*

I knew.

How I knew began one afternoon of heat. In Goa. He was one of those enchanting teenage boys that drive teenage girls and old men off their heads. Dark skinned for an Iberian though pale amongst Goans, the attraction of his face was in its perfect arrangement of all the parts beneath a particularly marked widow's peak. It was an elfin face. The eyes were so heavy with melanin that the pupils were indistinguishable from the irises and hinted at malevolence – but the high cheekbones and delicate pink rolls of the lips were too sensitive for those eyes to trouble you for long. The boy was a poet or at least an artist. There couldn't be any real ill-will, you told yourself, because that sort of puppy-torturing, evil-for-the-sake-of-it only came about through disappointment or frustration or lack of care. And which of these had ever impinged on Leon del Costas' short life? None of the above.

"That's an attractive boy – that Leon, I mean," I said to Martin.

"He's a pleasure to teach. Very bright. He's not got the complete grasp of syntax of – little Krishnan Choudray, say," he pointed at the dwindling figures, the brilliancy of the white shirts still shining out against the tree-shade of the drive, "he's the smaller of the two brothers. But Leon, he's got a sort of feel for the language the rest don't have. *And reads.* Puts the books away a couple a week."

We were standing, watching them out of sight: a quartet of boys that looked as though they'd stepped out of another century… Leon ruffles the hair of one of the others – but of course I see now it was probably a slap. The taller of the Choudray brothers intervenes. Tawny dust on a road devoid of motor-traffic is kicked up and swirls around them until nothing of what follows can be made out. Just a cloud where your mind tells you there are boys.

Although you could lay a huge amount of blame on Martin for letting my almost-complete book fall into Leon's hands, you have to give him credit for the quality of his teaching. On Leon he'd done the bizz. The narrative, my narrative, in neither particularly simple nor learner-friendly language, had been thoroughly absorbed. Only then could the boy have been able to get onto the task of editorship. There were a plethora of crossings out and alterations and revisions to my work: Leon's English was certainly up to the challenge. In this case the challenge was to fill every line break, every bit of margin and every indentation with his own commentary and additions. They were expressed in obscenities that, whilst never sacrificing clarity, were positively baroque. I have only fragments of it now – but one piece I know by heart. *Know* in the way the irritation of a simple tune gets into the head and can't be knocked out again (though this is years ago, as I've said).

It goes: **Mr Christopher sitting with Mrs Elly across very giant COCK, Mrs Elly bouncing on cock TWICE as big as Mr Kents shouting Cock Christopher, Saint Christopher Cock, oh better BETTER by much than that creep Kents tickle, More Cock Christopher Mr Christopher ace of cocks!**

Sub-Joycian, some of it. By luck? Hardly. My picture of Leon always had something of the gilded *leprechaun* about it – remembering that not everything small and cute needs protection and that gold occurs in some dirty declivities.

If only it could've been held onto, the Leon Version. Because it'll never come around again. On and on, page after page… a hundred and eighty-nine pages, to be exact and not one left unbesmirched. You had to hand it to the lad. Leon, as narrator, was a pretty original filter for the world. And that world was Goa, one small jumbled almost-island of a place, with its map held in his head. The bits he highlighted were those I'd been hardly aware of. For example, there was the outsiders' stupid acceptance of some elements of life in Panjim and beady-eyed dismay at others. Watching the young Western drifters, he had clocked a backpacker with filthy clothes and matted hair, how he carefully removed the cap from the beer bottle with his own belt-buckle rather than let the waiter do it; how to drink he arranged his lips as seal but only on the virgin glass the top had covered. If he hated the rangy foreigners with their improvisation of simplicity, his scorn for my Lakshmi went far beyond any standard sixteen-year-old machismo. She was desirable, easy and at the end of it all, and there was a lot of all, took it with a smile. Not that he could ever have meant it – could he? – but under Leon's sticky little fingers, *Lakshmi became Goa.* Enticing, grimy, giving: competed over so often and by so many you wondered if what was left would ever be worth having. And he put *me* in there with all the rest, just another female fetish to jerk off to.

But to get back to my book, once Leon had got his paws on it, what had it become? *Ruined,* I told Martin. He had to suffer, didn't he, for losing it? *Rubbished, trashed, violated,* I raved.

Between us, cooling on the table, sat a dish of rice and cashews and ginger that Ruth had taught me to make and I can never smell ginger even now without being back at that table. "Surely that's a bit over the top?" Martin reasoned. "Nothing's lost – we'll just go over it, type out a clean copy. I'll type you a clean copy if it'll help. Just give me a few days –"

Now another phrase could've sprung into his mouth. English – he taught English, the tongue of the infinite variation, the language with a dictionary vast enough to serve as a lethal weapon. *Another manuscript, a fresh one, a new script.* I don't think I'd have picked up any of these and run with them now. "A clean copy? What – you think you'll just plonk away at it for a weekend, picking your way round this – this graffiti? Oh and every now and again having to call me over. *This word that's crossed out? Here, just below where it says her face – her monkeyshit face – is that humour or horror maybe?* And I'll say *oh, I think it'll be horror, don't you?* This *clean copy.* How well will it've been cleaned? How will all this stuff that I've read get cleaned out of it?" And once you've got into this groove, this nothing will be right again nothing can be made better, it can't be.

Why did Leon do it? Why was the Leon Version made?

Here's one possible line: Martin had had occasion to tick off the boy – only mildly and for some minor physical misdemeanour. Leon, though a head shorter than most Northern European teenagers, was in the next weight category compared to the Goan kids, the Choudray brothers, for instance. But if Martin's honest, he has no real memory of any particular incident (mind you, you could fill an encyclopaedia with the things Martin claims not to remember). There was just *something,* he said....

One afternoon of heat. Twenty assorted boys reciting *Adlestrop* and a tiny plaque – "For Recitation" – awarded to Krishnan Choudray after three interminable hours.

Perhaps, in addition to a budding career as a fantasist, Leon was destined to be the bully, as much a tyrant to his fellows as he'd become to his parents... and to begin with the frail, match-wood puppet that was the smaller Choudray. *Perhaps* he'd been caught jostling the prize-winner and been humiliated by Martin's intervention. But this is a post-incident assessment, an adult's downgrading of the boy's strange nature. I guess a whole string of minor snubs simmered away inside Leon's puppy-fatted breast until rifling his teacher's stuff – as I bet the little turd did on a regular basis – he came across *On Cinnamon Street, a novel by Elly Kent.* And decided to try his hand at ghost writing.

Leon and I were bound together in something that was less collaboration than semantic contest... I think of it, now that it's lost forever, as a work produced not by mutual effort but by mutual hostility – and what's more promising than that? Leon, the little prince of his parents home, must've loathed Martin. And Martin's wife. A very creative force, hatred. There was all that unstructured filth oozing out between the puberty cracks and the nationality gap; it was a toxic brew I couldn't hope to cook up in an idiolect I couldn't hope to reproduce... and I was getting it for free:

"On the steps of the church of Our Lady of the Mount Christopher turned and snatched Lakshmi's bruised hand. Very deliberately he raised it to his lips while they stared out at the prospect of Old Goa's off-white towers and domes and campanile poking up though a malachite sea of branches and palm-fronds. **Girl open like coconut he** whispered brown mat open and inside the sweets! Oh, very soft to the tongue, I bet! In his head ran headfingers that pushed the way for handfingers...."

If visual artists made use of the unworked object, the naturally occurring litter of the city, why not writers? Leon's addenda could have been the sacred-cow dung, the rotting *caja* husks of my energised palette.... Imagine the reviewer: *In the character of Leon, Elly Kent faithfully itemises the miseries and uncertainties of the hormonally-ravaged, fresh male ego as it comes to consciousness within the pampered frame of a Catholic mother's only son.* And this is before Leon the Conquistador gets started on the rough colonization of Lakshmi's little body, the humbling of her parents. Leon was the one character I could never have invented for myself, and it was just what overly careful *Cinnamon Street* needed. He had hybrid vigour, this offspring of generations of mismatches.

Dear little Leon. It's always a mistake to discount beauty whether in fiction or anywhere else. And just to prove it – how he was so much a player – when he'd displayed his talents to the full, Leon got us kicked out of the place. I've no idea what really happened that long afternoon between *The Lake Isle of Innisfree's* last line and the car's depositing Martin on our veranda steps. The headmaster called out something – perfectly mannered as he was – before driving away. I didn't catch it, although the car's engine had already drawn me to the door. There was just the gracious, "And of course, I'm afraid I can't."

A Keeble man to the last.

What else went with it I'll never be certain. Martin told me, naturally, what the headmaster had said – and more. Too much about What Had Happened and none of it exact. And when, exasperated – this was before he was arrested – I demanded, "What made you do *that?*" he stopped mid-word, shook his head. It was as though just at that instant everything he thought he had clear, dissolved; he looked at me properly for the first time since getting home, looked at me with complete despair.

"D'you know what, Elly?" he said, "I don't know. I just don't. I can't think of a single answer to that one."

Let me invent it Martin. It's better for us both.

192

You see Martin had *marked* it. The relief at its return – it had been missing for forty-eight hours – must've been short-lived. Having found it back in his desk... being dumb*founded* at its transformation by Leon's unmistakable hand... having brought it home and been rewarded with my going into moult, he'd taken out his pen and set to work.

And then he'd kept the boy after class to discuss it: a pedagogic response.

Not shocked, Leon, if that's what you were hoping for. More surprised, really – and very disappointed in you. What d'you think your parents will make of it? And Father Giovanni – will he even understand some of these words you've used?

They'd gone though the first pages together: red streaks highlighted the condensations that had forced out many of the transitive verbs or, less heinously, articles and prepositions. Exclamations pointed to where random switches from first to third person narration flirted with incoherence (and yet also allowed some passages to deliver a surreal hit). In a miniscule, white void overlooked by the prolific Leon, Martin had pleaded *Surely the wrong word?* Hardly the actions of a man who, faced with juvenile smut scrawled across his wife's creation, is overcome with rage, seizes by the throat the little wanker (Martin's term) responsible for it and nearly chokes the life out of him. And the unfathomable depths of the event become bottomless when you consider this: somehow in the ensuing melee, Leon manages to escape with the better part of the manuscript – not to the boys' prep room either, but to the arms of his mother and a glass of Madeira. The complaint is made by teatime. Martin is escorted home, bearing the first three, violated pages. The prologue. Six months later, in Mr Shirdokar's intolerable office, the rest is solemnly handed over by the de Costas' lawyer's clerk. It is pristine, unfingered and perfectly typed on the same cheap grey-white paper I'd bought. Even my tiresome overuse of the dash is reproduced.

There was still the prologue, of course. A few unnumbered pages of joint authorship. But, "I do not think," Mr Shirdokar whispered to Martin while his eyes never left Marjorie's face (a rich matriarch was one character in the whole sorry business the lawyer could identify with), "I do not think it will benefit us in the least to have the writing on this so-called manuscript translated for His Honour. Trust me, Madam and Mr Kent and Mrs Kent. It profits us nothing to prolong the agony."

The period of imprisonment was fourteen weeks, every one lived through inside a furnace. Through July it dragged, if anything worse than the previous months. For now people told of the delayed rain that would certainly arrive any time now, but didn't.

Our little bungalow. Its olive shade. The solace of Ruth's visits. All unavailable.

"Tomorrow, rain," muttered the waiter over breakfast at the Mandovi Hotel; it was where I had been moved to join Marjorie. But in lieu of rain, the monsoon winds brought dusts in a medley of colours and particle size... dusts that deposited themselves along the Mandovi's terrace − so that on some mornings you crunched out to your table and crunched back as though you were on sandpaper and the tatty balcony a giant parrot's cage.

"Why on earth did you get Martin to come to this terrible place?" I remember Marjorie asking. Against the intensity of light and temperature and the brilliant fuchsia of a woman's dress passing behind her, it was difficult to believe in Marjorie's presence in Goa. Ever since her arrival she'd been my grey-haired, linen-clad stalker tottering from shadow to shadow on the street or huddled in the furthest corner of a room. She was inclined to flap anything to hand. Of course the incident that had her jetting five thousand miles to be constantly at my side, we never spoke about. This was because − to Marjorie's mind − Martin had done nothing wrong *and* the awful thing he had done was all my fault. Instead of teaching away diligently at his side, I'd idled away our time here by writing − and it was this writing that had caused her son to go uncharacteristically *off the rails*.

Overhead, high and rising, appeared one of the raptors that some Goans had to rely on to consume their kin. It was fixed for a long second against a painfully white sky.

"Look up," I wheezed.

And the rains came only on the day of Martin's release.

He was found guilty of assault but sentenced to time-served... and reparations to Leon of 200,000 rupees. Four thousand sweaty 50 rupee notes: Marjorie and I carried them from the bank to Mr Shirdoker's place of business, where the victim waited with his parents.

Oh Leon, brilliant ghee-boy, burn-free Leon, if only it could've been you out there in the sea.

iii

So, I thought, never again: no more writing. But it's our last night at *Tŷ Awydd*, at Richard's bijou House of Desire. Six days down, but none to match the first.

Supper is cleared away, our bags mainly packed. Martin has fallen asleep over *The Complete Short Stories of 'Saki'*. I'm holding a pencil. This has been prompted by a post-supper discovery in a drawer: a substantial pile of writing paper. Pale lemon in colour and fibrous, it's stiffly expensive. And personalised:

Tŷ Awydd, Aberhiw, Gwynedd, North Wales, UK.

Why had Richard stopped there?

Europe, The World, The Universe?

There was no one merited greetings from Wales. I sat at the table and began a list, noting how my own regular, forward-sloping hand was almost a match for Richard's chosen font:

Lost and Found

Findings

Pointers

This last I crossed out and then reinstated.

Lost, lost

Ring of Sand

The Rose Ring

The pencil point hovered of its own volition, scored it out... once, twice.

Salvage replaced it.

But while Martin dreamed of past or future travels I sat at Richard's table with Richard's expensive paper: underneath the list, I wrote *You don't walk a cat.*

And after that, after I've made the jump of a beginning, and the twist from I into Elly, it's falling off the wagon for a practised drunk, a well-oiled slide to the ground. Martin murmurs in his sleep something that sounds like 'Fine, fine' or *find*, perhaps… Richard's binoculars hang from a wrought-iron hook that pokes through the wall. Martin murmurs again. Log slips from log in the grate and reveals a hot heart. In this final flaring my face burns.

Out there walking the shoreline, an object had caught my eye. I'd grabbed for it, the tide's titbit, and when I opened my hand what I was holding *belonged to me*… because everything washed up has been either lost overboard or thrown away. If you're the victim of bad luck, bad company or just bad timing then you take what you can find and use it anyhow you can.

Start here, I think to myself. Get a file going for each of them. Just as once I'd kept exemplary notes: Maps of Old Goa, Portuguese Architecture, Hindu Festivals. Now the labelling will read: Martin, Pippa, Richard, AN Other. With Richard there was a continuing line of others – Pippa suspected me of being part of it. Near the front or near the back, I wonder? But Richard was my main man. Richard's cottage, Richard's beach, Richard's new girl in a succession of girls. Everyone's favourite. My motive force.

Though I knew by then, *What has Richard done?* I'd demanded for the last time as Martin us drove home.

I mean apart from *beaten* you on the tennis court. Did you think your bruises were unapparent – to me? The black sun in the middle of your chest, its corona seeping out across your heart for a week. Your lower lip split by that 'wicked volley of Richard's, well you've seen it, haven't you?'

What had Richard done, apart from presiding over our entire lives – until needed? Until the moment I'd asked for help. His response?

"This – bother, it involves a *child*, Elly?"

"The boy's fifteen, Richard. Fifteen going on thirty. In fact he might've turned sixteen now. He's a pretty knowing sort of child. And it's not as if Martin *actually hurt him*. You've got boys yourself so you must understand what they're like. Leon's making it all up. That's what he's good at, making things up. He's –"

"But a child," he interrupted as though I'd not caught it at half the globe's distance. Yet for once the line was clear. "Anything to do with children, it's just dynamite these days. You've been out of the country

196

too long. You have to be so careful. Reputation-wise."

"Well thanks for that – but as for now, Richard. As for right *now*. What about Martin? I can't begin to tell you what it's doing to him. They're going to get him to plead guilty. The lawyer the school recommended – he's turned out to be worse than useless. There've been some absolutely *hideous things* in the papers here. They're printing a pack of lies. They can make up anything. No way for us to refute it. But this boy's family seem to know how to get their side of the story told. Horrible things, that's what everyone's reading – either just plain wrong or sly. They're suggesting all sorts."

"No one who knows Martin would believe it."

"Yesterday there's a photograph of Leon coming out of church, for fucksake! I'm sorry – but I mean, *church* – and they just had to make the point about what a handsome boy he was. You get that, do you? Martin had seen it… when I went to the prison this morning."

"Not pleasant?"

"Richard, *please*. This is me. *I'm* begging you –"

"But Marjorie's on her way, I hear."

iv

The evening the body was reported on the news, as soon as could, I left Martin and Marjorie to finish whatever she'd spent an entire day cooking. I walked down on my own into Parkgate. I needed a place to sit and breathe.

Dazed, sun-touched families slouched along the promenade or balanced on the seawall. These massive sandstone blocks were now all pink and rosy in the slanting light, part of a fortification that was doggedly keeping back tides defeated a century ago. Acres of green marsh intervened now with mosquito clouds dense as dust-devils, audible larks – and the white forward slashes of cattle egrets. They'd patrolled the steamy, inland fields of Goa, or something very like them had: *The heron-billed pale cattle birds / That feed on some foul parasite.* Shocking to find them waiting for Martin and me when we'd arrived home.

There was a sparkle somewhere out there, as river and brine mixed… and beyond all this was Wales.

So who had gone into the water? My choice, I thought. *Horrible*

197

things, Richard, that's what everyone's reading. Only I get to write them now. It was a restricted company I had to work with – but I knew them with the sort of intimacy that Leon displayed describing *his* home, *his* people. I knew that well enough to let them speak for themselves.

"You don't walk a cat," I said to Martin when we finally made it onto Richard's beach.

I don't even like cats. They give me asthma, which started in Goa while Martin was locked up and never went. It was the dry season. Marjorie and I waited to get him out and the dust of Panjim got into my hair and eyes and lungs. The only way to breathe reliably was to sit by the ocean whereas Marjorie and I had to linger office-bound, waiting to see Mr Gonsalves and Mr Shirodkar – who had such fears for Marjorie's health. (Always someone has fears for Marjorie's health, in addition to Marjorie).

But at the cottage that night I had a single, perfect shell warming in my palm, the sole survivor from the whole length of the tide-line. And the paper was still virgin spread out across the table and I sat down… *to write a book.* Another book.

That's all.

My point about the cat being walked was this: Marjorie adores cats, whereas I don't. She'd have been the one to dash across, start making up to the creature. *Don't like cats, huh?* That makes my mother-in-law warm and fluffy and me a cold-hearted potential feline-filleter, so the answer is?

Fiction. Just fiction.

I never meant for anyone to die.

v

When the steaks had seared each side he swung them onto the blue plates they'd taken from the cottage: slabs of flesh manoeuvred with such skill hardly a drip of pink juices was lost, each transference achieved with a complete circle that brought the server back to his original place. A balletic movement, well-timed and executed on the uneven footing. There was only one other present to appreciate this performance. The rain-curtain was draped over the cave's entrance, utile as a drawn blind. And the worsening weather was a Do Not Disturb sign. They ate the meat without speaking and packed the plates and cutlery back into a fruitbox they brought with them. They drank from a bottle of Beaujolais l'annee that later someone would notice was missing.

No one else would ever remember taking a turn around the bay that wild afternoon. On several occasions before dark it did ease. But so fierce an offshore wind had got up by then that the covering of the beach dried each time only to be whipped into the air to face-height. This mix was hostile enough to keep even the dedicated dog-walker up above the splash zone.

All that wasted afternoon, waiting for a resolution to their confinement: talk was exhausted until each minute became more tightly wound than the last by the energy of outside.

"Look, look now – even that fucking sea's got it in for me. It's on its way up here. We should've moved already. We're going to drown now. The perfect end to a perfect shitty day. This is your fault."

"We're not going to drown. Drink your drink. Look where high tide comes – it's miles down the beach. I've been here before. Here, try these. And don't be a wus."

vi

On our travels if we've learned one thing, Martin and I, it's how dangerous it can be to rely on local knowledge. It's never impartial, never complete. Facts can be mishandled. And it's only human to turn them around, file them down and fit them forcibly into the gaps. That bit of sea or sky needs something to close it up. In Aberhiw they'll tell you the tide never entered one particular cave... and a dry piece of clothing, an empty wine bottle would seem to back them up. But from it, what had been a person and someone I knew, found his way into the water. With help, they think.

But coming up with the truth can also do damage. That stupid girl, Ruth, certainly did – another Ruth, not the Goan one. This was Aberhiw Ruth, the teenager, who'd *appropriated* a coat.

Aberhiw Ruth had picked up a handy-sized jacket in that cave. Why, after keeping it hidden under her bed for weeks, decide to tell? "The girl," according to Marjorie's *Daily Mail*, "only confided in her parents when she came to wash the missing man's jacket and wasn't sure if putting Gore-Tex through the machine might destroy its weather-proofing." She helped out at the local riding stables, up on the hillside, so it was a point worth clarifying. She'd already sponged blood off the brick-red sleeve and collar (well you would, wouldn't you?). Our Ruth was only presented with the ethical conundrum/hot wash dilemma after spilling Pepsi down the front of her find. A couple of scoops of biological powder and they could've all been left in peace, so Richard must've thought. Richard and his grateful line of those just-restored-to-life punters, stretching into the future. And there'd be Pippa and her boys, all comfortably growing out and up in the Donns' House (it's on the market: eight-hundred and fifty thousand, carpets, curtains and "many extras" included).

Hayley's the wild card. Royalty, obviously. I've seen her just twice: once, some while ago, when I didn't even know who she was.

The second and last time was at the funeral.

Blacon Crematorium, outside the city, filled up with hospital folk who nodded to Martin and stared at me. There were photographers at the gate, snapping the cars, hoping for a shot of Richard and Hayley, I guess, and being disappointed. *He'd* scuttled off to Tel Aviv to fulfil a "long-standing lecturing engagement." Hastily arranged would be more like it.

"You really don't have to come," Martin said that morning with just a vestige of hope left in his voice. I'd told him I'd be accompanying him the previous night. Here he stood on the hall's black and white floor looking quite extraordinary in his dark suit: a man in fancy dress. Fifteen years ago, he'd arrived at the Oxford Registry Office in jeans, DM's, and a denim shirt. I suspected the narrow black tie he was sporting now might have been his father's. "I mean, I'm off anyway and it's hospital, stuff – you know. But don't feel you have to. It's not as if –"

"It's OK," I said, "They're wretched things to do by yourself, don't you think?" I don't think he did. "D'you reckon they'll find who did it?"

"I believe they know who did it," Martin said, all stately as his suit.

"I mean *catch* who did it, then. Obviously when two people go on holiday and one turns up dead, you assume – I mean if *you'd* been washed ashore with your head smashed in, everyone's bound to think I've gone mental."

"Well I certainly would," Martin said, cheerfully. With a thumbnail he worked at a spot on a dead man's tie.

Of course I was mad to have another glimpse of the *infirmiere fatale* myself.

Hayley at the crematorium: she looked wonderful, behaved impeccably. Having arrived just ahead of Martin and me – in an ordinary car crammed with other nurses – there was no doubt who was the celebrity guest. One perfect black-stockinged leg had hardly planted itself on the paving when she was across to the sister, the other hand going to the faithful Phil's shoulder. Anyway Hazel, as I find the sister's called, together with the faithful and forgiving Phil seem to be the entire family. So touching, so consolatory is whatever Hayley whispers, they cling to her, won't let go.

A moment later Bernie is trundled forward to take his place at the head of the procession, and the sister and Phil keep her with them. Hazel grasps the thin sleeve of Hayley's very proper grey wrap-around. They follow Bernie's trolley: the supermodel flanked by a couple of dwarfish, ill-dressed designers. We and about thirty others fall in behind. I realize that I've had this down as a male gathering but we're about half and half, though youngish for a funeral crowd. We're positively sober. No Lycra, no outrageous dye-jobs, no multiple piercings – no flowers.

No flowers by request of the sister and Phil, although there are a half-dozen white lilies on the coffin. I smell them as we sing *The Day Thou Gavest Lord Is Ended* and, because we've been given a pretty accurate account of the corpse's condition when found (by both newspapers and TV) the *lilies that fester* line from Hamlet won't get out of my head. *Lilies that fester smell worse than – seaweeds*. As Bernie is conveyed to the furnace *Mad World* comes up from the sound system and ahead I see Hayley slump forward into Phil's arms, crying below the level of the volume. The sister remains composed.

Maybe there's a cathartic element to this carbonising finality. I find my own eyes filled with embarrassing tears. I've no right to them. I'm ashamed they might be noticed – and they can hardly be for Bernie. They're just a show of the Dunkirk Spirit, the shared misery of lives that are always going to be too brief. Each one of us sitting in the nineteen-sixties chapel attached to the Crem is feeling it now... that we're eking out our time on a tight strip of beach, getting shelled and picked off and then washed away. Seeing those we care for become a space, a nothing. Seeing their faces as they watch it happen to us.

Bernie got his twenty-seven years and now there's the fire – *My God!* What else could they do with something as far gone as this? I, more than anyone here, deserve to be conjuring up the look of him, complicit as I am.

Only from the public-spiritedness of Aberhiw Ruth could they know that Bernie had bled in the cave. Because there was nothing much left that bodily fluids could have coursed through – not when he came back ashore. Poor Bernie. And the sheer, fiendish injustice of it, Bernie. The gymnast's hard little body softening, becoming putty for the rocks' punches – until it flowed away from itself altogether... and became this unspeakable mass – just as quickly and easily as an aged, diseased, much-abused body could do. And that blow to the left side of Bernie's skull – to the "temporal lobe" as the pathologist insisted on informing us – was it this gave Ruth all the trouble with those dried-in stains? Blood gurgling from the scalp and down the face, soaking into the collar. Now it's smeared on the sleeve that, lacking co-ordination, attempts to clear whatever this stuff is... that's getting into the eyes, getting between Bernie and a sharper, more useful picture of what's going on.

I risk catching Martin's attention

(– so pretty soon there'll be nothing left of Bernie and if say sometime in the future someone wanted to clone Bernie but who'd do it not Phil from the look on his face he seems pretty composed but stupid no one'd ever want to clone Bernie nor me and Elly they'd only do scientists and politicians and rich bastards wouldn't they not poor Bernie here because all that expensive difficult stuff of getting him cloned doesn't seem to go with no flowers by request –)

We were meant to send donations to some sports trust, doing worthy things for kids on sink-estates.

All this was a full fortnight after the inquest, a full fortnight after the headline: **THE DOCTOR, HIS WIFE, THE NURSE, THE GAY NURSE AND 'MR ALDERSHOT'**

In name only, he was Hayley's invention. She it was who'd told the police and then the coroner how she'd given Bernie the key to *Tŷ Awydd* – to take "a friend" away for a couple of days... and been in no doubt who that friend was. She'd spoken to the murderer on the phone once. "Just put Ross on," he'd ordered her.

"Poor old Phil," Martin muttered as we made our way back to the car. There was a cold vegan buffet and drinks at the Boughton flat we were avoiding. "I can't see him wanting to clone Bernie can you?"

"*What?*"

Martin side-stepped nimbly to avoid the excessive tributes from an earlier cremation that were now lining our exit route. "And I bet that buffet – I think we'll give it a miss, huh? – but I bet that's all down to Phil, as well."

Poor Phil, faithful to beyond the end.

vii

And once, some while ago when I didn't even know who she was.

This was the party we *did* get to. It was at the Donns' House, in the spring. Can you imagine it? To a drinks-do given in his own home – together with his own wife – the arrogant one invited his lover? How enjoyable would that have made it (for me, I mean) if only I'd known?

Pippa, I can picture now – flustered, ill-at-ease. She was jittering across the Donns' House's elegant and new-decorated hall, hoping fervently that people had been able to find them all right... and if they had, whether they had been able to park... hadn't been caught in the last shower... hadn't had to put off something else they always did on Sundays. Each arrival was treated to the full story of how their trusty caterer had been taken ill – this complete with an extended lower lip, the better for the blowing of a lifeless fringe away from her forehead. Each time it revealed two tramlines of distress. Then came the rueful half-grimace that Pippa usually saved for the boys' rowdiness.

Richard was dispensing red, white or Bucks-Fizz from the morning room table. Pippa's contribution was trays of barely heated-up, well-dried out cheese savouries that you could've balanced on a two-pound coin, spring-rolls the size of a decent spliff.

There must've been a hundred packed into the drawing and dining rooms, and then there were the awkward few that couldn't be got further than the hall and blocked doorways – *and* the doctors and lawyers that wouldn't budge from the vicinity of Richard and the drink. I thought Richard must be fuming, surely, at this poor showing. For Richard, entertaining had always been a competitive sport. Martin pointed out a tubby greaseball of a man as the hospital's Chief Executive and I watched him pause, mid-pronouncement as a gummy morsel attached itself to the roof of his mouth.

"This is one of the benefits of a big house," I said to Richard when I'd shouldered my way through assorted solicitors and oncologists.

"What's that?" He was instantly suspicious.

"Well, you can have *everybody* you know round. The economy of scale, isn't it? Get 'em all done at once." I looked at the plate of cooling, pastry medallions abandoned next to the lines of clean glassware. His gaze followed mine.

"Septic food," he said pleasantly. It was going to take more than this to ruffle him. The shirt was a careful two shades darker than the khaki chinos, the hair a touch too long – the whole a very Richard riposte to those poor saps getting a first look into the Donns' House, and jacketed for the occasion. "I wouldn't touch it if I were you." He was speaking as though to a fellow guest who was also a complete stranger. My glass was refilled. Stray drops picked up on a white linen napkin, turned it red and then just rosy. He threw it aside and chose another.

"We're not going to serenade them, then?"

A baby-grand stood in one corner of the morning room. It was where Pippa attempted to interest Adam and Thomas in learning to play.

"Apparently not."

"D'you remember I got Pippa to do the Eurythmics that night? I sang and you and Martin –"

"What?" He saw beyond me into the crush of guests. "No."

Distance – but of course, that's how Richard did everything. Don't go in for ensemble pieces... make sure you're never upstaged and *never* in the way of collapsing scenery.

But it turns out I was at an entirely different play.

"This is Bernie," Pippa said. Bernie was head-to-toe in black, but then so were half the women in the room, including me. Pippa certainly *should* have been, instead of that ankle-length, vilely-patterned garment from which her silver feet protruded like a pair of fish-slices. If I had Pippa's money to spend on clothes, I'd shop in different shops.

"Oh, I've met Elly before," he said. There was a kiss for both cheeks, properly and accurately planted. A lovely, exotic smell. "So-called Christmas party at the Jade Garden. She's lived *everywhere*. Can't impress her. Mind you, since then I've been to Tibet! To visit the monks. (No thanks, Pippa, I'm on the Atkins diet). Can't you see I've got this aura, now?" He invited us to look down the modest length of him to patterned loafers, "Come on, you must see how it's just oozing out of me. I've got more top quality karma than I know what to with."

Pippa's expression was doubtful but, "You certainly look well," she managed.

"That'll be the communing with yaks," I said.

Bernie gave something between a tut and an exhalation. "What was it gave me away?"

"Gave what away?" someone else asked. I realised there was another, taller, slimmer figure behind Bernie, her orange sweater providing a backdrop to Bernie's silhouette. He turned and at the same time extended our circle of three to include her. "Do you know Hayley?"

Here it was. What I almost missed.

"Hayley's new in High Dependently," Pippa said.

"Dependency," Bernie muttered. He polished his own pearly head with one palm – in stress, feeling for her.

"What did I say?"

Hayley just laughed, "Not so new anymore," and raised her glass. Now I see that, far from the front-page Jezabel she's been cast as, she had a portion of weak-decency about her, just like the rest of us. If she was quick to raise her glass to lips that were impeccably defined with mere gloss, it was to hide her blushes on the wretched wife's behalf... but at the time I just thought *Bucks Fizz* and *here's a girl that's going to manage to enjoy herself anywhere.*

A wonderful occurrence: coming across, when you weren't expecting it, absolute physical perfection. Twice it's happened to me. Firstly Leon, now Hayley. Never underestimate the significance of beauty. Stendhal claimed the vision offered us "the promise of happiness"... well, he *was* a man. He was going along the lines of pursuit – acquisition – possession – smuggery. For a woman who witnesses it, the promise is reversed. Especially when you see a girl as flawless as this. I had a little green bile-bug hatch out in my middle. Stendhal's right about the happiness-thing, but it's all hers – or it's going to be hers... as long as the looks hold out.

There were streaks of cochinealy red just starting to fade from her dark, sharply-cut hair – although she could've gone pure auburn (brows, the lot) and got away with it: the skin so blossomy and those fresh, see-through, pink cheeks. Perhaps it was a new material they were trialing: looked like skin, felt like skin, but lacked pores. Her eyes were big but not so deeply set as to even suggest at menace. They were a very warm brown-with-olive, though half-lidded, now, resting on Pippa with what I just took to be boredom.

Of course, it was pity.

Then she turned away. "You're Martin's wife," she told me.

"It's a fair cop."

"Oh don't say that. Where is he? Everybody at the hospital likes Martin! But – oo-oh, I get it. You do too, don't you? I can tell." She gave me a playful nudge with her free hand. "And it goes both ways. He talks about you a lot. You work for a charity. And you used to write stories for magazines but not for things like *Cosmo*. And one day, he says, you're going to write a whole book."

"Are you, Elly?" Bernie asked. "What'll it be about?"

Martin walked up just then with Marjorie in tow. One of Pippa's boys caused some sort of incident out in the hall and the thing sort of fizzled out as she went to investigate.

But she must've known.

She can't have watched Hayley, moved gently by Bernie from group to group, from couple to singleton, everywhere except where Richard was hiding behind his battlements of bottles – and even when he did come out, everywhere except the bit of the huge drawing room where Richard was holding forth… she can't have seen that and not known, can she?

All that business in the cafe: 'I think he's seeing someone else.' Come on.

You didn't need Aunt Dulcie's second sight. All you had to do was look at the Girl, walking across the Congreve's heirloom of a carpet: her glowing sweater draped over shoulder bones tantalising as wing-buds, the nape of the white neck exposed as she bent to catch Bernie's low-down sentence… naked blue-veined insteps flexing in black court shoes – and Richard turning his back on her progress, bursting into sudden laughter at the joke Pippa didn't realise she'd just made.

viii

If Richard's dossier filled of its own accord and Pippa's needed closing down to prevent the overflow of her *perfectly understandable hurt*, Martin's is still like a misplaced piece of luggage. His is that battered, well-loved holdall you confidently claim – only to find that, yes, there's the broken handle, scar of its fall from the Chopdem ferry, but within it are another traveller's belongings, a stranger's change of clothes and holiday read.

I love Martin.

At thirty-six I realise it hasn't withered away. I do love Martin, whoever he is; that's something else I found on Aberhiw beach. "If we are to stay together," I had my mouth open to say to him. But as I did, I felt myself become estranged from the old animosities and the current niggles that we'd dragged over the border into Wales. I got a glimpse of what God was meant to feel about us all, once. Love with interest: a puzzled but dedicated partisanship. I was touched by it even as I mentally cursed my husband with a plague of boils. And that meant love for the entirety of him – his separateness, the inconvenience of his nature and complete lack of any familial traits that could correspond with mine. Just like the grit of Goa to which nothing living nor inert was impermeable, love for Martin was ground into me. *If we are to stay together* dissipated like a dud line, blocked out only to be replaced by the more telling phrase: the best three, single-syllable words in the English language.

For Bernie, someone had it acutely. I never found out anything like enough for a Bernie file – but it was easy to picture him as an object of desire. People would remember Bernie. Even Martin (who's unreliable on things like whether ex-President Chirac's still alive) can tell you the what and the when of their last conversation. It fitted neatly between Cal Brinkley's death in the early hours of the morning and meeting Richard for lunch, with the offer of the cottage: two things from a single day managing to stick in Martin's head.

If that was her dad just gone, I'm sorry I missed him, that was from Bernie. From Richard it was, *Up to you dull boy – I'm only providing the venue.*

Already Richard's eyes are sweeping the room for a new target. But before this there is Bernie with his good-quality information, making Martin feel the complete simpleton he sometimes seems to be, but isn't....

Only a few weeks ago – we're coming up to the first anniversary of the crime – Martin had a researcher ring up out of the blue, having blagged his way through to him at the hospital. Could they talk? Gareth Somebody: he was examining a number of unsolved murders and unexplained deaths in North Wales: Bernie's was one of them. He had a hunch there was a pattern. *(Oh yeah,* I wish Martin had thought of saying, *and I'm Mr Chips).* He just needed a few more – you know? Could they perhaps meet and go over a few details?

No, Martin had the sense to tell him.

What you won't find in back copies of the *Chester Chronicle* is how bloody lucky Mr Aldershot was as to timing. Hayley had given Bernie a key to *Tŷ Awydd,* safe in the knowledge that she and the cottage's owner were off to Edinburgh for a long weekend. Not a successful one, though: its finale turns out to be their first huge row. Hayley returned to the hospital on the Monday morning, organised herself a week's leave and popped across to Newcastle for a whinging session with an old friend. Back home again, you can count on the loss of a few days more in make-up sex before she notices: not only no key, no Bernie.

There's a reason for Martin's so swift brush-off of newshound Gareth. Phil reports Bernie missing. The hospital reports Bernie missing. His sister, unvisited in her Saltney council house, reports Bernie missing. But only Richard and Hayley know missing from where – and they're not saying. What's the betting she was all for coming clean and Richard wouldn't have it? This is not the sort of thing to get associated with. Who'd want to see Tŷ Awydd on the six o'clock news if it could be avoided? Why get sucked into a set of events that were beyond his, our (he means Richard's) control?

I'd heard it all before: *You have to be so careful. Reputation-wise.*

And later, to the police: "Of course, I went immediately to the cottage in Wales when we realised. There was a remote possibility that Mr Rosco had gone there or was still there. But it was completely undisturbed. I understand now that it had probably been cleaned. Thoroughly. But at the time it was just in good order. Nothing suggested to me that anyone had been inside the place since my previous visit with Miss Ford. Go to the authorities – but with what? Nothing. A lack of evidence. As I've said there was no indication –"

Well actually there was the one, Richard dear. That little glass vial – with whose fingerprints? Yours? Bernie's – or whoever was with Bernie? I found it and like an idiot I lobbed it into the sea.

Bernie certainly had gone where nothing mattered. Not the way gentle, uncomplaining patients died on him, whilst hostile, near-psychotics recovered. Not that four pounds put on during the winter, despite the Atkins diet, and now refusing to budge. Not even the terrifying rise in Chester house prices that would leave him and Phil with the prospect of life in a two-up, two down terrace... *if only* they'd bought last year.

All resolved in a moment and forever.

But a missing scene came just before that moment in April. Each one of us has his or her own draft: the clichéd, the melodramatic, the confused. Probably they're all equally inaccurate. In my mind it's a production that is kindled out of nothing – but it burns, fierce as phosphorous. There's the violence of words to begin it. Then Bernie's head, that beautiful smooth-as-a-Benin-bronze head, receives one appalling blow. Which is enough. As Richard instructed me a long while back: people watch it on the screen and think the victim just clambers to his feet, while the attacker, sportingly, waits around. Wipes his mouth. Then the thwacked-one fights back. People see it, believe it. Get shocked and angry when it doesn't happen. Mr Aldershot, he was the angry sort.

... *all his own fault. This is not playing fair. This is not bouncing back as he was meant to do. Why must he insist on just lying there? Why has he gone and ruined everything, saying what he said – then laughing when I – when he – and now just lying there... dying on me, all his own fault....*

As though the place didn't already reek of death.

ix

--How could you *Elly*? And you've called me Marjorie! (He let me see it, though he wasn't going to. I knew you wouldn't mind). How could you? It's not for myself – I mean that's obviously not me, I'm not complaining on my own behalf. But the others! Isn't *Richard* meant to be a friend? We've known them for years, the whole family. I thought they were both supposed to be your friends – and hasn't he been so good? Coming up with the job when – well, least said, soonest mended. Then that holiday you were going on about needing – I'm right, aren't I? You didn't pay for it. Or rather, this is how you repay him – anyone who reads it will recognise the surgeon. He's an eminent man. You'll be raking it all up again, all that unpleasantness, just when it's died down in the press. Unless that's part of it? Based on a true story – isn't it what they put when they're trying to sell these things? As if calling us all something else was going to do any good. "Names have been –" you know – to protect the innocent. Bunkum. Everybody'll guess it's you and my son in here. Oh you've been very crafty. I don't think there's anything you can be sued over. Apart from about that poor man who died, and they say you can't libel the dead. That's another thing. Somebody died! Nobody can be sure how – and it's useless you pretending you do. You don't. He might not even have been quite dead when he went into the water. Without the lungs, and everything being so badly – you know, they weren't able to tell. I mean it could always have been some sort of terrible accident. They've never found who was with him. Mr Aldershot, you called him but who really knows? He's not going to come forward now. It'd look suspicious, now. Maybe you should think twice. I wouldn't be comfortable myself, not with him still out there – maybe taking offence at you in particular, because you're the one dredging it up. If he's done it once, well –

What d'you have to say to that, *Elly*?

x

I say --There's a new series of *Celebrity Shootout* starting in five minutes time. Another half-dozen candidates: a disgraced children's entertainer, a warned-off jockey, the flabby TV chef among them. (Let's hope *he* falls into one of those traps they do). But who could resist the justice of degradation for any of them? So why don't you go and switch it on? I know you want to, though you pretend it "sets such a bad example it shouldn't be on the television." And I agree with you. It's absolute mind-filth. I'd go for just checking on *Shootout Update*. Every night after the news. It's no fun on your own though, is it? I could come through, if you like.

I say --Isn't it a thrill to watch some people cut down?

I think: at least I've changed your name, and with only two mouse movements and four keystrokes, I can change it back.

xi

We'd been home from holiday in Aberhiw for – no, you got me there. To tell you how long, I'd need to be able to pin down when it was we went. But I know my best friend had *definitely* disappeared. It wasn't a literal decomposition, not at first. The process began by his becoming an elusive shape – something I thought I could just make out ahead of me in a corridor – or at the wheel of a car speeding away. Never caught up.

Once, it shames me to report, I went along to try my luck with his secretary. I'd actually got one buttock onto to her desk, next to the photograph of the musically-gifted grandchildren – and suddenly there's the sound of her boss, in the next office, an armful of files being dropped unceremoniously onto a desk.

I call out to him.

"No good!" he hollers, "have to catch you later. I'm already –"
His phone goes off.

The outer door slams.

I tried ringing him once but all I got was the wife. More humiliation.
I can hear their youngest screaming in the background. "Sorry?"

I say again, "It's me – I just wanted to say thanks for the cottage.
I can't get hold of himself –"

"Oh, yes?" she shouts when we've got over the identity-of-caller
hurdle. "Go out? Yes, that'd be really um, nice. Just one moment,
sweetie-pie. *Plea-s-se.* Oh, it's the little one. He's got an ear infection. It's
awful – it's giving him no sleep. And he was being *so* brave weren't you?
Till about an hour ago and then – It must hurt him *so* – Yes, sweetie,
have it, have it if you want it! Lovely to – go. Somewhere. Maybe next
– not too much though! *Not all of it, though!* Could you arrange with
– at work? A week, say? In a week – it'd be lovely to –"

The line actually went dead while she was still talking, which was
novel. Usually when a woman puts the phone down on you, it's you.
But there would've have been no ill-will towards me, no desire to
belittle. I like her and she likes me. Never a word of reproach from
that quarter.

Happening, or rather non-event, number two was that neither of
us had mentioned the holiday. It's positive effect, I mean: how right
I'd been to accept it, the whole restorative process of being alone.
Good, on the whole. I think. Sex on Monday night, Tuesday and *twice*
Thursday (rain assisted). Soon, quite soon, I was going to sit down
with my mother and get some sort of understanding about the Debts.
Could it be in the interests of any of us, I was going to demand, to
carry on with this pretence of future repayment hanging over us like
post-insolvency syndrome?

But what had prevented our enjoying a holiday review was taste.
Bernie had run aground not long after our return – although of course
he wasn't Bernie then, just an anonymous, pitiable huddle of bones
and bits. Then came the x-rays of teeth, an ornate buckle on display,
a few cells in a nutrient medium. At last, a grainy photograph on the
local news. There was a plea for information to track down the killer,
delivered by his partner, a paramedic from the same place he worked.

Same place I work.

Obviously we'd need to leave the whole subject for a cooling-off period – a decorous interval between The Bad Event and The Up-Side. You'd be sure to leave a gap between the news that someone has died on a cycling holiday in Spain and speculating (aloud) if you might be able to get your hands on that strip of garden you've always coveted: "It's just occurred to me that we might approach –"

It's like clearing a cheque, an emotional IOU. So just as I was thinking, Right, any evening now, she'll save me the trouble of starting off myself, she hits me with the bloody story. Been banging on at it during working hours, apparently.

You don't walk a cat, I read. There were a lot of pages under that one. The last finished mid-sentence.

"Well? What d'you reckon?" she demanded. Too wired to sit, she was back and forth on imaginary tidyings: a glass picked up, taken next door to the kitchen and returned still in her hand. "It's nowhere *near* finished yet." I'd skimmed the first few chapters. It had taken me three quarters of an hour.

"I – I'm astonished. Absolutely amazed."

"What about the dolphins? D'you like the dolphins?"

"Dolphins."

"It starts with the dolphins."

"They looked like the prologue."

"Of course – *and* a bit of scene setting. *And* a way of kick-starting the plot."

"But I never read the prologue. You know that. I always leave it till after. I started with the cat."

Scene setting: we were in the small room at the side of the house that had probably been intended as the under-butler's overspill pantry. We used it as a sitting room. We'd had the end of the Scotch and a purloined bottle of my mother's Dry Ginger between us. A few broken cashews fragments in the bottom of a dish seemed to have spread out over the sofa cushions, my fingers, my trousers, the rug and the folded face of last week's *Observer*. It was turned to the crossword, still with its sad couple of no-shows. (Six across: *Girl goes wild at this sparkler.* Eight letters. Blank blank blank M blank N blank E). I had had it, the solution, just on the cusp of my frontal lobe, when the typescript had been thrust at me. Now it had rolled right off again.

Although still only late September the gloom was pressing in on the leaded lights. The gas fire and Channel 5 were on.

"Have you noticed they don't seem to do Five Facts About anymore? I used to quite enjoy a bit of forcible education. Five Facts About Cancer, Five Facts About Fish."

"You hate it, don't you? I've a lot of work towards the end to redo – on account of this awful thing about its being Bernie. I got the idea for it at the cottage – well, on the beach. *Finally* I get an idea – it was going to be the stunning nurse… You hate it."

"Of course not. But – you know I thought you really liked little Ruth?"

"Ruth?" Not like her to be slow on the uptake. "Of course I did."

"It seems a bit cool, what you've written. A bit patronising."

"I'd have thought," she said with her eyes doing that narrowing business that's always a red light, "you'd have been more interested in what I had to say about that boy at the school. I've had to be really careful. With the stuff about that boy – and you."

"Oh, *I* come across as a total bag of shit. But apart from that –"

"No you don't! I tried to *explain it all*, which is more than you've ever done. *Where* do you come across as –?"

She wedged herself in beside me on the economy-class sofa. She tried to snatch the typescript away but I was onto that. I'd had that done to me before. I held it out over the carpet on the side farthest from her, although this was a position from which I was unable to rifle through the sheets. All I could do was flap them a bit for emphasis.

"Then there's all that about not understanding about *Marjorie*. Of course I understand. I understand like buggery. It's just nothing I can alter. Just can't get over the fact she's on the other side of the wall."

"Yes. I needed to write it. That'll have to come out –"

"And that thing where I don't say 'I'd take you into The Grosvenor looking like that'."

"You didn't say it. That's the truth. You didn't fucking say it."

"I know! But it makes me out such a – rat-bag, then."

"*Really?*"

"I know one thing. I wish I *had* found a fucking finger with a fucking ring on it." Well why not? We'd entered the fucking-this, fucking-that stage. "And then we'd have the prospect of – I don't know. Something. Anything. Instead of having fuck-all. Less than fuck-all."

I felt her jump up and I thought it best to be looking again at the manuscript, as though I was giving it another go. I could at least bone-up on the bloody cetaceans… but even before she'd sighed deeply, dropped the glass onto the table-top, stalked to the window, just managing to avoid a chair, I knew I'd blown it. Homed in on the weaknesses, in the way that only couples do – no, make that couples and parents. Not just by cutting straight to what you have to whinge about, but by actually going out looking for receptacles for your whinging and, if these aren't immediately apparent, if they won't spring to the hand, then manufacturing them. On the spot. Just because it was *her* weakness. It's as though the closeness of marriage acts like an over-scale fence. Built too near the house, the only way you can see what you think you crave, is to look beyond it. Now the really big deal about this fence is that it separates a world not giving a toss for you from the one person who does. So what do you do? You ignore it, you stupid bastard. You piss off this one person good and proper every time you get the chance, because pissing off those other fuckers, the ones outside the fence, means getting kicked in the nuts, sacked, evicted, thrown into jail, humiliated to an extent you just wouldn't believe.

With anyone else, *anyone in the entire known Universe that hadn't previously swindled me out of a fortune or given up bathing*, I'd have come up with something. I'd have found an affirming word to say about the proffered opus.

I read on. Get to the end of the dolphins. Look up. I'm alone. Outside a car engine is being turned over. Any second now there'll be the spit of gravel from the front wheels. I heave at the rain-swollen sash.

"Come *on*," I shout, "I've read the dolphins, now. Dolphins are good. I do actually like the dolphins –"

Thanks to Gwen Davies from Alcemi for editorial assistance.

To Malcolm and Ceri Lewis for all sorts of useful stuff as well as their longstanding friendship.

To Geoffrey Gilling-Smith, Iola Williams and Renate Johnson for much medical information.

To Michael Andrews for the quotation from "Mad World".

And finally, apologies to the inhabitants of the real Aberhiw whose village I've not only shifted along the coast but also renamed.

Gee Williams is a poet and the prize-winning author of two short story collections. Numerous full-length plays and short fiction pieces of hers have been broadcast on BBC radio. This is her first novel. To find out more, go to www.academi.org and click on *The Writers of Wales*.

ALCEMI ✡

voices

fiction

stories

contemporary

new

authentic

vulnerable

diverse

international

original

ironic

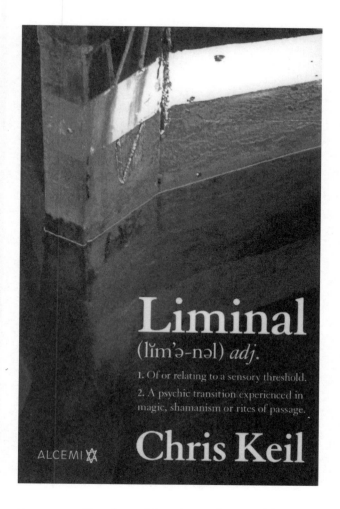

Liminal

(lĭm'ə-nəl) *adj.*

1. Of or relating to a sensory threshold.
2. A psychic transition experienced in magic, shamanism or rites of passage.

ALCEMI

Chris Keil

Set among Greek marble ruins and a crumbling Welsh estate, this novel looks at relationships – father and youthful son; son and elderly mother; fiancés, lovers, colleagues – and how none of them ever stay static.

£9.99
ISBN: 978-0-9555272-1-0

ALCEMI✡

www.alcemi.eu

TALYBONT CEREDIGION CYMRU SY24 5AP
e-mail gwen@ylolfa.com
phone (01970) 832 304
fax 832 782